The Regan McHenry Real Estate Mysteries

The Death Contingency
Backyard Bones
Buying Murder
The Widow's Walk League
The Murder House

Other books by Nancy Lynn Jarvis

Mags and the AARP Gang

**Cozy Food: 128 Cozy Mystery Writers Share Their
Favorite Recipes**

The
Widow's Walk
League

A Regan McHenry Real Estate Mystery

Nancy Lynn Jarvis

Good Read Mysteries
An imprint of Good Read Publishers

This is a work of fiction. Names, characters, places, and incidents are either
products of the author's imagination or are used fictitiously.
Any resemblance to actual events, locales, or persons, living or dead, is
entirely coincidental.

**Good Read
Mysteries**

Good Read Mysteries © is a registered trademark of Good Read Publishers
301 Azalea Lane, Santa Cruz, California, 95060

Copyright © 2011 by Nancy Kille

Library of Congress Control Number: 2011927913

ISBN: 978-0-9821135-9-2

Good Read Mysteries, First Edition, June 2011

Printed in the United States of America

www.GoodReadMysteries.com

Books are available at special quantity discounts through the website.

To Pat and the Bonny Doon ladies who walk.
I promised you a book; here it is.

Acknowledgements

When I think my stories are finished, my husband Craig reads them. I write the books; I know what I mean. He makes sure you will, too. His comments make the characters come to life and Regan's adventures more interesting.

A huge Thank You goes to Warren Atwood, the president of our local Woodies club. He knows everything there is to know about Woodies and the annual Santa Cruz event, Woodies on the Wharf, and generously shared his knowledge. He even told me which model Woodie Mike McAllister should be driving and where he should park on the wharf.

To Douglas Kay (Gallagher), who thought Regan should have a run in with a psychic reader. He was right.

And to Morgan Rankin for her copy editing skills.

The
Widow's Walk
League

Nancy Lynn Jarvis

A widow's walk is a railed rooftop platform, often with a small enclosed cupola, frequently found on 19th century North American houses. Originally they were probably built to facilitate chimney sweeping, but popular romantic myths hold that the platforms were used to look for vessels returning from the sea. The lore states that as ships became overdue, wives would spend time looking out to sea and praying for their husband's safe return, while hoping their mariner husbands had not perished and that they were not widows.

Halloween in downtown Santa Cruz is always a monstrous event — not monstrous as in frightful, but monstrous as in enormous. The celebration starts innocently enough in the early afternoon when Pacific Avenue store owners hand out candy to costumed little ones parading through town with their parents.

Many of the parents wear costumes, too, using their children as excuses, props for their own dress-up fantasies.

Older children and a few teenagers join the party in late afternoon after school lets out, and some older adults venture downtown, too.

Stores run out of candy around 3:30 or 4:00 and young children are taken home. For a time, Pacific Avenue and the surrounding streets become almost vacant again. This is not an end of the celebration — it is the ocean receding before a tsunami.

Last year, Halloween night in downtown Santa Cruz began innocently, but it didn't end that way — innocently, I mean. And it was just the beginning.

Regan McHenry

Halloween in Santa Cruz coupled unbridled creativity with people freed from their normal inhibitions. The night was festive and exhilarating, but with so many people anonymous behind masks, there was always the potential for trouble. Police officers worked in pairs; it was safer that way. They let the crowd party — Halloween was everyone's favorite holiday — but they were vigilant, ready.

Spontaneous parades started as merrymakers followed the giant steps of stilt-walkers striding up Pacific Avenue. Spicy aromas of food from many nations emanated from sidewalk stands opened for the hungry. Face-painting and party-hat-making stalls sprang up to help revelers with personal adornment. Other booths offered decorations to carry: magical wands, glitter-covered stars and moons on sticks, and feathery batons to wave and bounce up and down. Music came from volunteer bands performing on every street corner.

As the night progressed, ever more people crowded on to Pacific Avenue. The street became a crush of resplendently costumed hordes.

A number of women braved the October night's chill

dressed as harem girls with bare midriffs and gauzy leg coverings. Most strutted with attitude, certain their role was to provide titillating entertainment for the throng, although not all were young or svelte.

Imaginative ideas were expressed in costume. Pizza boxes were stacked high and akimbo to surround a woman and turn her into a leaning tower of pizza; a thick covering of purple balloons transformed another reveler into a bunch of grapes. Many costumes were inspired by fanciful imaginings of sea creatures that might be lurking, undiscovered, in the deep submarine canyon of nearby Monterey Bay.

One group of friends formed a multi-headed dragon, which was capable of playfully snapping at several passersby simultaneously. An oversized big bad wolf, his jaws open menacingly and his teeth already bloody, snapped, too, until a still intact and very much in charge sweet Little Red Riding Hood produced a whip and warned him to stop or he would be punished.

The night brought out many shadowy black figures with rubbery masks portraying Edvard Munch's *The Scream*. Without exception they bounced and scurried and waved to friends. It seemed incongruous that they were so engaged and having such fun when their masks portrayed only despair and misery.

Halloween brought out other black-clad figures, too, some carrying bloodied scythes. Most tried to walk silently and slowly enough that the hoods covering their heads fell forward to obscure their skeleton-masked faces.

If asked who they were, their ghoulish presentations were often ruined by a returned question: "Dude, can't you tell?

I'm Death."

Some did manage to stay in character long enough to murmur menacingly that they were Death. Usually though, they couldn't resist following their whisper with a laugh, as if they were driven to keep some separation between their portrayal and their person by making light of it.

On this Santa Cruz Halloween night, one such solemn phantom set a higher standard. It seemed to have no human face to hide. Black scrim, the kind used in stage productions, obscured a barely visible death-head set deeply under the hood, leaving the details of what was behind to the imagination of Death's beholders. It was over six feet tall, towering, and thin enough to suggest there might *be* only bones under its dark robes.

It moved soundlessly and evenly, its shroud obscuring its feet so completely that it seemed to float. If spoken to, it remained as silent as the grave and responded not at all, as if it were truly otherworldly and oblivious to the commotion around it.

Occasionally it raised an elegant black gloved hand and tapped a costumed reveler on the shoulder. When its chosen target turned to face it, Death handed him a small piece of paper. Death's note held a future date lettered in a bold typeface that resembled hand-written script. Recipients quickly figured out their messages ... they were the dates Death would return to claim them.

Reactions to receiving a death date were curious to watch. Those made aware of their mortality knew it wasn't real, but most, even the young, reflexively drew in their elbows to protect their midsections and twittered nervously. Then they laughed too exuberantly, dismissing their future death by making it a joke and an event too distant to warrant any more of their attention, especially not on a festive Halloween night.

One elf-costumed man had a very different reaction to his death-date.

"What kind of crap is this?" he confronted Death. "Is this supposed to be funny, because I don't think this is a bit funny!"

He shouted loudly enough that those near him stopped and took notice.

"What is it, Walter?" a smallish woman in a matching elf costume asked.

He shoved the card at her, narrowed his eyes to angry slits, and tilted his head back to glower up at the lofty Death.

"This jerk says I'm going to die tonight."

Death, its delivery made and the elf-man's displeasure clear, bowed slightly, backed away from the couple, and then turned and began silently retreating into the surrounding crowd.

The elf-man shook his fist in the direction of the withdrawing grim reaper. "Are you smiling under your mask, you creep? You think this is a joke? Come back here!"

The elf-wife took the note from her husband's hand and read it. She sighed and shook her head, "What a sick sense of humor, and on a night that's supposed to be fun."

She wadded up the note and dropped it into her pocket. She looped her hand through her husband's arm and pulled him close. "That disturbed individual is not worth getting worked up over," she smiled up at him. "Umm, can you smell cinnamon? Let's tempt fate and get something to eat that's greasy and loaded with sugar," she said as she tugged her husband toward a nearby churro stand.

With a final huff, the elf-man turned his head for another look over his shoulder. He wanted to give Death a final annoyed stare, but Death was gone, banished it seemed by the high spirits of the milling swarm.

Neither the elf-man nor his mate gave the note another thought as they enjoyed their treat. Certainly no one in the crowd who witnessed the elf-man's outburst took any further notice of him, nor did any of the patrons at the popular churro stand — that is until he lay crumpled on the ground with his bright green and gold costume darkening from the blood that pooled around him on the sidewalk.

The elf-man's mouth worked helplessly. He tried to speak but the death closing around him had already taken his voice.

His elf-wife dropped to the sidewalk next to him.

"Walter!" she screamed.

She was aghast but not hysterical. She turned him on to his side and touched the wound where his blood oozed near the small of his back. She covered one of her hands with the other and pressed hard in a practiced way, but she couldn't staunch the bleeding.

"Help me, please," she commanded the surrounding crowd with surprising authority, "someone call 9-1-1."

Cell phones appeared from the most incongruous places: from the paw of an oversized Dalmatian dog, from under the fronds of a light-covered strolling Christmas tree, from the unseen pocket in the folds of the Statue of Liberty's gown. The phones chirped out in harmony as all dialed the same three digits.

A man dressed in green hospital scrubs came forward and announced he was a doctor. The irony of his profession matching his costume was lost on most in the crowd.

He dropped to one knee and felt the elf-man's neck at the carotid artery. He looked closely at the elf-man's open and unblinking eyes. The doctor spoke barely above a whisper but the surrounding crowd had fallen silent … they heard his words.

"He's gone."

The elf-wife wailed, "Death stabbed my husband!"

One by one the surrounding bystanders began to squeal as the growing pool of blood around the elf-man reached their toes. What they were witnessing was real, not a Halloween show, not performance art done well.

The mass of people, who had been slowly pressing closer for a better look, moved back a step in unison, seemingly of one body and mind. A black-draped grim reaper backed away, too.

The elf-woman's eyes searched the crowd until she saw the threat. She pointed an accusing finger at the dark-clad figure. "Death killed my husband!"

Death no longer seemed towering and reed-thin. He seemed diminished in stature, but fuller, as if in the act of claiming his quarry, he had sunk into the earth with the weight of his victim's mortality.

Death did not like being the center of attention; he did not like the accusing finger of the elf-wife pointing at him. He turned and pushed through the growing throng.

The troubled witnesses stepped aside willingly, glad to see him go. Some might have thought they should stop him —

but no one dared lay hands on him or interrupt his leaving, not after what they had just seen.

Within a heartbeat, no one was looking after Death any longer or wondering if his black gloves camouflaged fresh red blood. They were silent in the presence of the newly dead, and looking only at Death's newest acquisition.

Dr. Walter Henshaw's memorial service, held two weeks after his death, was minutes from beginning when Regan slid into the wooden pew two rows behind his bereaved widow.

Considering she had met Dr. Henshaw and his wife only briefly at their crowded Fourth of July party, the pew she selected seemed embarrassingly near the front of the chapel, but it was the only pew left with an empty aisle seat.

Regan was a real estate agent. She knew how challenging parking would be in the tiny exclusive neighborhood of Depot Hill where the service was being held. They should have left their home in Bonny Doon ten minutes earlier, but her husband, Tom, had changed his mind and his clothing a couple of times before finally realizing they were at risk of being late.

Tom slipped into the pew next to Regan, angling himself to test where his long legs could protrude into the aisle in case the memorial service ran long and he needed to stretch. After some discrete investigation, he put his feet under the pew, sat upright and faced forward to keep out of the way of other last-minute arrivals.

Two grey-haired women sat in front of them, in the pew directly behind the widow. Regan guessed the older woman was past seventy. The younger woman, clearly the more vigorous of the two, leaned against her so their shoulders touched. It was obvious the younger woman was whispering intensely to the older woman — her sassy pixie-style hairdo bobbed as she spoke — but her words were delivered so quietly, Regan couldn't hear them.

She squeezed Tom's knee as she whispered in his ear with a voice as soft as the woman's in front of her, "I know it's a somber occasion, so this probably isn't the time to say it, but I'm glad you decided on your dark suit. It makes you look decidedly hot."

"Hot?"

Tom's eyebrows went up dramatically and he gave her a wickedly crooked half smile as he turned his head toward her, his intensely blue eyes twinkling. He kept his voice as low as hers had been, "Mrs. McHenry, are you flirting with your husband at a funeral?"

"Flirting?" She leaned toward him and brushed his ear with her lips. "At least."

"Could you sling it over a bit?" The questioner began wiggling herself onto the pew next to Tom before he had time to respond. She flashed him an impressive large-toothed smile made even more arresting by the slight buck of her front teeth. "I'm five-feet-thirteen inches tall," she elbowed Tom to emphasis her joke, "and have such long legs, I like an aisle seat," she burbled.

Regan and Tom slid over hastily but not quickly enough to keep the large rigid brim of the new arrival's hat from raking

11

Tom's ear.

"Sorry," she said with her smile unwavering.

She gave her hat a sharp pat on the crown to return it to its proper position and announced, "I'm Olive. Who are you two and how did you know the dead guy?"

Her question was delivered with enthusiasm; unlike Tom and Regan and others in the chapel, she didn't make an attempt to modulate her voice.

The younger woman in the pew in front of them spun in her seat. "Olive, show a little respect! Keep it down, will you?" her forceful whisper came out as a hiss.

Olive waved a dismissive hand at her.

"Oh, Tika, Walter won't care if I don't sound mournful," she turned to Tom and Regan making them co-conspirators, "now will he? So?" She beamed at Tom, ignoring the woman's interruption and ready for his answer.

"I ... we," Tom cleared his throat and continued in something louder than a whisper, "we played golf together and my wife and I," Tom nodded toward Regan by way of an introduction, "well, mostly me, are Walter and Susan's realtors."

Regan reached across Tom and offered her hand to Olive, "Regan McHenry and Tom Kiley."

"Oh, good," Olive's voice rang out, "the real estate brokers! I want you to talk to Susan as soon as Walter gets planted. She's going to need to sell her house once the estate is settled, so she can move in with me as part of my marvelous co-op in Woods Cove.

"I've purchased a terrific house there with five bedrooms en-suite. Being realtors, I'm sure you know how difficult it is to find a house in this community with so many bedrooms, each with its own private bathroom, so five widows can share it and look out for one another in our golden years. We'll be just like that old TV show, *The Golden Girls*. I'll be in charge like Maude was."

Both women in front of them turned as best they could to face Olive. Tika frowned disapprovingly, her eyes, the color of coal, glowered over her sharp high cheekbones, but it was the older woman who confronted Olive this time.

"Olive, you are obsessed with your commune, your grim league of widows. This isn't the time or place for such matters. Give it up, at least for now, and please be quiet."

"Helen, you should be embracing my co-op. Your Henry can't last much longer. I don't know why you even try with him; he doesn't even recognize you half the time. You should be putting him away somewhere and selling your house, too, before the stress of taking care of him destroys your health."

Helen's reaction was a soft gasp, close to a sob; she was wounded by Olive's words. "Oh, Olive, how can you say such cruel things? You have been such a good friend. You've helped me take care of Henry so many times, more than any of the others in our walking group.

"You may try to make it seem like it's just your nursing background that makes you so good with him, but I know better … you are a truly caring person and Henry feels that."

"Pssha," Olive pulled in the corner of her mouth and rolled her eyes. "Henry 'responds' to me," she made little quotation marks with her index fingers, "because I know how to work with him better than most, that's all. I can still get him to do what I tell him to do, but he has no idea who I am or if I care about him or anyone else."

Tika issued a dagger-sharp stare at Olive. "You, of all people," she imitated the disdain in Olive's voice, "shouldn't be telling Helen what to do about Henry."

"It's all right, Tika. I know she doesn't really mean what she says." Helen's voice broke and she had to quickly search her purse for a hanky so she could catch an escaping tear.

Tika put her arm around Helen's shoulders. "Don't listen to anything she says, my dear friend." She lowered her voice but still spoke loudly enough that she was certain Olive would hear what she said, "She can be such a bitter old thing."

"I don't have a bitter bone in my body. I'm just a realist," Olive muttered. "Granted, I was the first to be widowed, but we're all getting older, and mark my words, it's not just me and now Susan who are widows. We'll all outlive our husbands. It's just a matter of time." Olive crossed her arms over her boyish breasts to add finality to her pronouncement.

Regan peered at her around Tom and reflexively put her arm through his to pull him away from any accidental contact with Olive.

🏠 🏠 🏠 🏠 🏠 🏠 🏠 🏠 🏠 🏠 🏠

"Well, that's over at last." Olive's perpetual smile took on an added boldness as the memorial service concluded. "At least it wasn't one of those new style services where everyone has to get up and say something charming about the dead person.

"My husband had the decency to die before that sort of

thing became fashionable. He was a fine man, too, and had accomplished more in his life than most, so it wouldn't have been difficult to find interesting things to say about him, but now *everyone* seems to think each little detail of their generally uninspiring time here deserves to be publically flaunted and fawned over ... waste of everyone's time, don't you agree?"

Regan displayed a polite but noncommittal smile. Tom searched for the right words to remind Olive that his golfing friend was an accomplished man as well, a cardiac surgeon who had saved lives with his skill and was highly respected in the community.

Neither of them needed to bother. Olive moved on swiftly.

"Nice meeting you, Regan and Tom, wasn't it?" she asked as the assemblage began to leave the chapel. "I'll be seeing you again ... I'll be bringing Susan by ... moral support ... that sort of thing," she announced crisply, "sooner rather than later if Walter had their affairs in order. One can only hope."

She turned and marched down the center aisle without another word to Tika or Helen.

Olive's broad hat brim, held high because she was taller than many of the mourners, was still low enough to menace some of the people crowding into the center aisle as she recognized acquaintances and turned and swayed to greet them.

Tika hoisted Helen out of her seat and propelled her into the aisle so quickly that the women passed Regan and Tom's pew before they could leave. Tika aimed a comment in their direction when they passed Tom. "Crazy old bat," she derided as her eyes followed Olive's careening progress toward the back of the chapel.

Regan smiled at Tika in amused agreement.

Tom followed Olive with his eyes until she was almost out the chapel door before his glance moved to a man slouching near the doorway, out of the way of people leaving the memorial service.

He was making no attempt to exit; instead he seemed intent on studying each person as they left.

Tom frowned and asked Regan, "Is that Dave ... at the back ... to the left of the door?"

The chapel doors were wide open to a dazzling November afternoon and the bright light streaming through made her blink a couple of times before she could clearly see the figure Tom was indicating.

"It is. Did he know Walter?"

"I'm pretty sure he didn't."

"What do you think he's doing here?"

"From the looks of him, from the way he's surveying people, I'd guess he's working," Tom speculated.

Regan and Tom sidestepped toward Dave as they reached the chapel door. He flipped his hand up at the wrist in acknowledgement; but Tom was right, Dave was working and not ready to chat with his friends.

They slipped behind him and waited silently while he continued to survey people leaving the chapel.

As soon as the last group had left, Dave turned to Regan. "I didn't expect to see you here ... sure, this was a murder but there's no corpse for you to find, and given your history, I thought ... oh, maybe I'm missing something. Did you already come across the body? Tom, was Regan on Pacific

Avenue on Halloween night?" he chuckled.

"Nope. She was home passing out goodies to little trick-or-treaters. I can vouch for her whereabouts all night."

"What I want to know is why you're here, Dave," Regan quizzed.

"I've told you at least once before that sometimes police like to have a look-see at a murder victim's funeral. You'd be amazed how many times killers take a little victory lap to admire the effects of their handiwork. You getting forgetful, Regan?"

"I do remember you mentioning that ..."

"Yeah. Well we decided who better to scope out this event than a one-eyed public relations meet-the-press-guy like me. We figured I'd have laser focus with my good eye, be able to make nice with the mourners if they wanted to know what we police are doing to find good old Doc Henshaw's killer, and even be ready to field questions if the press turned up.

"See?" He pulled a colorful collar up from under his jacket lapel. "I wore a nice conservative dark jacket over my Hawaiian shirt so I wouldn't stand out at the service, but I can lose the jacket before any cameras get rolling so my fans will know it's me."

The prosthetic eye Dave had worn since he lost his in a years-ago police shootout matched and moved perfectly with his functioning eye. The only thing it didn't do, Regan noted, was twinkle with mischief the way his real eye did whenever he teased her or reminded her that as Santa Cruz Police Ombudsman — the job he'd created for himself after his forced retirement from active duty — he got to wear trademark clothing and be a regular TV interviewee.

17

"Did you notice anyone suspicious here today?" Tom asked.

"Nah. It's been a pretty disappointing show. I was hoping someone would be acting a little off, you know, there'd be somebody who didn't seem to know anyone else here standing by himself, or someone would look extra fidgety or smug ... those are obvious things to look out for ... or that maybe the killer would be here overacting how grief-stricken he was."

Dave seemed ready to say more but his narrative was cut off by the widow leaving the chapel.

Regan had observed her seated in the middle of the front pew during the service. A young woman and a man barely old enough to be labeled a man, the dead man's grown children she guessed, sat to the widow's right. There had been enough space between the widow and her stepchildren that the deceased could have fit between them. A couple, who seemed to be there for her support, sat to her left.

The stepchildren, looking a bit stunned but dry-eyed, had held one another's hand and fled the moment the service was over; in fact they led the procession out of the chapel.

But the widow had remained seated until the chapel had completely emptied. Now, she slowly made her way outside, supported physically as well as emotionally by the couple who had remained with her.

Except for the bright white handkerchief she crushed in her hand, she was dressed completely in black. Even with her high heeled boots that added inches to her stature, she still looked like a tiny figure, seemingly overwhelmed in equal parts by her loss and by the head-to-toe hue of her widow's garb.

She clutched the arms of the woman on her right and the man on her left. Her face was barely visible under the dark veil of her hat.

Regan thought of Jacqueline Kennedy as the widow approached. She had seen photos of Jackie following JFK's funeral cortege; Jackie had worn a similar hat with a dark veil. Jackie Kennedy, who, like this widow, had watched her husband die a sudden and violent death, carried herself with dignity and composure. At the time, news correspondents said she had to; if Jackie had collapsed under her grief, the nation would have followed. But no one watched Walter Henshaw's widow; she had no need to be strong for the sake of watching eyes and she freely expressed her grief.

As the trio passed by, Regan was able to make out the widow's words.

"Linda, my dearest friend," she said to the woman, "and Mike, dearest," she turned toward the man on her left, "however would I have made it through today without you both?"

"Poor woman," Tom whispered as the widow left the chapel.

Dave's only comment was a protracted sigh.

"You got a few minutes Monday afternoon, Tom? You're not a high priority but your name is on the list of people we'd like to talk to about the deceased. I took it off the master list and put it on mine."

Regan smiled to herself. Dave, though his job title suggested he should be completely removed from murder investigations, had once again managed to put himself in the middle of one.

"Oh, and Regan," Dave flashed a broad teasing grin, "you don't have to be there; I'm seeing this as just Tom and me — a guys only little get-together, OK?"

"Of course," she replied sincerely.

She had no friends or clients connected to this crime, thank goodness, and except for the fact that Tom had been a golfing regular with the victim, neither she nor her husband had any particular stake in solving it. There was absolutely no reason for her to get involved with a murder — not this time.

"You two have your little talk. I'll be busy doing something else while you do."

3

A few minutes before 11:00 the following Monday morning, Tom came by Regan's office carrying his laptop and poked his head through her open doorway.

"I've got a couple of visitors in the conference room. I think you'll want to join us."

"Who are they?"

"The recently widowed Mrs. Susan Henshaw and her dear friend and apparently constant companion, Olive, whatever her name is … the woman from the funeral, the one with the toothy smile and the hat."

Regan pressed save on her computer and closed the folder she had open on her desk.

"Sounds too interesting to miss."

She followed Tom down the central corridor to a glass enclosed conference room.

Amanda, their receptionist, had seated the women in the listing conference room, the one with the round table. The table's shape was meant to convey camaraderie and a sense that everyone was on the same team and subtly suggest that the kind of creative collaboration necessary to sell the client's property had already begun.

The women sat next to one another in the two seats farthest from the door. Olive, wearing the same effervescent smile she sported at the funeral, spotted them through the conference room glass and gave a cheery wave.

Susan Henshaw saw them, too, but she didn't move. Regan would never have used effervescent to describe her. Although the widow was not the distraught creature she had been at her husband's memorial service, her face told tales of missed sleep and held no enthusiasm for the meeting that was about to take place.

Olive jumped into the conversation as soon as Regan and Tom sat down and said hello, even before Susan had a chance to answer Tom when he asked how she was.

"Walter was a reliable man when it came to arranging his estate. Isn't that marvelous? Everything may be settled within a couple of months, maybe sooner. Isn't that grand? Susan won't be able to sell the house until then but she can put it up for sale right now, can't she? It usually does take a bit of time for a house to sell, doesn't it?"

Olive fired questions enthusiastically; Susan sat silently as if she were muted by the force of nature seated next to her.

Tom answered Olive's questions methodically and suggested that Susan should have inspections done and any needed repairs made immediately. "That way," he said, "when I advertise that the house is in turnkey condition and ready for a discriminating buyer, I'll be stating fact."

"Oh, Susan, doesn't that all sound just so sensible?" Olive gushed.

Susan nodded wordlessly; her attempt at a smile came out as a mere twitch at the corner of her mouth.

"Susan, how many times do you think you offered me a beer," Tom reminisced, "while Walter and I rehashed our games after we played the Rio del Mar course?"

Susan didn't answer; she blinked back tears.

"I've seen your house, inside and out, so many times over the years that I already had enough information to select comparable properties."

Tom turned his laptop toward the women to display the first property on his list.

"The location, ocean front in a gated community like your house on Via Gaviota, Susan, is so singular ..."

Regan watched the new widow as Tom continued his presentation. She seemed present in body only.

"Excuse me for interrupting, but Susan, selling a house, even when you're looking forward to the move, is a stressful thing to do. You've just lost your husband ... wouldn't you like to stay where you are for a short time, stay where everything feels comfortable and familiar, and ... and not rush into any other lifestyle changes just yet?" Regan looked intently at Olive as she mentioned lifestyle changes.

"We're coming up on the holidays and gray, winter weather, not the best time of year to be selling a beach house. Why don't you give yourself a few months and list your house in the spring?"

Susan glanced at Regan but avoided making real eye contact with her. "Won't it take a while for my home to sell? I mean it's not like I'll have to leave my home in a couple of months, is it, even if I sign the papers to sell it today?"

Tom had been referring to Susan and Walter's property as "the house" or "your property" as he discussed comparables. To Susan, her house was still "my home." Regan heard a woman who wasn't ready to move on, no matter how hard Olive pushed her.

Tom answered Susan's question. "That's true most of the time, but there's always a chance someone is out there who's been waiting for a house like yours to come on the market ... someone who might make an immediate offer. Our goal will be to get your house sold as quickly as possible and we'll be marketing it aggressively even at this time of the year."

Regan posed another question about Susan's future. "Susan, what would you do if your house did sell quickly?"

"Well, I guess ... I guess ..."

"That's easy," Olive burst in, "she'd move in with me sooner than we expected. Susan plans to live with me in Woods Cove. She'll be the second member of our co-op, my second in command, as it were," Olive crowed.

Regan tapped her lips as Olive continued to exuberantly describe her plans for what she called her widow's league, the same plans she outlined at the funeral.

Regan rolled her eyes in the direction of the door. Her motions were a restrained signal; she hoped Tom understood.

"Olive, I've heard you can hike into Woods Cove from Henry Cowell Park. Is that right?" Tom asked.

"It certainly is. I discovered my house when the group was out walking one day and we did just that."

"I've never figured out how the trails work." Tom was all curiosity and warmth. "I have maps in my office; may I show them to you? Would you be willing to point out the entrance trails to me while Susan fills in the disclosure forms with Regan?"

He smiled grandly at Olive and then said in a soft stage whispery voice, "That part's so boring but it has to be done."

He leaned toward Olive, who was seated on his right, and continued in an intimately friendly tone of voice, "Maybe we'll be able to figure where in Woods Cove your house is if we look carefully at my maps. Perhaps I've seen it. I saw several of the houses when they were being built."

House-proud that she was, Olive was on her feet before Tom could get up to pull back her chair.

He motioned toward the door with a sweeping gesture.

Olive grabbed his arm as she passed him and pressed both of them out of the conference room so quickly, Tom was only able to manage the quickest of winks at his smiling wife before he was whisked away.

When she turned her attention back to Susan, Regan was surprised to see she was smiling, too.

"I wish I took as much delight in life as Olive does."

"It's a difficult time for you right now," Regan soothed. "Give yourself some time, things will get better. In the meantime, don't let Olive push you into anything."

"Oh no, really, it's all right. She's not pushing me. I do want to sell the house … I need to sell the house. Walter has two grown children from his first marriage. His divorce was messy to say the least. His ex did her best to poison his children's minds against him. She largely succeeded and he was estranged from them for years. Recently though, they were … well … the three of them were trying to reinstitute some family ties.

"Walter would have wanted ... I know he would have wanted them to have some sort of immediate legacy ... at least enough to pay for college and get established. I want to be able to do that for them. Selling the house will let me help them."

"I'm sure you're right. If Walter were here, I know he'd tell you how pleased he was to hear about your generosity toward his children."

Color flushed Susan's cheeks for the first time during their meeting. "So, you see, Olive isn't pushing me. I'm just letting her be in charge, or at least think she is. Her heart is in the right place and I don't have the energy to take care of details right now, and she's only too eager to take care of everything," Susan offered an almost imperceptible smile.

"Why just a couple of days ago she was so wonderful. The car insurance was due just about the time Walter ..." she didn't finish the sentence. "Well, it turns out I didn't pay the bill. It lapsed and so did the roadside assistance coverage.

"I was determined to get some exercise, I thought it would help me sleep better, and it was such a beautiful November day, cold but brisk and clear. The walking group Olive and I belong to was going to do an easy walk along West Cliff Drive from Lighthouse Field to Natural Bridges and back. I was determined to go, but when I tried to turn on the ignition, my car refused to start.

"I just broke down and started to cry. You understand ... it was like no more, please ... not right now."

Regan nodded sympathetically.

"I called Olive to let her know the group shouldn't wait for me, and do you know what she did? She drove all the way

26

to Aptos, to my house, to pick me up. Then after our group walk, she bought me lunch.

"When she took me home, she even figured out what was wrong with my car. It turns out it was a fuel pump fuse, an easy fix. I guess it had worked its way loose somehow. My car started right up after Olive reseated the fuse.

"If she hadn't helped me, if she didn't know about engines," Susan shook her head. "She tried to say it was no big deal, that she learned all about how vehicles work when she was a nurse in Vietnam — killing time between crises, I guess — but if it weren't for her, I would have had to have my car towed and deal with mechanics. I sometimes wonder if they treat women fairly; I wouldn't have known if they were telling me the truth. At this time in my life, I wouldn't have been able to cope.

"So you see, Olive isn't forcing me to do anything. She's just looking out for me."

Nancy Lynn Jarvis

Regan made Tom promise he'd tell her what Dave had to say about Walter Henshaw's murder. Once she had his word, she truly put Tom and Dave's meeting out of her mind.

She was, therefore, quite surprised to find herself engaged in a pantomime with Dave late that afternoon.

She was coming out of an associate's office when Dave caught her eye, rolled his, shrugged lackadaisically, crooked his finger to beckon her, and then pointed into Tom's office.

She shook her head to indicate a firm no. She pointed to the papers she held in her hand, and silently mouthed the word "busy."

"Ah, come on, Regan," Dave finally ended their silent communication, "you know you want to."

Before she could muster a challenge, he shrugged again, this time in defeat. "As it turns out, I've thought of a question or two I want to ask you, too."

"If you really need me," her voice was honey-toned, "I'll make time to join you."

Tom was the designated broker of Kiley and Associates, the small real estate company they co-owned. His added responsibilities got him the building's biggest office and a sofa. His sofa was Regan's favorite place to sit; she made a beeline for it, still smiling with satisfaction at being invited to participate in Dave's investigation.

She kicked off her shoes, curled up with her long legs under her, and rested an elbow on the sofa's arm.

"Isn't she a picture, Tom?" Dave chuckled as he sprawled into one of Tom's slouchy client chairs and turned it from facing Tom's desk to halfway toward Regan.

"I tell her I have a question for her, and she's here in a flash, all settled and comfy and ready to listen in. I hope you're not going to be disappointed; I'm here today to collect information, not to tell you all about the case."

"That's exactly what I'd expect you to say."

Regan's grin was mischievous; she wondered if he realized her statement could be taken in more than one way.

"In murder cases, we like to talk to people who knew the Vic. Sometimes people know things without even knowing they know. It's routine."

"What do you think I might know without realizing it?" Tom asked.

"Finding that out is where real professional police work starts."

Dave's voice held a great deal of pride; his pointed look toward Regan spoke volumes: in his mind, the fact that she had been instrumental in solving past murders didn't change her amateur status.

"For openers, did your pal seem different recently? Did he seem worried about anything, you know, his finances, his marriage, his practice?"

Tom considered momentarily and then shook his head. "No. He didn't mention anything out of the ordinary. In fact, he was pretty positive about his finances and his practice recently. He had lost some money in the stock market after 2008 like everyone else did, but he was bragging that he had fully recovered. He had more patients than he could handle. He said he was considering bringing in a partner, maybe backing off his busy schedule a little."

Dave nodded repeatedly while he arranged his mouth into an upside down smile. "And his marriage?"

"It seemed solid. Walter could be a pain-in-the-neck occasionally — he did have an ego commensurate with being a cardiac surgeon — but I think things were good between Susan and him ... better recently, in fact."

"Are you saying there was a time when things weren't great between them?"

Dave and Regan both leaned forward ever so slightly, their body language betraying their interest.

"No. I'd say not great is an overstatement. Susan was a cardiac nurse — a good one, I hear — that's how she and Walter met, but recently he'd pressed her to give up her career.

"He didn't like her in his operating room — he said it was distracting to have her there — but he was possessive in an odd way and didn't want her working with other cardiologists in their operating rooms either.

"There was some tension between them about that because Susan liked nursing, but it didn't seem to be a big deal. Susan finally acquiesced. She stopped working earlier this year, so her career wasn't a cause for friction anymore."

"What did the little lady do to fill her spare time when she stopped nursing? Any hints about a special friend, stuff like that?" Dave asked.

"Susan? No way. She started doing volunteer work, something at the hospital, I think."

Tom's brow puckered. "The police don't think Susan had anything to do with Walter's death, do they?"

"We don't have anything specific that makes us think the widow was involved. The spouse always gets a real close look-see. It's standard police procedure because a pretty high percentage of the time, it is the spouse who did the deed."

"Dave, the story is that Susan Henshaw said a man dressed like Death killed her husband. I understand several people witnessed the murder and reported that a darkly costumed man ran away when she started screaming. Isn't that what happened?"

"That's the media version, all right."

"But not the right version?"

Regan couldn't be quiet any longer. "Don't be shy, Dave. What do the police think happened? You can tell us."

Dave squirmed. "I'm trying to tone down my detail sharing, especially with you, Regan, since you have a history of meddling ..."

"I don't meddle." Regan stiffened her back and sounded indignant.

"You just turn up in the midst of things, is that it ... just accidentally find bodies, start poking around, and get people worked up enough they try to kill you?"

"I have no reason to get involved here, Dave. I hardly know the Henshaws; besides I'm sure you'll figure it out. The

31

police must have a lot to work with, since so many people witnessed the murder. Isn't that what you said when that local TV personality cornered you after the memorial service and you got to show off your Hawaiian shirt?"

Dave's foot started tapping but he didn't seem to be aware of it. "I think that's what I implied."

"Dave, you didn't mislead the media did you?" she teased.

He tugged at his chin and raised his eyebrows. "We've really got nothing to go on except the note Susan Henshaw kept," he said finally.

"We wouldn't even have that if she wasn't such a compulsive anti-litterer. When her husband gave her the note, rather than wadding it up and dropping it on the street, she put it in her pocket, saving it until she could find a garbage can, so she still had it after her husband's murder."

"That's right," Regan breathed, enthralled as she recalled the details printed in the *Santa Cruz Sentinel*. "The newspaper said Walter Henshaw had been warned about his impending death. That's what made his murder so creepy."

"Yeah," Dave clasped his hands and leaned toward Regan with his forearms on his thighs, anxious to relay the best spine-tingling details he knew. "This death guy was handing out notes to lots of people on Pacific Avenue on Halloween. Several people remember seeing him; some even remember getting a note from him and remember what it said.

"A couple of people came forward who still had theirs. One guy said he kept his note because he thought it was cool that the death guy put real effort into his performance."

"What do you mean? What did he say about the man's performance?" Regan tried to hold her level of interest in check to sound only mildly curious.

"The notes were printed, not written by hand, but the typeface he used looks like handwriting, like Death had written out the dates personally, and he said the guy's grim reaper costume was better than most. He said it made the death guy look tall and thin, like a dressed skeleton.

"Most people threw the notes away after they read them, but what they remember is that the notes had a date: a day, month, and year on them, always in the future."

"Ooh," Regan whistled, "that is creepy."

"Yeah, it is. But the note the Vic's wife kept was even creepier. It had a time on it, too. It read October 31, this year, and then 9:58 p.m. As near as anyone can remember, that's real close to the time Walter Henshaw was murdered.

"Like the media reported, when the Vic's wife started screaming and pointing at the death guy, he took off running. A couple of cops arrived at the scene right after that and gave chase. They collared more than one Death look-alike — it turns out there were a number of guys dressed like Death on Pacific Avenue that night. The police rounded up all of them they could find, but we think the killer got away."

Unlike his wife, Tom wasn't fascinated by macabre details. He only wanted facts and a straightforward understanding of why the murderer hadn't been caught. "Why do the police think that? Why don't they think one of the costumed people they rounded up was the murderer?"

"The way Henshaw was killed was bloody. There's no way the killer could have done it without getting blood on his hands, maybe not without getting blood all over himself. None of the death guys we rounded up and questioned had

33

any blood on them."

"Couldn't the murderer have thrown away his gloves and replaced them with new ones? If I were the murderer, I might have thrown away my whole costume and had something else on underneath," Regan offered.

"There she goes, Tom. I worry about her on so many levels. It's not enough she gets involved in murder, she's got a criminal mind, too." Dave taunted, "Nope. It doesn't look like your death guy planned ahead like you would have, Regan.

"We did a careful search of all the places near downtown where someone could have disposed of a costume or even just gloves. Lots of cops got lots of overtime lookin' in garbage cans and dumpsters, checking tossed out boxes behind stores, and just picking up trash in general.

"We even brought in a tracker dog and had him search for the scent of the Vic's blood. Nothing. That's why we figure the death guy got away."

Tom listened pensively. He was as engrossed by what he was hearing as Regan was, but less titillated by the facts Dave was relaying than Dave or Regan seemed to be.

"We think the killer took his costume with him. It's probably been destroyed by now, unless the Perp wanted to keep it as a gruesome souvenir."

"Did the police search for a knife as well," Tom queried.

"Oh, yeah. We didn't find a murder weapon, either, so the Perp probably took it with him, too. FYI the coroner says the weapon may have been a scalpel; the wound was a nice, tidy one like a scalpel might make."

"Does that mean whoever killed Walter Henshaw was a

surgeon or worked in an operating room?" Tom was quick to ask. "Is that why you were questioning me about Susan Henshaw?"

Dave shook his head, "Scalpels aren't hard to come by. You can buy them in college bookstores; students use them for dissection. That could make anyone attending UCSC a potential suspect. By that standard, maybe even kids attending Cabrillo College could be killers.

"Henshaw died because he bled out quickly after he was cut. The thing is lots of people think a kidney stab is a way to kill someone fast, maybe even before they can yell for help, but it's not true. People watch too many old prison movies where a guy gets shived in the back and dies right away. It doesn't work like that. A kidney stab is instantly incapacitating, but if that's what happened to your pal Henshaw, he probably would have survived."

"What caused him to die so quickly then?" Regan queried.

"What got him was a completely severed renal artery. That kind of wound will do you in real fast. It might be possible that the killer got in a lucky stab, but the coroner says it's unlikely. A cut like that probably takes some pretty specialized medical training, more and different from what a cardiac nurse would have."

Dave's attempt to use his good eye to produce a wink didn't work terribly well. His prosthetic eye partially mimicked his good eye's closing, so his knowing wink became a knowing squint. "We may not be looking for Mr. Death here; we may be looking for Dr. Death."

"I'm confused," Regan said. "Does that mean Susan Henshaw isn't a suspect after all?"

Dave raised his hands heavenward and shook them dramatically. "Again she jumps to the wrong conclusion," he said with mock exasperation.

"What we think is even though Susan Henshaw was close enough to her husband to have stabbed him, if she was involved in her husband's death, she got someone else, someone like the missing death guy, to do the actual killing.

"That's why I wanted to know if there was anyone else in little Susie's life. If she did want to bump off her hubby but wasn't the type to have a special friend, like some Doc she met at work, then maybe she hired a pro. We'll be having a close look at her recent finances before we decide anything about her for sure."

Regan sat in silence while Dave asked Tom several more questions about Walter Henshaw, only offering her comments when directly asked.

When Tom told him that Susan Henshaw had come in earlier to list her house, Dave snapped to attention, sitting upright in Tom's slouchy office chair.

"What's the Henshaw house worth?"

Tom told him the listed price. Dave's reaction was a protracted, "Whew! That much! Yeah, we'll be looking at the widow's finances all right. That kind of money could be a murder motive for lots of people."

Regan felt the need to explain Susan's actions, "She's giving some of it away, Dave. It wasn't in his will, evidently, but she told me her husband would have wanted his children from his first marriage to have some of the proceeds."

His comment was acerbic, "Ahh, isn't that sweet?"

Regan didn't respond to Dave's poke. That was unusual

for her, but her thoughts were elsewhere and she hardly even heard what he said. The beginning of an idea was forming in her mind.

Suppose Susan's marriage was as good as Tom thought it was. Suppose Susan wasn't involved in her husband's murder at all. But suppose someone close to her was, someone with a medical background ... someone who wanted to start collecting widows.

"Dave, the police aren't only considering Susan Henshaw for her husband's murder, are they?"

"No, the investigation is very preliminary at this point. Like I said, the spouse always gets a look-see but she may not have been involved at all. The killer could have been a whack-o and Henshaw a random victim. Or the killer could have been someone with a grudge against Henshaw, someone like, oh, say, a relative of a patient who had a bad outcome under the Doc's knife, for example.

"Having Henshaw die at a prescribed time and by a knife, well, it might be a message ... kinda' like 'my dad went under your knife at 7:00 am and didn't survive, and you're not going to survive my 9:58 knife,' that sort of thing."

Regan nodded abstractedly, not looking at Dave as she did.

"OK, where is your mind off to?" Dave sighed as he asked.

"Nowhere ... I was just thinking," she frowned.

"I know I'm gonna regret this, but why don't you think out loud?"

"We sat with a woman at the memorial service. She's ... um ... I can't quite put my finger on what it is about her. She came in with Susan Henshaw today. She seems pleasant enough, although strong willed and outspoken ..."

"So other than the fact she sounds kinda' like you, what's suspicious about her," Dave teased.

"Nothing specific really," Regan conceded. "Let's just say she struck me as a woman with a goal, a mission, who seems able to control Susan Henshaw. And she has a house she wants to fill with widows ..."

"Sheesh, Regan, even for you. The way your mind works!"

He rolled his eyes — the long-suffering skeptic — but his next words belied his grudging respect for her people-reading skills. "OK, just to keep you from racing off on one of your wild imaginings, do you know her name? I'll put her on my list and take a little look at her."

Tom marketed the heck out of his new listing. He developed an online presence for the property, had slick brochures produced, and advertised the Henshaw house heavily in a number of print venues.

His efforts produced a nibble just before the first of the year that went nowhere and one in early February that looked promising until the potential buyer's company became embroiled in a securities scandal and he no longer was focused on buying a house.

Tom kept Susan Henshaw apprised of his latest efforts. She was appreciative and patient, frequently repeating that she was more than satisfied with his efforts and realized that the process, especially in the current market and in her price range, might take time. Besides, she said, she was in no hurry to sell.

It was Olive who expected — badgered — for quick results. She became a regular drop-in at their office. Tom was always polite but discrete; it was inappropriate for him to discuss Susan's business with her.

Regan watched Olive through the conference room glass

when she met with Tom. What she saw made her uncomfortable. Olive smiled at Tom with affection as he spoke, but she seemed to always be taking his measure. She reminded Regan of the wicked witch poking Hansel and Gretel to see if they were fat enough for her to eat.

After the third time Olive stopped by, Regan, hoping to end her visits, took a turn explaining privacy issues to her in harsh terms. Once she set a course, though, Olive wasn't easily sidetracked. She didn't give up. She merely tried a different tack.

Olive took to delivering small presents as an excuse for her drop-bys. They were inconsequential gifts; Olive always called them small tokens of her affection. She presented them beaming with childlike innocence, but with conspicuous ulterior motive. It was as if she expected little gifts might cause Tom to work harder on Susan's behalf, or at least might unseal Regan's or Tom's lips about any progress being made on the sale. And offering gifts gave Olive a chance to see Tom, to look at him with hungry eyes.

The gifts began in early January with the delivery of a homemade fruitcake. It was festively wrapped in red paper printed with dancing raccoons and addressed to both of them. Olive said, while fruitcake was usually a holiday gift, she planned the delivery of hers so it wouldn't be considered a Christmas present.

Regan wrote Olive a thank you note: her way of acknowledging the fruitcake as a gift and not a bribe. In it, Regan confessed that, while they both enjoyed the treat, she had eaten most of it because she was one of the few people in the world who deliberately sought out fruitcake and relished every bite.

Olive's next gifts, delivered in mid February, were distinct and separately directed. Tom, a man whose office walls displayed not his professional awards and credentials, but photos of bygone era train engines, was given a train whistle from one of the gift stores at Roaring Camp, the Felton tourist attraction that offered rides on genuine steam trains.

Regan was given a delicate silver pin made from the skeletonized remains of a leaf that Olive found in the gift shop at Henry Cowell State Park.

Olive watched with delight as they opened their presents and announced she wouldn't leave until Tom tooted his whistle and Regan pinned the leaf on her jacket.

After they complied, Olive explained she thought of them when she went for a hike from her house in Woods Cove, first through Henry Cowell and then across the train tracks into Roaring Camp, because she had pointed out that very trail to Tom on the day Susan listed her house. Olive continued clumsily, "And speaking of Susan …"

Regan could barely hide her amusement when Olive, in her singularly focused and happily determined way, attempted to segue into a question about Susan's sale progress. But by the time Olive reminded them that she was only following up on Susan's behalf because she was so eager to have Susan join her at her widow's house, Regan was no longer amused.

Olive suggested in her perpetually jovial way that if Tom didn't get Susan's house sold soon, she was going to have to start looking for other widows. The way Olive smiled at her, as if she too was being assessed, and then devouringly at

Tom, made Regan apprehensive.

When Olive followed up with a joking pronouncement that she was growing rather fond of Regan and asked Tom how his health was, he laughed at her implication. He told Olive he was in excellent health and advised her that she shouldn't get her hopes up.

The exchange, lighthearted as it was, made the hair on the back of Regan's neck stand on end.

🏠🏠🏠🏠🏠🏠🏠🏠🏠🏠🏠🏠

Susan Henshaw delivered another of Olive's gifts in the middle of April, the same day she first started seriously pushing to get her house sold.

Their receptionist had left for lunch and one of the agents in the office was taking a turn filling in at the reception desk for her, hoping to capture an unattached buyer calling about one of the office listings. He buzzed Regan in her office to say that a Mrs. Henshaw was at the front desk looking for Tom, but that she was willing to talk to Regan since he was unavailable.

"Could you send her back my way?" Regan asked.

"Will do."

Regan stepped to her doorway to reconnoiter and saw Susan walking slowly in her direction, peering into offices as she passed them. When Susan saw Regan, she smiled and quickly walked down the hall.

"I assume I can talk to you as well as Tom about my house?"

"Of course," Regan said as she ushered Susan into her office, "although I may not be up on the very latest details of your listing since Tom is handling it."

Susan sat down in one of the chairs facing Regan's desk and put her purse and a small parcel wrapped in red paper with dancing raccoons at her feet. She sat upright and exuded determination and decisiveness.

"I want to lower the price on my house. That will make it sell soon, won't it?"

"It might cause a sale but there's no guarantee it will."

Susan looked crestfallen. "I really need to get it sold by June. I know I said there was no rush, but … circumstances have changed. I had no idea how much money Olive was going to need in July."

"Olive?" Regan puzzled. "Olive needs money? I don't understand."

"I hate to gossip," Regan could see Susan's decisiveness falter as she twisted her hands together in her lap, "but Olive … well, she was never a rich woman. Oh, she and her late husband always had decent jobs … and I think she has some sort of a pension as a result … and Social Security, but she has a good heart and has always been very generous with charities and friends. And then there were all the medical bills before her husband died; I don't think she ever rebuilt much in the way of savings after paying them.

"The house she bought in Woods Cove … it was expensive; she put every penny she had into it. Even so, I thought she had a large mortgage. I wondered how she got one, especially a big one, since she's no longer working and is living on a limited income. I asked her how she'd manage;

43

we go way back so it didn't seem like I was overreaching by asking.

"You know how optimistic she is. Olive said she assumed she'd only have to squeak by for a short time before she'd have other women like me buying in and sharing expenses with her. She thought she could fake it, that's the phrase she used, with credit cards for a while if she had to. She told me that's how she paid her property taxes last December and earlier this month.

"I moved a few pieces of furniture into her house, things Tom's home stager said detracted from the look she was going for, and I've been giving Olive some money since December, calling it a storage fee so she wouldn't feel bad about accepting it, but I had no idea she didn't have a normal mortgage.

"It turns out she hadn't qualified for a bank loan and got herself into an installment sale with the house builder. Her second installment is coming due at the end of July. I'd help her but I just don't have enough ready cash to give her what she needs.

"Olive has been making light of her situation. She just flutters her hands, keeps her big smile as broad as ever and says, 'Don't worry; I'll just have to find another widow soon, one with some capital.' She jokes about it, but I know she's worried and she's really in a tight spot. That's why my house has to sell soon."

🏠🏠🏠🏠🏠🏠🏠🏠🏠🏠🏠

Regan stayed in her office and tried to work after Susan

left, but she couldn't concentrate. Susan was gone, but the parcel she brought, another gift from Olive, remained. This present was addressed solely to Tom.

She tried his cell phone and got his answering message rather than him live; he must be with a client rather than at lunch.

She tried his phone every few minutes — obsessive behavior. She reproached herself when she did it, but the small parcel covered with red colored paper and dancing raccoons kept insinuating itself into her mind and creeping into her line of sight, even though she tried to ignore it.

The parcel seemed to have power over her. It was the package, surely, and not her curiosity, that caused her to repeatedly ignore the shame she felt when her finger hit the redial button on her phone.

Regan was once again glowering at the package when a smiling Tom walked into her office.

"So many calls; I feel so loved and desired," he grinned. "What's up?"

She nodded at the package, "Special delivery for you from Olive via Susan Henshaw, who was just here lowering the asking price for her house.

"It seems she now needs a quick sale because Olive is about to go belly up, financially speaking. Susan feels the need to help her hang on to her widow's house."

Regan handed Tom the price reduction document.

"Wow! She really must want the house to move. This is a huge drop."

"She says it's a sale or Olive will need to find a flush widow before the middle of July ... which brings me to the gift for you from Olive. It's addressed to you. I hope it's not a bomb."

Regan's smile was tentative; she half believed it might be.

"Open it, please, and get rid of those raccoons. They're starting to unnerve me."

"What, these cute little things?" he laughed as he picked up Olive's package and gave it a shake. "They're dancing and smiling. They're cheerful and happy, just like Olive."

"That's my point. Raccoons are adorable. People feed them and think of them as clever little dog-like creatures that can use their paws like they were little hands. They're really related to bears. They're smart, strong, and dangerous. Maybe they are just like Olive: all smiles and guileless on the outside, but with something potentially treacherous hidden deep inside."

"You really think Olive is dangerous?" Tom chuckled as he finished opening the package.

"I don't know exactly what I think about her, but what you see is not what you get when it comes to Olive. She's hiding something; I'm sure of that."

There was a card between the wrapping and the plastic container, the disposable kind which, from Regan's angle, appeared to be filled with a muddy-colored substance. His chuckle grew into a full-blown laugh as he opened the card and read the note inside.

"What?" Regan pressed.

"They're morels ... a kind of luxury mushroom. It seems Olive is not only an avid hiker but also a fungus fancier and a member in good standing of the Santa Cruz Fungus Federation. She found these mushrooms on a hike in Sonoma

County and prepared them especially for me.

"She says she knows the difference between Morchellas, which these are, and false morels like Verpa and Hellvella, so I don't need to worry about being poisoned. She says she got all the natural toxins out of them, too."

He raised an eyebrow and grinned at Regan. "I'm not supposed to share them with you, though, since you ate most of the fruitcake.

"When I call Olive to thank her for *my* mushrooms, should I empathize with her financial situation, tell her all our money is tied up in real estate and let her know that even if I died today, you couldn't possibly become a rich widow with liquid assets by July?"

Tom's levity left Regan unsmiling. She was dour and serious. "Tom, there *is* something about Olive that bothers me. I get such a strange vibe from her. I know I'm being silly, but please, humor me. Don't eat the mushrooms."

"What am I going to say if she calls and asks me what I thought of them?"

Regan's brow furrowed. "Tom, please?"

He took a deep breath and exhaled noisily. "I won't eat the mushrooms, not if you don't want me to. But I do think you are being silly. Murderers don't announce their intentions, or leave such an easy to follow trail."

The epicenter of Santa Cruz as a tourist town is the Santa Cruz Beach Boardwalk. Its century-old carousel features a 342-pipe organ built in 1894 and a "new" companion Wurlitzer acquired from San Francisco's Playland-at-the-Beach after it closed in 1972.

Like their predecessors did more than a century ago, carousel riders stretch precariously to grab an iron ring and toss it into a clown's grinning mouth as they pass by, no easy feat given the rider is both whirling and galloping up and down on one of the merry-go-round's brightly painted mounts.

More adventurous riders with a historical bent head for the Giant Dipper. It's a 1924 wooden relic, and like the carousel, a National Historic Landmark. Before it ascends, the roller coaster plunges into darkness and makes a heart stopping left turn that throws its unseeing and unprepared riders sideways as the wooden structure vibrates and creaks. Those who don't know that the entire coaster is walked and repaired daily, scream and worry that they may have made a dangerous choice in riding it.

The Beach Boardwalk is also home to the famous Coconut Grove where Artie Shaw, Benny Goodman, Xavier Cugat, and Lawrence Welk played in the heyday of big bands and where entertaining events are still held today. The San Francisco Giants 2010 World Series Trophy made a stop at the Coconut Grove on its national tour; and a local favorite, the Clam Chowder Cook Off, is held in February in the structure's ocean-facing arcade.

Past the western end of the Boardwalk and separated from it by a stretch of beach, the Santa Cruz Municipal Wharf juts out half a mile into Monterey Bay. The wharf is home to several annual events, too. One of the best is Woodies on the Wharf, which takes place every year on the fourth Saturday in June.

Some locals think the Clam Chowder Cook Off should be held at the same time as Woodies on the Wharf. Steaming bowls of clam chowder, welcome as they are at the ocean in February, would be just as welcome in late June because, on most early mornings during the summer months, the fog at the ocean is so dense that Santa Cruz resembles a pea-souped London.

Even with the cold and thick drizzly fog, Woodies on the Wharf is a vibrant event. More than two hundred '20s to '50s cars cram on to the wharf for the day. All, if not brightly painted, glisten with high polish on their chromed bumpers and their wooden sides.

The most competitive Woodie owners shrug off their Friday night welcome party hangovers to line up at the pier entrance before dawn. When the wharf gates open at 6:00 a.m., they crawl their cars, guttural engines droning, down the structure through the morning mist in the hopes of securing one of the few places known as "power parking" spots. The spaces, located at the ocean end of the wharf where a bump-out that doubles the wharf from two lanes to four lanes ends, are the best places to show off cars.

After all the power parking spaces are taken, drivers go past Stagnaro's to the end of the wharf and compete for one of the eight spaces in the second most desirable location.

Drivers carefully back into their parking spaces, leaving just enough room between their Woodie's rear end and the wharf railing to set up a lawn chair. Owners hold court from their seats, watchful of their cars and the surfboards and other gear they have set up to stage their pride and joy, and spend the day talking with admirers who come out to see the cars, wistfully hoping they may own one someday.

🏠 🏠 🏠 🏠 🏠 🏠 🏠 🏠 🏠 🏠 🏠 🏠

On the drive to Woodies on the Wharf, Tom sang along loudly and slightly off key to his Beach Boys CD. He found a spot to park on the down-slope between the Dream Inn and the wharf, and still singing, parked to strains of *Little Deuce Coupe*.

"Just a little deuce coupe with a flat head mill
But she'll walk a Thunderbird like it's standin' still
She's ported and relieved and she's stroked and bored.
She'll do a hundred and forty with the top end floored."

Regan joined in for the chorus,

"She's my little deuce coupe, you don't know what I got."

Tom jumped to falsetto and repeated the chorus,
"My little deuce coupe, you don't know what I got."

Regan laughed and reached over to touch his cheek.

"I think we both better keep our day jobs; we're sure never going to make it as singers."

"I don't know why we haven't gone to this event before; I think it's going to be fun."

"We haven't gone because Saturdays are busy days for us. We're not even going today; we're here as a courtesy before our office opens. We just have to find Susan, have her sign some papers, and then go to work. The event doesn't get into full swing until 10:00. We'll be long gone by then and miss most of the cars ..."

"But we'll still get to see a lot of them," Tom interrupted gleefully. "Positive attitude, here," he grinned. "Susan said her friends will be trying for one of the spots all the way at the end of the wharf, so we're going to be forced to look at cars all along the way — coming and going. Ahh, the sacrifices we make for our clients."

They walked out onto the wharf with arms around one another, snuggling against the cold that was penetrating all the way to their bones.

"Oooh," Regan shivered, "you have to be dedicated to be out here so early. It's going to be hard to spot Susan; everyone looks like a ghost in this fog. We'll have to trip over her in order to recognize her."

Regan tried to drag Tom quickly to the far end of the

wharf where they were to meet Susan, wanting to move fast to stay warm. He tried to stop for a long look at every car. Their stuttering progress toward the end of the wharf took many minutes.

The concession stand across from Stagnaro Brothers was crowded with now-settled early arrivals buying coffee and hot cocoa for warmth and to help them pass the time until the crowds descended. Regan pointed out a petite figure at the stand dressed in a dark hooded sweatshirt and long sweatpants.

"Is that her?"

"I can't tell," Tom said. "She seems about the right size for Susan, but between the mist and her clothing, everyone looks alike."

"Regan, Tom?" a voice called from behind them.

They turned to see Susan smiling at them through chattering teeth. Her hands were stuffed in the pockets of her buttoned-to-the-neck dark navy jacket and her hair was covered by the hood of a sweatshirt she wore underneath it. The hood was pulled tight around her face by its drawstring.

As she got close, Susan slid her hands out of her pockets, squeezed between Regan and Tom, and looped an arm through each of theirs.

"Come on. I'll buy you coffee," she said, pulling them toward the concession stand.

"My friends and I have been making coffee runs all morning. I've already had three cups and had to go to the ladies room. I wouldn't have come out except for expecting you two — it's such a miserable morning and it's a lot warmer in there than out here."

She released them and opened her jacket pocket with one hand, peered into it, and then reached in with her other hand. It took a few seconds before she produced a handful of loose bills and gave them to the concessionaire.

"Two coffees for my friends, please.

"We got here before dawn so we'd be among the first on to the wharf. I don't know why Mike cares so much about getting the right parking space, but he does. All this pain and he still had to settle for second-from-the-end by Stagnaro's.

"He's desperate for one of the corner spots and his wife is crazy enough to encourage him, but those spots always get taken by an organized group that comes up from southern California; he never has a chance.

"And speaking of Mike's enabling wife ..." Susan said as she introduced them to a similarly clothed woman.

"Tom and Regan, this is my best friend, Linda. Linda, Regan and Tom are my ..."

Before she could say more, Susan was silenced, first by a pronounced bang, then by the sound of wood being torn apart, and finally by screams. All eyes turned toward the uproar at the end of the parking area past Stagnaro's.

Susan dropped the cups she was holding and clutched Linda. But Linda, her hand outstretched toward the spot where she had last seen her husband, tore free of Susan and ran to the edge of the wharf where the railing was smashed apart. Tom raced after her.

Linda threw herself against a remaining section of railing and leaned over to the water below calling her husband's name, "Mike! Mike!"

Only the shining chrome front bumper remained above the

53

water as seawater swamped Mike's Woodie. Within a few seconds, even the bumper disappeared in a froth of swirling ocean.

Two middle-aged bystanders jumped into the water, one sensibly feet first and the other saying, "We'll get him," before he plunged head first into the water twenty feet below in a practiced and showy dive.

Regan was still with Susan who was frozen where she stood and silent. Suddenly she collapsed to her knees and began a moaning wail that built to an agonized scream.

"Death," she cried. "I saw him! I saw him!" She bent forward and put her head on her knees and sobbed hysterically.

Regan dropped down, covered Susan with her arms, and pulled her close. She rocked Susan like a mother might do to comfort a terrified child awakening from a nightmare.

"I saw him," Susan howled and sobbed inconsolably. "I saw Death again."

Regan's eyes searched the crowd.

A woman nearby yelled, "There!" as she pointed down the wharf toward the beach.

Regan saw a tall figure dressed in dark clothing moving up the wharf away from the commotion even as others came toward it, but the figure she saw seemed very human; she would not call him Death. She soon lost the darkly clad form as it disappeared into eddies of fog.

"There he goes," a man called out, pointing in the opposite direction.

Regan spun her head to follow his finger but found herself staring into a sea of legs. She could see nothing.

The would-be rescuers surfaced more than once, gulping air before going underwater again. They were joined by a younger man, who shouted, "I'm an EMT," before he leaped off the wharf.

He, too, surfaced empty handed.

"I can't get a door open," he yelled up at the crowd. "Throw me something I can use to smash the windshield!" he pleaded.

A bystander high on adrenalin flung his lawn chair down at the EMT who had to dodge the contraption to keep from being clobbered.

A more clearheaded man reached into his Woodie and produced a heavy crescent wrench. He tugged on a knot of the rope he had wrapped through his Woodie's open windows and up over his car's roof to lash down a surfboard. As soon as it released, he pulled the rope free, forced one end through the hole in the wrench's handle, and tied it tightly. He leaned out over the railing and tossed the wrench off the wharf, being careful to make sure it dropped a couple of feet in front of the EMT.

The young man grabbed the wrench as the rope-holder let go, took in a huge slug of air, and disappeared once more.

He resurfaced after what seemed to the anxious crowd like several minutes, gasping for air and dragging Mike's limp body with him.

Bystanders, Tom among them, had used brute strength to break into a locked shed that held rental boats and lowered a rowboat over the wharf's side.

The two would-be rescuers in the water struggled into the rowboat while the EMT got Mike into position next to it.

55

With a supreme effort, they managed to roll him, his unresponsive body a dead weight, up and into the boat.

The EMT pulled himself onboard and immediately began to administer CPR.

Linda watched from the wharf. She clung to the splintered railing with one hand while mindlessly rubbing her other hand over the edges of the rough, broken wood until it was raw and bloodied. She seemed unaware of her injury as she repeated her husband's name over and over and pitifully begged him not to die.

In the world of cell phones, someone had called for help. The crowd heard the siren blaring with ear-splitting authority well before they saw the blood-red fire truck emerge from the mist, opening a path through the bystanders out on to the wharf. Gold lettering on its side proclaimed it was equipped for emergency response.

Susan gulped air; her crying became less hysterical with each breath. Finally she looked up at Regan and said, "Please, I want to leave here. I need to get away."

"I'll drive you home ..."

"No. Please. Call Olive. I want to go to her house. Call her and ask if it's OK."

Regan pulled her cell phone from her jacket pocket. "Do you know her phone number?"

Susan said each number slowly but with assurance. Regan tapped in the numbers and pressed send.

The phone rang four times before a breathless Olive answered with her usual cheer. "Helloow," she sang out a protracted greeting, "Whoever you are, I'm sure I'm delighted you called."

"Olive, it's Regan McHenry."

She could hear Olive breathing rapidly, trying to catch her breath.

"There's been a terrible accident. Susan is here with me ... she's quite upset and says she wants to come to your house. May I ..."

"Yes, of course. I'm walking in the woods near home, but I'll turn around. I'll be home before you get there."

Tom left the crash scene and was standing over Susan and Regan by the time she ended her call. Regan looked up at him in wordless inquiry.

He shook his head slowly, his mouth tight. "It doesn't look good. They're still working on him, but he was in the water so long."

Tom helped Regan raise Susan to her feet and the three of them moved slowly along the wharf toward shore. At the entrance to the wharf, they passed a silent ambulance turning on to the pier. Regan stared at it over her shoulder until it disappeared, another apparition swallowed by the sinister mist. She knew what its silence meant; there was no need to hurry on Mike's account.

By the time they reached Tom's car, Susan had stopped crying, but still looked dazed. She didn't say a word as she climbed into the back seat; she sat in a catatonic stupor, staring out the window while they drove.

🏠🏠🏠🏠🏠🏠🏠🏠🏠🏠🏠

Olive was standing in her driveway dressed head to toe in black — sweats, running shoes, and fanny pack — when Tom pulled in next to her car.

She opened his back door, scooped Susan out, and enveloped her in a tight embrace.

"There, there, you poor dear," she cooed to Susan.

"Regan, you said there was an accident? What happened?"

"There was a mishap on the wharf. One of the Woodies went over, went into the water."

"Oh my. Is the driver all right?"

Olive drew her face into a wince as she realized her gaffe. She mouthed the word "killed" silently.

Tom nodded.

Susan buried her head against Olive's chest and began to sob softly. "I loved him. I've always loved him. He and Linda were my best friends, and now he's dead. I know Mike's dead because I saw Death there."

Regan noticed the fleeting expression that crossed Olive's face. It could have been a checked grimace … or a slight smile.

"Our Linda's Mike?" Olive asked.

Susan's voice quavered as she spoke, "Yes, our Mike."

"Well then, as soon as you're up to it, Susan, we better go see the new widow. She'll need consoling, don't you think? We'll want to let her know she's not alone; we'll let her know she can join us here."

Olive's genial, toothy smile blossomed. "I'll take it from here. You two can run along."

She turned Susan toward the widow's house, and with her arm still surrounding the smaller woman, began slowly moving her toward the front door.

Tom's eyebrows rose. He leaned toward his wife and

whispered, "I guess we better go; we've been dismissed."

As she started walking between the cars to Tom's passenger door, Regan had to step over a puddle of water on the driveway coming from under Olive's car.

She puzzled. *Is that air conditioner runoff?*

She put a hand on the hood of both cars; both were equally warm. Olive had just come home from somewhere, but from a walk in the woods near home? Regan thought not.

Local media had a field day with the way Mike McAllister died. The enthusiasm of the Saturday night TV newscasters was palpable. Usually relegated to reporting less newsworthy weekend stories, the not-yet-prime-time broadcasters excitedly enticed audiences to stay tuned for more details after the commercial break.

Teasers teased: "Stay tuned for the latest Woodies on the Wharf death toll." Alliteration abounded: "Woe on the wharf, local man dies in wrong-way Woodie."

The Sunday morning *Santa Cruz Sentinel* used alliteration, too, and added a surfing connection for their banner story: "Woodies on the Wharf wipeout."

By midday Sunday, one diligent reporter was running a video of a woman who claimed she had seen a person dressed as Death fleeing the wharf right after Mike's car disappeared under the sea. A new wave of attention and speculation exploded from the media.

The story continued to have legs, especially after it fell to Dave, in his role as police spokesman, to acknowledge that the Woodies on the Wharf calamity hadn't been an accident.

Regan usually tuned in the local news on their small kitchen TV at night while she prepared dinner. When she recognized Dave's voice, she stopped chopping tomatoes to give him her full attention.

"That is correct," he stated calmly into the microphone held by the young blonde reporter.

"The vehicle has been recovered. At this time, the police are declaring the death of Michael McAllister to be under investigation as a possible homicide."

"Are the police saying his car was tampered with?" the correspondent asked, thrusting the microphone back in his direction.

"No, they are not. I have no further details for you today," Dave signaled the end of his interview.

She persisted, her voice keen, "It's been reported a death figure was seen at the accident. Do the police think this murder is related to the homicide of Dr. Walter Henshaw on Pacific Avenue last Halloween, since a death figure was reportedly seen there as well? Do we have a serial killer in Santa Cruz whose signature is impersonating the Angel of Death?"

"The Angel of Death?" Regan questioned the TV screen and chuckled. She watched Dave's reaction closely.

When he hesitated to scratch the side of his nose before answering, she knew he was stalling, battling for cool and self-control before continuing.

She could practically hear the sarcastically snappy answers he must be rolling around in his mind. But at this point in his career, he had become the consummate professional and was beyond being baited by one of the local

61

station's newest hires. He smiled and remained civil.

"As I said, I have no further comments for you today. Thank you, Brittany," he said with finality, leaving the eager cub reporter to come up with her own speculations for her TV audience.

🏠🏠🏠🏠🏠🏠🏠🏠🏠🏠🏠

It was one day shy of two weeks since the wharf accident. Linda McAllister, the new widow, sat in the conference room sipping coffee that was loaded with sugar and cream, listening inattentively as Regan concluded her listing presentation.

"Whatever you think," she said nonchalantly before draining her coffee. "You don't have to convince me to hire you, you know. Susan said you and your husband are the best. So do whatever you do, whatever you think is going to work.

"Susan said there would be papers for me to sign." Linda looked at Regan expectantly and held the fingers of her writing hand as if she were holding a pen.

Physically Linda and Susan resembled one another so closely they could have passed for sisters, but that's where the resemblance ended. Linda seemed distracted, Regan decided, but not rattled like Susan had been when Olive shepherded her through her listing appointment with Tom.

Linda came across more like a busy woman, one who wasn't interested in house selling details, preferring instead to turn them over to a recommended professional. She didn't seem to be still in a state of emotional turmoil after the loss of her husband.

Even so, though Regan wanted to hold her tongue, she couldn't in good conscience let the meeting go forward without giving Linda *the talk*.

"Are you sure you want to do this now, Linda ... make another major change so quickly ..."

Linda cut her off with a harrumph.

"Susan said you'd tell me to wait a while. Aren't realtors always supposed to be anxious for business?"

Linda charged on before Regan could reply.

"No, I don't want to wait at all. I miss my husband, you have no idea how much, but I won't miss," she rocked her head from side to side as she pronounced each word distinctly, "the old family home, especially if my selling it causes my mother-in-law grief.

"The house got turned over to Mike and me for tax reasons; I bet mom is sorry now for taking that tax advice," she snickered. "The house is mine, free and clear. Imagine that. I'm going to sell it because I can."

"Linda, your house has so much history. It won't be easy to replace should you have a change of heart after it's sold."

"I'm not going to change my mind." Linda shifted in her seat to cross her legs and fold her arms across her chest. Her body language seconded her determined words.

"Mike and I were married for twenty-three years and that old biddy has done her best to make my life miserable from day one. She liked Susan and wanted her son to marry her, a fact she has reminded me of at least once a week for all these years. She thought I stole him from Susan and never forgave me for it."

Linda rolled on.

"OK, they were going steady for a while and all that — Mike even said one time that he and Susan were each other's first — but it was high school, for goodness sake.

"The old witch thought Mike made a mistake choosing me, which is ridiculous. Mike and I had so much in common. I mean, take Woodies and antique cars for instance. I was into those as much as Mike was even before I met him. Oh sure, Susan tried to be interested — I think she even took a mechanics class with Mike in high school — but she did it to please him, not because she liked working on cars or wanted to be a hobbyist like Mike and I did."

Another harrumph escaped Linda's lips.

"Then there were her plans for the future. Susan was a great student — she even skipped a year and graduated young. All she wanted was to go to college, become a nurse, and work. It was really important to her to do that; she said she wanted to make a difference in the world. Mike didn't need a working wife. He didn't want a career woman for a wife — he made that perfectly clear.

"He needed a help-mate. He needed someone to schmooze, to help the family business. I was terrific at that. I didn't want a career, so I had time to be on all the right charity boards, have all the right people over for dinner, and throw all the right kind of parties.

"I networked like mad for him and helped grow the family business like it was my own, but did that old battle-ax appreciate what I did? Never.

"I did steal him all right; she was right about that. Who

wouldn't have if they could? He was cute and rich and important, a big man on campus, and I knew he was going to be important in town, too, considering his family connections."

Linda undid all her crossed appendages.

"Why, he might even have had a political future — and I loved the idea of being a politician's wife — but sheesh, Susan forgave me. We've been best friends since we met in kindergarten at Westlake Elementary School. She got over it. If Susan could, after twenty-three years of me making Mike happy, I don't see why mother-in-law-dearest couldn't let it go."

Regan hadn't expected an intimate recitation of how much Linda disliked her mother-in-law. Hearing it made her uncomfortable. She tried to steer Linda back to business.

"Are you planning to stay in Santa Cruz after your house sells or will you move away and get a fresh start somewhere else?"

"Oh, I'll stay here. I may not be sixth generation Santa Cruz like Susan is, with a street named after her family, for Pete's sake," Linda drew the sides of her mouth down disparagingly, tilted her head up, and flipped her upturned nose with her index finger, "or fifth generation like Mike, but thirty-six years of living here makes Santa Cruz home."

"Are you planning to downsize or simplify?" Regan tried again to move the conversation in another direction.

"Oh, no. Not with my volunteer work. I'll still need a big house for the kind of charity events I host. I just want to get away from the grand Victorian I've had to put up with for all these years.

"I'm planning to move into Olive's house in Woods Cove. You've met Olive, haven't you?"

Regan nodded slowly but her thoughts raced: *Olive has another widow.*

"It's a great entertaining house. The grounds need help, but I gave Olive money to get some work started. She agreed we'll need a sizable outdoor area for entertaining and a complete outdoor kitchen for the caterers my events need. Even so, she was reluctant to start groundbreaking without a firm commitment from me. Maybe she thought I'd change my mind and make her pay me back. Who knows? She asked me to buy in immediately before she ordered any work done.

"I told her I'd like to do that, but while I have access to plenty of money to keep me going for the time being, I don't have anything like what I'd need for buying a fifth of the house.

"She seemed upset by that, so yesterday, just to prove how serious I was, I signed a letter of intent saying that if I didn't buy into her house as soon as mine sold or the estate settled, whichever came first, she could keep the landscaping money I gave her."

Regan was relieved Linda had moved beyond talking about evening the score with her mother-in-law. How Linda planned to settle old scores was of no interest to her. She wanted to know about Olive, and she worked to keep Linda talking about her.

"That was very considerate of you, reassuring Olive like that, but then, since you're going to be moving in with her, I assume she's been a close friend of yours for a long time, so you'd naturally want to put her mind at ease. Susan mentioned she and Olive go way back. Have you known Olive as long as Susan has?"

"Oh, no. Susan and Olive were military nurses together during the Gulf War. I only met Olive when she started volunteering as a Pink Lady at Dominican Hospital.

"I've been volunteering there for, let me think, six years, no, seven years, and coordinating the volunteers for most of that time." Linda sounded self congratulatory as she brought up her volunteer history. "Olive only joined our group within the last three years.

"Of course, I don't have day-to-day contact with the individual volunteers. I didn't really get to know her until the Widow's Walk League started, and that's just a little over two years ago."

"Both Susan and Olive mentioned the league but neither explained what it was about," Regan smiled guardedly. "The Widow's Walk League, the name sounds vaguely ominous."

Linda chuckled. "Far from it. A group of us get together to walk. We change the route every week, starting from wherever we've agreed to meet and walking until someone spots a widow's walk.

"You know what those are, don't you, being a real estate broker and all: one of those fenced places on the tops of old houses where wives used to go to watch for their seafaring husbands' ships coming home? Oh, of course you do."

Linda didn't allow Regan more than a nod before she rolled on with her opinion.

"I always thought they should be called wife walks, but I guess the big deal was that the wives would really use them when their husbands' ships were overdue or when they began to suspect their husbands had probably been lost at sea and weren't coming home. I think those overlooks got called widow's walks because the women who spent the most time on them were already widows — they just didn't know it yet, or didn't want to believe it because they still hadn't given up hope."

"I think that's the way the lore works," Regan agreed.

"We dubbed ourselves the Widow's Walk League because of that spotting game and because one of us — and yes, I do mean Olive — who thought the group needed an official name, is a tad over-dramatic.

"You should join us some time. You could make some good connections in the group. And we have fun with our walks, especially since once we spot our widow's walk, we go have lunch … or a picnic if we're walking in the country."

"How does that work, walking in the country? I don't imagine you come across many houses with widow's walks once you're away from the ocean."

"You'd be surprised how many homes have them just as a decorative feature. Of course, the hungrier we get, the more we broaden our criteria. If we're starving, a high deck with a rail will do." Linda offered the first merry laugh Regan had heard from her since they met.

"I remember the day Olive found her house. We elected the house across the street as our official sighting because we were so anxious to eat. Woods Cove is such a pretty place and we all were famished. We plopped down in one of the open space fields and had lunch right there. I remember Olive just kept staring at her house — it had a For Sale sign on it. She was fascinated by it, especially after she collected a flyer from one of those realtor boxes. She said the house had five bedrooms and five bathrooms. By the time we finished lunch, Olive said she was going to buy it and populate it with widows.

"I remember it all clearly because she said it was too bad none of the others in the League were widows and then paused theatrically and said, 'Yet.'

"Helen, who has a ... well, her husband isn't doing well. Helen thought the comment was aimed at her and took offense. It was quite a scene. As I said, Olive has a flare for the dramatic.

"It is kind of spooky if you think about it, though. Now two of us are widows and are going to live in her house," she sighed. "Two down and two to go."

The quick involuntary breath that Regan took was loud and obvious.

"Oh, Regan, forget I said that. What must you think of me?" Linda's face flushed. "I didn't mean ... Olive wouldn't have expected two of our husbands to die — especially not to be murdered — when she said that! It's just a coincidence ... even if it is kind of an eerie one.

"And I ... I," Linda's voice faltered for the first time, "I'm not usually so vindictive. It's just that if I don't stay angry at someone — and my mother-in-law is such a huge target — if I don't over-schedule myself with volunteer work, I'm going to fall apart. I've been talking nonsense since Mike died ... I loved him so much ... please ... please, don't pay any attention to what I say."

But by the time Linda left, Regan couldn't keep her suspicions under wraps any longer. She dialed Dave.

Dave sat center-back in a round six-person booth. He was already half way through a bowl of warm tortilla chips and salsa when Regan slid into the booth at El Palomar and wriggled along the seat until she was next to him.

"You're right," Dave greeted her, "the acoustics are terrible here. No one can eavesdrop, not even from the next table. So, from what you said on the phone, you've got some juicy info about who's been offing husbands, right?"

Regan nodded eagerly.

"No wonder you didn't want anyone to hear what you have to say," Dave gave her a laconic smile. "But you know how excited *I* am to hear all about your latest murder theories." He added, "I feel so special," under his breath.

"Dave, if you don't want me to tell you what I've uncovered … if you don't appreciate how helpful I've been in the past … how I've solved murders before, just say so. My lips will be sealed."

Regan drew her fingers across her mouth in a confident tease, but their relationship was such that, as she pretended to zip her lips, she hoped he wouldn't say that was fine. She didn't expect him to, but he might, just to get a reaction out of her.

Dave made a great show of pondering. He moved his tongue around the outside of his teeth. His mouth bulged with his tongue's movement.

"Whatcha got?" he asked finally.

"I've got a suspect with motive, opportunity, and I think with the necessary knowledge to commit the crimes." Regan had a slightly triumphant tone in her voice.

"This killer you got in mind? You back to the widow collector — Tom's mushroom lady?"

Dave leaned back in the booth seat and popped another salsa-laden chip into his mouth. He chewed it deliberately, smiling as he did.

"Tom told you about her giving him suspicious mushrooms?"

"Tom told me about missing the opportunity to taste some great mushrooms because you jumped to one of your wild conclusions," Dave corrected.

Regan was used to Dave mocking her — she gave as good as she got — but if Tom did the same thing when he and Dave were alone — she was hurt to think her husband would laugh at her behind her back.

"Well, he may not have said it quite like that; you know how sappy he can be about you. He mumbled something about you not wanting him to take any chances because you kinda' like him — but I got his drift."

"That's you, all right," Regan shook her head, "man of subtleness and a skilled reader of nuance."

She vowed to give Tom a huge kiss the next time she saw

him and forgive him completely for something he hadn't done.

"You know I did do a quick look-see at your mushroom gal, what's her name? Some kind of fruiting tree isn't it? Cherry or apple or ..."

"Olive."

"Right," he smirked. "Olive. Yeah. I did a wee bit of research after you said she creeped you out."

Dave held up his hand as Regan started to protest his choice of words. "OK. Let me rephrase — after the last time you said she seemed suspicious."

"And?"

"And nothing. She's a nice older lady who served her country as a nurse during Vietnam and again during the Gulf War. Now she does volunteer work, is a little kooky, and totally harmless."

Regan threw out the question she wanted answered, hoping she could use what Dave said to strengthen her case against Olive. "Why are the police calling Mike McAllister's death a possible homicide? I saw your interview on TV. You were coy and didn't answer the reporter's question."

"Nope. Not goin' there, Regan. I knew you'd want to nose around sooner or later, especially when I heard you and Tom where there when the McAllister guy died, but you don't have any skin in this game, so no sharing this time around."

He folded his arms over his stomach.

There was nothing subtle or difficult to read about his body language. He was telling her not to bother asking again. Regan allowed herself a tiny sly smile, no more. He may have made up his mind not to tell her anything, but his decision wasn't about to stop her from probing.

"Something happened to Mike McAllister's car, didn't it? That's why the police think he was murdered, isn't it?"

"The Angel of Death messed with it — isn't that what the rumor is? You and Tom were there that morning; didn't you see him?"

Regan knew him well. His snide answer was a typical Dave diversionary comment. She held her ground with silence, confident she could win the round.

After a few seconds of mutual silence, he uncrossed his arms and shifted in the seat — he was itching to talk — he just needed some encouragement.

"Dave, you said Olive served in Vietnam and the Gulf War. Did you know she spent some of her free time during those wars learning the ins and outs of how vehicles work? I understand she's an accomplished mechanic.

"What happened to Mike McAllister's car?" she asked again. "Someone did mess with it, didn't they? Not the Angel of Death, someone very earthly."

Dave sighed. He grabbed his paper napkin and unfurled it flat onto the table. It had a small spot of red on it; one bit of salsa hadn't made it all the way to his mouth and he had wiped up the spill with the napkin. He decided it was clean enough for his purposes.

"Got something to write with?"

Regan produced a pen from her purse and handed it to him.

"Great."

Dave drew a large rectangle, put two small circles that didn't touch in the center of it, added three sides of a small

73

rectangle to the bottom of each of the circles, and topped each off with a triangle. Then he drew parallel straight lines slanting off to the left from the tops of the triangles.

"Pretend these are shift linkage rods on the bottom of McAllister's car," he said as he finished his illustration. "The two I drew should attach like this to first gear and reverse, but somebody crossed them." He drew a new set of lines over the originals to form an X.

"Now we know it had to have happened after the Vic parked his car because his missus and her friend, the Doc's widow, rode to the wharf with him and said the car worked just fine.

"I've been told it would be easy to cross the rods. All it would take is a crescent wrench and a pair of pliers — things probably every car there had in its tool box — a little knowledge, and maybe some practice time to get the hang of it."

"Dave, when Tom and I were walking out on the wharf, we saw lots of drivers tinkering with their cars; no one would think it odd if someone slid under his car for a few minutes. The fog was so dense that morning and it was so cold outside … people were wearing jackets and sweats …" Regan saw Susan Henshaw in her mind, with her sweatshirt hood obscuring part of her face.

"Someone could have watched Mike McAllister leave his car to get something warm to drink and then … the Angel of Death could have been almost anyone on the wharf."

"That's right," Dave nodded. "We think the killer set the Vic up, too. The guy in the parking spot next to him says he had just gotten back in his car with a cup of coffee when he heard the Vic's cell phone buzz.

"The neighbor said he had his windows down, driver side and passenger side, and that McAllister had his driver's side window down. I guess most of those owners roll down at least a window or two and some open up the back of their Woodies, too, so people can get a good look inside.

"The guy said he thought the call was a text because he says the Vic looked at his phone rather than putting it up to his ear, let out a whoop, and held the phone up to show him the screen. McAllister yelled, 'See ya! I'm moving to the power row!' Then he gunned his engine.

"It's maybe five-six feet from where the Vic was parked before he would have smashed the railing and his rear wheels would have been rolling off the wharf. McAllister would have tail-ended into the water below. The back of his Woodie was open, top flipped up and bottom fully down, with a surfboard stick'n out, and he didn't bother to close up. My guess is he figured he didn't need to since he was just going to move across the wharf and down a couple hundred feet. Maybe he figured someone else would grab his spot if he didn't hurry up." Dave shrugged, "Who knows.

"Then, as if that wasn't enough, he drove a '49 Ford. Woodies got their name because most were partly made of wood, but that car was all steel with wood just bolted to the sides for style and show. His car was heavy … sank like a rock.

"Yeah. Once his rear wheels went off the wharf, he was a goner. He was probably still leaning forward with a big smile on his face when he hit the water. Force of the water from the back and his left side through the window, not to mention the loose stuff in his car — autopsy said he drowned, but his head showed internal signs of a concussion and he had a gash over his eye. You get the picture."

Regan put her hand on his arm to emphasize her next words. Her grip caused him to hesitate as he was raising another salsa-laden chip to his mouth. Red salsa splattered over his napkin drawing.

"Dave, Olive knew enough about cars to have switched the transmission links."

"I bet she did," he said as he finally got the chip to his mouth. "And so did the Vic's wife and lots of other people on the wharf that day.

"You or Tom see your mushroom lady lurking around? Oh, wait. You wouldn't have known it was her if you did see her because she would have been dressed like Death."

He raised his arms above his shoulders and wiggled his fingers. "Ooooh," he said with a shivery voice.

"I've got more, Dave." Regan glared at him and crammed as much disparagement into her tone as she could.

"Susan Henshaw was borderline hysterical — she's the one who first said she saw Death, and then other people said they did, too — and said she wanted to be taken to Olive's house.

"I called Olive to ask if it was OK to bring Susan there. She said she was out walking nearby but that she'd get home before we got there."

"There you go. Proof positive she wasn't at the wharf — dressed like death or not."

"Listen for a minute. First, I never told her where we were. How would she know she'd get home before we'd get to her house? It was like she did know where we were … maybe because she had seen all of us at the wharf."

"That's a stretch, even for you," Dave belittled.

"When we got there, her car hood was warm. She drove her car from somewhere; she wasn't out for a nearby walk."

Regan stopped mid-thought.

"Did the police find Mike McAllister's cell phone? Do they know who called him? If Olive called him …"

"His phone's probably still in the muck under the wharf, but we don't need his phone. His carrier was able to supply us with his last incoming phone number."

"Who called him?" Regan asked, her voice barely above a whisper and her eyes open as wide as they could be.

"The phone belonged to someone who paid cash for it. It's a pre-paid one; impossible to know who bought it."

"Someone planned this pretty carefully, didn't they?"

"Looks like it."

"They planned this murder as carefully as the murder last Halloween was planned, didn't they?"

"You're not getting ready to ask me if I think we've got a serial killer on the loose who thinks he's Death … like that reporter did?"

"No. I think we may have a serial killer, but not one who thinks she's Death.

"Suppose I told you Olive needed a serious amount of money by the end of July? She was buying her house from the builder in an installment sale and was due for another big chunk of the purchase price then.

"She could have seen how the Henshaws lived, seen where the Henshaws lived, and assumed if she made Susan a widow and convinced her to live in the widow compound, her troubles would be over."

"OK, you got my attention."

"According to Susan Henshaw, she's been giving Olive some money, calling it a storage fee, but it wasn't anything like the amount Olive needed for her second installment. Susan had us reduce the asking price on her home because she said without a sale she didn't have the resources to keep Olive from losing her house.

"When Olive killed Walter Henshaw, suppose she didn't realize Susan wouldn't have access to most of her inheritance until after her house sold, or that the sale could drag on past her second installment due date in July.

"I told you Linda McAllister just listed her house as well, and is also planning to move into Olive's house when it sells. Maybe when Olive asked Susan for more than small monthly payments and Susan said she couldn't help yet, she added something offhanded like, 'too bad I'm not flush like Linda, who has plenty of ready money?'

"Olive knew Susan and Linda were close friends — maybe she assumed Linda would want to join her friend in the widow's house. As it turns out, that's exactly the way things are working.

"Olive could have decided to make a second widow in a hurry. The only problem for Olive is that Linda can't do much for her right now either.

"You always say murder is usually about sex or money, don't you, Dave? How am I doing so far for a money motive?"

"For an amateur who spends too much time listening to

gossip and worrying about her little *feelings*," Dave mocked her with the word, "about people like your mushroom lady, not too bad, I guess. 'Course, if you used factual information, maybe you wouldn't come up with so many wacky ideas."

"What are the facts, then? Where is my reasoning off?"

"Reasoning?" Dave issued a hearty laugh. "First thing is you're off in calling your wild guesses reasoning. Olive making widows to keep the big bad lender away? Hah!"

Regan knew it was a stretch, but she was so sure Olive was involved, she grabbed at the first idea that popped into her mind.

"OK, what about this, then. You said police always look at the spouse when there's a murder. I remember you suggested, too, that widows who want their husbands dead sometimes pay someone to kill them. Olive needs money. Maybe Olive is the means but not the brains here. You said the police always check the widow's finances. If Susan or Linda, let's even say Susan and Linda, wanted their husbands killed … when you were taking your little look at Olive, did you happen to see any money put into her bank account by Susan Henshaw or Linda McAllister?"

"You mean more than the little bit we discovered the widow Henshaw says she gave her as rent and more than the twenty-grand the widow McAllister says she gave her for landscaping?" Dave licked his lips. "Well, now that you mention it … we did uncover some interesting relationships."

Dave looked around furtively and then leaned close to Regan, not trusting even El Palomar's poor acoustics to ensure privacy.

"It seems Olive, who can trace her ancestors to Russian

aristocrats, had a granddaughter who was kidnapped and brutally murdered, and Susan Henshaw was the little girl's nurse, and Linda McAllister was the little girl's aunt, sister to the mourning father who killed himself after his wife died from a miscarriage caused by the shock of their daughter's death ..."

"You can stop now. I've read *Murder on the Orient Express*, too."

Dave burst into raucous laughter.

"You and your theories, Regan. I'm sorry, but sometimes I just can't help myself — you leave me no choice."

"Have you calmed down enough to listen to me yet?"

"Just one more heh-heh and I should be good," he chuckled.

"Wonderful. What I'm concerned about is that if I am right about Olive needing money and widowing Susan and Linda hasn't solved her dilemma, she's going to need another widow. And soon."

Regan gathered her hair up into a ponytail and clipped it with a wide clamp. She bent over and began tying the laces on her running shoes as Tom came into the bedroom. Her tee-shirt separated from the cropped pants she was wearing. He smiled appreciatively and ran his finger along the skin just above her pants.

"Nice view," he crooned. "You look like a woman getting ready to go for a run; and here I thought you were an avowed non-runner."

"I only run when I'm being chased, and then only if it's by someone I don't want to catch me. I'm going for a walk," she said as she straightened up and turned to face him.

"You want company?"

"Sorry, not today. This is a women-only walk. I'm taking up Linda McAllister on her invitation to join the Widow's Walk League at least for one day. She says it's a good way to do some business networking."

"And some sleuthing?" He flashed a knowing smile. "If you happen to see Death, run like crazy."

"I won't have to since I'm female. Death seems to prefer

men right now."

"That's right!" Tom feigned a sudden shock of realization and clasped his heart. "Death goes for the husbands of women who walk. Are you trying to get me bumped off? What did I do to deserve this? Spare me; I'll try to be a better husband."

Regan giggled and put her arms around him.

"You bravely eat my experimental meals and don't complain when they don't work, you do dishes and take care of Harry and Cinco's litter box without any prompting, and you have the most amazing blue eyes I've ever seen. What more could I ask for. I think you're a perfect husband already."

He smiled down at her, "I bet you say that to all the men you think are about to get murdered."

Regan's expression changed to one of uneasiness. "Tom, don't make a joke about that. There was something about Olive that made me uncomfortable from the first time we met her. Now that I think it's possible she's involved in a couple of deaths ... the way she looks at you ... it's not funny to me."

Tom stroked her hair, "Sweetheart, pleased as I am to see how much you care, I don't want you worrying about me needlessly. I agree with Dave. Olive is an oddball, but a harmless one. Besides, she likes me. Even if she's Death, she's going to pass right over me." He smiled as he said it, but his voice was soft and he spoke soberly.

"Anyway, this whole death thing ... I don't think it's real. Granted Walter Henshaw got a note saying he was going to die on Halloween night; that doesn't prove anything. It could still be a coincidence."

"But his note was different from all the others."

"It was different from all the others that the police know about. Don't you think it's possible other people got specific notes, too, maybe with the hour of their death on them but at a future date?

"People may have thrown them away or didn't let them register and spoil their Halloween fun. The Henshaws probably wouldn't have given Walter's note a second thought if the date and time on it hadn't been so immediate. Even so, they probably would have tossed it if Susan wasn't so consciences about not littering."

"What about Susan seeing Death at the wharf?"

Tom shrugged. "What about it? We were there; did you see anyone you'd say looked like Death, other than some of those Woodie owners who partied too hard the night before and then got up so early?"

He smiled broadly but was still serious. "You looked for a death figure when people started pointing and screaming; that's what you said, isn't it?"

She nodded, "Uh-huh."

"But you didn't see anything, did you?"

"No."

"I think Susan is still pretty fragile after what happened ... her husband bled to death in her arms, imagine what that must have been like for her ... and she ... her imagination got the better of her on the wharf, that's all."

Tom's voice grew clear and almost harsh, "And then some of those people, the people around her ... you majored in behavioral science ... you tell me if mass hysteria can be a real phenomena or not."

"It can be real," Regan agreed. "You think Susan is seeing the Angel of Death because she's so traumatized?"

"I think she's seeing death all right, but the lower case garden variety, the death of two men she loved.

"If I recall correctly, it was one of our eager young news people who originally started all the fuss about the Angel of Death visiting Woodies on the Wharf, not any of the people who were there. Once the suggestion was planted, though, people started thinking about it and convinced themselves they'd seen Death, too.

"Some of them came forward to swear to it on TV. The promise of fifteen minutes of fame can make people see lots of things.

"Go on your walk. Network like mad. Spy. Have fun. And just to be on the safe side, in case I'm mistaken, remember to let Olive know we're not rich, and making you a widow won't help her out," he chuckled.

The Widow's Walk League was meeting on West Cliff Drive in front of the Surfing Museum at the lighthouse. The location challenged the Boardwalk for prominence as Santa Cruz's most recognizable monument, and there was no way Regan could find parking nearby at the height of summer tourist season.

She had to park near Columbia Street and make a half mile sprint to be on time. She was slightly disheveled and could feel a single bead of sweat rolling down her face from her hairline as Linda greeted her and began introductions.

"We're waiting for Olive who, as usual, is late. Susan won't be joining us today because she volunteered to sit with Henry so Helen could come."

Linda leaned close to Regan's ear and whispered, "Henry has Alzheimer's and needs an attendant."

She returned to her normal voice and announced, "Everybody, this is Regan. I invited her to join us today."

Linda began introductions with a humorous, if not original line, "Pay careful attention, Regan. There will be a test."

Regan made a quick sweep of the other six members of the group. She recognized Helen, the oldest woman present, and Tika from Walter Henshaw's memorial service.

Mary Anne, who was more pointed out than introduced, stood at the periphery of the group. She had ear buds in both ears which she didn't remove and seemed to be bouncing to a tune none of the rest of the women heard.

Joyce had a nervous air about her. Regan bet she would be an anxious handwringer if she weren't extending one of her hands for a handshake.

Leslie and Karen were introduced as one. Leslie was sinewy and athletic, and past fifty, Regan guessed. She seemed not to belong in the same phrase as Karen, a baby-doll blonde who could still be in her thirties and was as pudgy and soft as Leslie was firm and fit, yet the moment Linda finished her introductions, Leslie piped up with her own proud definitive link, "Karen is my wife. We got married at City Hall in San Francisco the very day then-mayor Gavin Newsome said we could."

Karen said nothing but beamed lovingly at her spouse.

"Can you believe her luck?"

The group followed Linda's gaze to the parking lot. Olive was turning her car into a just-vacated parking space.

"How does she do that? How does she manage to arrive just as a space opens up." She shook her head merrily in wonder.

Olive got out of her car and discarded a dark sweatshirt and shimmied out of matching dark sweatpants to become resplendent in a lime green outfit. She plopped a broad-brimmed sombrero-like hat on her head with one hand while she locked the car door with the other. Her hat provided so much shade, she didn't need sunglasses.

Olive turned toward the lighthouse and saw her walking friends. Her face broke open at the lips and formed into one of her notoriously toothy smiles. She waved and hurried toward them.

Her greeting was a protracted and sunny high pitched "Helloow," just as it had been when she answered her phone after Mike McAllister's tragedy.

"Oh, Regan, I'm delighted you'll be joining us. Have you met everyone? Have we decided in which direction we want to walk?"

Leslie answered for the group. "We thought north toward the park at Natural Bridges, but we'll make a right at Swift Street and walk up to Mission. Some of us are interested in Thai for lunch and there are several restaurant choices along Mission Street. We are confident we will have spotted a widow's walk by the time we get there," she giggled.

"We don't want to walk south and have lunch at

Stagnaro's on the Wharf?" Olive asked.

Heads turned toward Linda who looked like she had been slapped.

"Oh, Linda dear, I'm so sorry, how tactless of me," Olive apologized and her smile diminished ever so slightly.

Tika said nothing, but the cold glare of her dark eyes did. She put an arm around Linda's shoulder and the group began a protective walk in the direction of Natural Bridges, leaving Regan, the outsider, and Olive, the offender, to bring up the rear.

"Well, this is awkward, isn't it?" Olive smiled jovially but her words were spoken by one who knew she had been soundly chastised.

"Are you willing to walk with me? I'll understand if you don't want to. I try to be pleasant at all times but I am *so* skilled at saying the wrong thing and offending, worse, hurting people I care for."

"Sure, I'll walk with you," Regan answered.

Olive heaved a huge sigh. "Good. Now, let's change the subject and talk about something pleasant like that charming husband of yours."

Regan regretted her offer immediately. Her reaction to Olive wanting to talk about Tom was almost as severe as Linda's had been at the mention of where her husband died. Her stomach clenched. For a fleeting moment she felt afraid that if Olive even said Tom's name, something terrible might happen to him.

"You do know why I'm so fond of your dear Tom, don't you? He reminds me so much of my own wonderful Paul. I thought it was his eyes at first; he has such intense, beautiful

87

eyes just like my Paul did, although his eyes were green rather than blue.

"Tom is very much like my darling Paul was: all tall and attractive and so obviously intelligent, but now that I know Tom better, I see it's so much more than just those physical similarities between them. Both were ... are ... caring, sweet men, too.

"Your Tom and my Paul; well, if I had to use just one word to describe them, I'd say they were Galahads, the noblest of men to sit at King Arthur's Round Table. Wouldn't you agree?"

Regan hadn't thought of Tom in quite that way.

"I bet he's good in bed, too," Olive laughed and looped her arm through Regan's. "That's probably something else they have in common."

Her words were playful — she seemed perpetually good-humored and jolly — but when Regan, startled by what Olive said, looked into her eyes, she saw something there that didn't match the smiling countenance that Olive presented to the world. She saw pain and loss.

"Do you still miss him?"

"Every minute of every day. It's one of the reasons I want to open my house to widows. I know first-hand how terrible it can be to have to go on alone, without someone you loved so much that, even after you made a vow ..." Olive stopped.

For the first time her smile faded. She swayed, and had she not been holding Regan's arm, she might have stumbled.

"But one shouldn't dwell on things that it's too late to change, should one?" Olive pulled herself rigidly upright. Her militarily perfect posture returned and so did her eye-catching smile.

Regan looked again at Olives eyes. She still saw raw pain and the sadness of loss, but now she was aware of something else in them, too. The ancient proverb said eyes were the windows of the soul. If that were true, what Regan saw when she looked into Olive's eyes was a heart that held guilt.

They caught up with the rest of the League walkers. Tika had released Linda from her protective care and was by Helen's side gesturing and rolling her hand as they walked and as she asked her questions.

"You've been giving him ginkgo biloba and lemon balm?"

"Yes," Helen nodded.

"What about vitamin E? Have you been giving him the dose I recommended?"

"Yes, I've been giving him ten milligrams a day like you said."

"And you're giving him natural vitamin E, the ones labeled d-alpha-tocopheral, because the synthetics aren't any good. If the vitamin E label doesn't have the d on it, they're synthetics."

"I've been careful to make sure I get natural vitamin E."

"Have you noticed any improvement?"

Helen hesitated, stuck somewhere between not wanting to disappoint Tika and not wanting to admit her husband's condition hadn't improved. "I ... I don't think so."

"Why don't you raise the dosage a little, maybe give him two capsules a day?"

"His doctor says too much can cause internal bleeding."

"Then add turmeric to his food. The doctor shouldn't have any complaints about turmeric."

"OK, I'll try that."

"I have something else for you to try, too."

Tika reached into her pocket and produced three large lavender crystalline stones.

"These are amethysts. They help clear the sixth chakra which controls the brain. I've dedicated them so they have specific healing energies. I'll come home with you after we walk and show you how to use them with Henry."

"Thank you, Tika."

Olive and Regan had been quietly listening to Tika and Helen talking. Olive could be quiet no longer.

"All that mumbo-jumbo and new agey stuff you push, Tika, really. Henry has Alzheimer's. Your diet and mysticism aren't going to do a bit of good for him. What's become of the scientist in you?"

"It's nice of Tika to try to help, Olive," Helen said. "We've tried everything else, maybe …"

"It can't hurt," Tika overrode Helen.

"There's a widow's walk!" Mary Anne proclaimed in a shout loud enough to compensate for her music induced lack of hearing.

"Oh, good; I'm starving," the anything-but-starved Karen gushed. "Now we can all have lunch."

🏠🏠🏠🏠🏠🏠🏠🏠🏠🏠🏠🏠

They abandoned their quest for Thai cuisine and settled in at Upper Crust Pizza instead, because it was so close to where Swift Street came into Mission Street, and once spotted, had been decided on unanimously by the walkers' grumbling stomachs.

Mary Anne's ear buds were gone but she looked no less distracted as her fingers furiously tapped text messages on her smart phone. She was good at multitasking, though, and able to join the conversation in spite of never looking up.

Tika's phone blasted music just as the pizza arrived at their table. She glanced at the caller id and ignored the call. The phone sang out again a few seconds later. She repeated her maneuver.

When the phone began playing *We Are the World* for the third time, Olive sputtered impatiently, "Decide, Tika. Answer the damn thing or turn it off."

Tika looked to the others at the table for support. When their expressions indicated they all sided with Olive, she pressed the screen and held the phone to her ear.

"Ola."

Tika listened for a long time without saying anything while the color drained from her rosy cheeks, still extra pink from their walk. The coloring of her face became so ashen, it began to take on the hue of her grey hair.

Finally she said, "Estoy en la pizzeria Upper Crust en la calle Mission en Santa Cruz. Tu sabes donde queda? Cierto? Porfavor me puedes buscar? No creo que puedo manejar."

"That was my housekeeper. She's coming to pick me up," Tika announced matter-of-factly. "The police are at my house. Charlie's been shot. He's dead."

For all their bickering, it was Olive who jumped up and threw her arms around Tika in time to stop her from falling as she dropped her phone and fainted.

91

🏠 🏠 🏠 🏠 🏠 🏠 🏠 🏠 🏠 🏠 🏠 🏠

They all stayed until Tika's housekeeper came. Olive silently climbed into the back seat with the new widow as she was taken away — whether to her home or the police station was unclear.

Once she was gone, the remaining members of the Widow's Walk League started back toward the lighthouse by the most direct route they could find. Regan didn't join them; instead she ran down Swift Street to her office.

She didn't stop to acknowledge Amanda and she almost collided with Jim, one of their agents, who happened to be in the hallway, as she barreled past him to Tom's office.

Tom was on the phone when she burst through his doorway. Her distress was so obvious, he interrupted the person he was talking to with, "Let me call you right back," and hung up abruptly.

She closed his office door before saying anything so she couldn't be heard, but her overexcited entrance had drawn the attention not only of Amanda and Jim but also of two other agents whose offices she raced by on her way to Tom's.

By the time she flung herself down onto his sofa, four sets of eyes were peering unabashedly through the corridor window into his office. Tom's warning glare didn't disperse them.

"Take a couple of deep breaths and give me a second," he instructed as he closed the blinds on his hallway windows and sat down next to her on the sofa and took her hand.

"What's going on?"

"There's been another murder." She breathed heavily —

there was urgency in her voice.

"Tika's husband was shot this morning. Tom, that's three — three widows in Olive's walking group. That's got to be too many to be a coincidence, doesn't it?

"I've got to let Dave know that Tika is part of the Widow's Walk League. Do you think I should tell him Olive was late getting to the group? She didn't show up until well after 11:00, and when she did, she was dressed in black again, like she was when we took Susan to her house after Mike's murder."

"I'm not sure I see the importance of either of those …"

Regan's words rolled over his.

"Don't you see? If Tika's husband was killed this morning, especially late this morning, Olive wasn't with the group. Where was she? Does she have an alibi for when Tika's husband was being murdered?

"I wonder if anyone witnessed the murder, or more importantly, if anyone saw a darkly-clad person leaving the scene — maybe even someone they'd say looked like a figure of death?"

🏠 🏠 🏠 🏠 🏠 🏠 🏠 🏠 🏠 🏠 🏠 🏠

By the time she reached Dave's answering machine and left her message, her questions had become statements of fact, delivered calmly by a clearheaded woman volunteering potentially useful information in the police investigation of Charlie's murder.

Even her speculation about whether or not Olive, since she was a nurse in the military, would have been trained in how

93

to use a gun, seemed like a sound topic of investigation.

She had Tom to thank for her composed message — Tom, her rational Galahad — who had listened quietly and then insisted she take several more deep breaths for good measure before she picked up her phone.

"Tika Smith wants me to stop by and talk about selling her house. The interval between widowhood and selling is getting shorter all the time," Regan told Tom.

"If she's planning to move in with Olive, should I tell Dave about it? Should I push him?"

"You can push all you want, but he was pretty definite that Charlie Smith's murder didn't have anything to do with Olive."

"I don't think the police even tried to find out how she spent her morning the day he was killed. Dave was borderline hostile acknowledging that, yes, as a former military woman, Olive would know how to fire a gun."

"Sweetheart, I think this time Dave knows something significant and isn't at liberty to tell us what it is. Let it go."

🏠🏠🏠🏠🏠🏠🏠🏠🏠🏠🏠

It was a short drive from their Swift Street office to Tika's house at the end of Rudolph Street on the upper west side of Santa Cruz. The house last sold four years before, so it was still in the realtor database and Regan was able to see pictures of it and get the basics: square feet, number of bedrooms and baths, and lot size; but she didn't have time to do a title search.

She also hadn't seen the house since its sale, so she needed to have a careful look at it inside and out before determining comparable houses that had sold recently to arrive at a sensible market price.

Rudolph Street was in a desirable location and had features that would appeal to many buyers, but when Regan pulled up in front of the 1960's house, she was disappointed. The roof had moss at the shingle edges, the house was in need of paint, the yard looked like it was overrun with gophers, and the windows looked as if they hadn't been washed once during the Smith's ownership.

None of those problems were insurmountable; spending a modest amount of money would have the house exterior looking sharp. Her concern was that house interiors usually match their exteriors. If that was the case with Tika's house, there would be a great deal of work to be done before the house was likely to find a new owner.

When Tika opened the front door and ushered her inside, Regan was pleasantly surprised. The house was a charming single level which had an open and flowing floor plan. It had gleaming hardwood floors, a new kitchen, bathrooms updated with expensive fixtures and the latest designer colors and tile patterns, and furniture worthy of an appearance in *Architectural Digest.* The house wouldn't need cleaning or staging; once the exterior was corrected, people would line up to buy it.

Tika punctuated Regan's house tour with, "Nice, isn't it?" comments; she was clearly proud of what they had done inside the house.

The tour ended in the living room where Tika invited Regan to have chrysanthemum tea and some cookies.

She poured the tea and handed Regan her cup, then rather than letting her guest have first choice of the cookies, Tika piled half a dozen on her own plate and began shoveling them into her mouth.

"I've been eating non-stop since Charlie died. You'd think I'd be gaining weight, but I've lost seven pounds. It's probably the stress and the searching."

Regan looked quizzically at her hostess. "The searching?"

"Where should I start?" Tika pondered her answer as she devoured another cookie.

"I guess you're going to have to sit through it all because I have several questions and issues you're going to have to sort out for me; but then, solving problems for their clients — that's why realtors make all the money they do, isn't it?"

Regan smiled. Tika wasn't going to be her first client who seemed slightly hostile to her profession.

"I'll help you with everything I can."

"Well put, although you have no idea of why that is, yet."

Tika took a deep breath and said, "In the beginning ... oh," she chuckled, "don't worry, my history may be an epic, but it's not biblical in length. In the beginning, I was a nice half-Navajo girl on my mother's side named O'teeka Sanchez, who, like so many of my tribe at eighteen, decided I'd rather be mainstream than Navajo.

"When an opportunity to go to college in New York came

up, O'teeka, Navajo for Sun Maiden, became Tika, the slightly exotic looking college freshman — who was very slim and trim at the time, I might add.

"I graduated with a degree in art history but it didn't suit me. The little Navajo girl, so used to open spaces in New Mexico, didn't thrive indoors in New York art galleries like she thought she would.

"I made another radical change in my life direction and joined the Army. That didn't last long either.

"When I got out — I'd had my great adventure and was beginning to miss home — I went to nursing school, thinking maybe being a nurse would make me useful if I went back home to New Mexico and the Big Reservation.

"But before I graduated, I met Charlie Smith, or I should say Konstantin Kola. He was my physical opposite: tall, blonde, blue eyed — wow, did I ever fall hard for him — we were married and making a beautiful baby daughter six months later.

"He was also a run-away like me. Konnie's father was a big deal in the Albanian Mafia in America. He was a real gangster before that word became gangsta, as in rap music, but Konnie didn't want any part of that life. At least that's what he thought at the time.

"I should have known better. My past was calling me; why would I think his wouldn't eventually call him?

"Konnie was an accountant and worked for one of the big stock brokerages in New York. I was a school nurse, so I could have days off when our little girl did. We were happy … at least I was.

"I have no idea when my husband decided we needed

more money or when he got bored with his job, or even if either of those things happened. All I know is that at some point, he started working for his father — and he didn't tell me.

"He surprised me with a big new house. It was glorious and seemed way beyond our means, but he was our money manager and he said he had made some really good investments. He told me to enjoy our new lifestyle, and I did.

"Our little girl had just gone off to college, Brown no less, when everything fell apart. Konnie said he had become involved in the family business, and after his father died, had been embezzling from the mob.

"He was worried he was about to be made and said he had gone to the FBI and offered to turn state's evidence if they would put him into witness protection and ensure his safety.

"The Feds were only too happy to help. The only kicker was, he had to turn everything over to them, including his little nest egg, the one he had stolen.

"I should have left him. I thought about it, for sure." Tika sucked in her cheeks until her prominent cheek bones looked like they might burst through her skin. "The only problem was I still loved him — I couldn't do it."

She sighed. "So he turned over five million dollars to Uncle Sam and a little over five years ago the two of us became Petrika and Charlie Smith of Santa Cruz, California.

"I haven't seen my daughter in five years. She could be married by now. I could be a grandmother. I hated Charlie for what he did to us, to me, but I still loved the big idiot. How dumb does that make me?"

Tika refilled her plate and asked Regan if she wanted more

tea. Regan had been so engrossed in Tika's story, she hadn't taken a sip from her cup. "No, thank you, I'm fine."

"We got new jobs with our new identities. Petrika wasn't a nurse and Charlie wasn't an accountant. He was provided with a job, a fairly low level job for the Social Security Administration, and I was expected to be a housewife. We were given some supplemental money in addition to his income, but not much, and expected to live within our means. We were supposed to be renters.

"The kicker is that Charlie hadn't embezzled five million dollars like the Feds thought. He said he made off with close to seven million, the last two million all at once and in cash. He really overstepped to do that, and that's why he thought he was going to be caught.

"The thing is, Regan, I don't know how Charlie did it, but he managed to get the cash here, to Santa Cruz, but it's not like he could go to Bay Federal Credit Union and deposit it. So he hid it. He hid it right here, somewhere at this house.

"He'd never tell me more than that, but every time he thought I was getting down or we had an anniversary or I had a birthday, and especially when I complained about how badly I wanted to see our daughter, he'd produce a little gift for me, something for inside the house that no one else could see, except for my housekeeper, Rosa. She's undocumented and quiet because of that. She's also my friend, loyal, and well paid for her services — paid in cash — he paid cash for all our treats.

"He'd laugh about it and say we lived like recluses who had no friends or company, but at least we lived alone in a nice place."

Regan downed her tea in a gulp. Tika refilled her cup as she continued.

"So, that's my story. Now here's the first problem I have that I need your help with: tell me about disclosures. Charlie has been coming to me at night. He waves his arms a lot but so far he's been unable to speak, although I do think he's trying to tell me where he hid the money. Do I have to disclose the house may have a ghost?"

Regan downed her second cup of tea like she had the first, but this cup was still so hot it burned on the way down. She struggled but managed to maintain a semblance of professional composure.

"I'm going to have to think about that, Tika. There are so many disclosure forms that the state requires and our company has separate forms, too, but honestly, that question, whether or not the presence of a ghost has to be disclosed, hasn't come up until now."

Tika added tea to Regan's cup for the third time, and thinking that she seemed enthusiastic in finishing her first two cups, paused with the teapot aloft ready for a fourth refill.

Regan was afraid to pick up her teacup this time until she heard what Tika had to say next.

"I guess you noticed the holes out front on your way in?"

"I did. It looks like you have a terrible gopher problem."

Tika chuckled, "I hope that's what the neighbors think, too. I started looking for the money in the backyard, to be discreet of course, and because I assumed Charlie would have been as well. I made a grid and started digging systematically everywhere there was loose dirt. I mean, I probably would have noticed if he had dug in the lawn back there because, believe me, I was paying attention. Nothing. No buried treasure.

"That's when Charlie started coming to me. I thought he was trying to tell me to stop wasting my efforts in the backyard and to look out front. There's only sort of lawn there and it's not nicely kept like out back, so that seemed reasonable. He could have disturbed it and I wouldn't have noticed. The holes you see in the front lawn — Super Gopher — that's me! And still no luck."

"Do you think he hid the money in the house, then?" Regan couldn't believe how casually she tossed out the question, especially given the sum involved, where it came from, and Tika's mention of nightly visits by a dead man.

"He must have. I've started looking, but I'm really at a loss as to where the money is. It seems to me like something over a million dollars — I figure we've spent the rest — even in bills of a fairly big denomination would take up a lot of room and should be fairly obvious; but I've looked in all the easy places, like the attic and under the house, and no luck.

"That's why I want to have a séance — so Charlie can tell me right out where to look."

Regan was glad she waited on the tea, but after that last announcement, she thought Tika couldn't have any more startling revelations, at least during the time it would take her to have a sip. She was just bringing the cup to her lips when Tika added another zinger.

"I'll want you to be there, of course, because I think a narrative written by you would work well as a disclosure document. And then, having another pair of ears present when Charlie tells me who killed him seems like a good idea, don't you think?"

Regan put the teacup down so quickly it rattled, but at least it didn't spill. She was speechless; no one would have accused her of answering Tika's question like a polished professional.

"Uh, um, I, uh."

"The police say Charlie was shot twice in the chest from some distance and then the killer got close and put a final shot in his head — the coup de gráce — execution style. I think his identity was discovered and that he was killed in a mob hit, but the way he was shot wasn't consistent with a hit. Usually all the shots would be delivered at close range; mobsters like their victims to know they've been made and to understand why they are about to die.

"The police are looking into it; I'd like to know for sure. If the Albanian Mafia killed my husband, I'd like to put Konstantin Kola on his tombstone and call my daughter.

"The Albanians aren't vicious like the Russians, and they usually don't punish family members for the transgressions of one of their own. If they killed Charlie, that's probably the end of it: double-crosser punished with death. But if it turns out they didn't kill Charlie, I'm not sure I should do either of those things. I wouldn't want to take any chances."

If Regan was knocked for a loop before, she wondered what she should call the impact of Tika's newly revealed dilemma.

"The other thing I need to know is which papers I can sign and which Olive needs to sign, since she's on title."

Regan thought since she was focused on mobs and hits and had only been half paying attention, she must have misunderstood what Tika said.

"What? I'm sorry. What did you just say?"

"I asked if I can sign papers, at least to list the house, or if Olive has to …"

Regan missed the end of Tika's question this time but it didn't matter, she had heard it correctly the first time.

"Olive owns this house?" Regan tried to sound nonchalant.

"Yes. Like I said, we were to be renters."

"Tell me, Regan, is being a real estate agent like being an attorney? Is there something like attorney-client privilege between realtors and their clients?"

"We have a fiduciary duty to our clients, yes. It's essentially the same thing." Regan embellished the definition of fiduciary duty considerably and she was certain if anyone heard her do it, they would not only correct her, they would cite her for an ethics violation.

Tika nodded and seemed reassured. "I guess it's OK to tell you the rest, then."

There's more? flashed through Regan's mind.

"We had the money to buy the house, but we couldn't without alerting the FBI to Charlie's stash. So Olive … You know, I'm not sure I should be telling you this, after all. I don't think what Olive did matters anyway; I don't think it's related to selling the house."

Tika was withdrawing; Regan was desperate to keep her talking.

"Please, let me be the judge of that. There may be some disclosure or some legal technicality you're not aware of. Why don't you tell me about Olive and let me sort out whether or not anything matters. Like you said, that's what I'm getting paid to do."

"Yes ... yes, you're right. Well ... Olive kind of did a little money laundering for us. At the time, I'm not sure we thought about it much."

"Why was Olive willing to ... help you like that?"

"That's a long story. How far back do you want me to go?" Tika asked. She was back on Regan's track.

"All the way back, all the way to the beginning."

Regan smiled with her best calmly reassuring professional face. Inside her head she screamed, *Tell me everything about Olive,* so loudly she was afraid her thoughts would burst through her skull and Tika would hear them.

"I was attached to Walter Reed Army Medical Center when I was in the military, and Olive worked there as a civilian nurse, at least until she had to quit to spend all her time taking care of Paul before he died.

"That's how we met. She's the one who inspired me to go into nursing.

"We were close, but after she left I lost track of her — you know how that happens. It had been, oh, twenty years maybe since I'd seen her, when the first week Charlie and I were here with our new identities, who should I run into in the grocery store, in Shopper's Corner, but Olive. She recognized me as readily as I recognized her.

"At first I didn't know what to do; I was afraid I'd ruin our newly created identities, but then I realized Olive didn't know anything about my life after Walter Reed. I could simply present myself as Tika Smith and introduce Konnie as my husband Charlie Smith. I didn't even tell her I had a nursing

105

degree or that we had a daughter.

"Funny how that worked. Olive and her husband never had children — they were afraid to, what with her husband's family history — and assumed maybe we had similar difficulties. It made Olive very sympathetic toward me.

"Over time we became close; so close we shared our deepest darkest secrets. I told her about us and she told me about Paul and how she broke her vow to him — Oh, I shouldn't go there. That's private and really doesn't have anything to do with the house."

Tika looked flustered. It took all the self control Regan could summon to feign lack of interest.

"We still are close. I'm going to move into her house after this sells, at least for a bit, while I sort out who I am now that Charlie … Konnie … see what I mean?" She sighed with frustration, "I don't even know what to call my dead husband."

"I'm surprised," Regan frowned. "You and Olive seem to …"

"To disagree all the time?" Tika smirked. "When I came to Santa Cruz, I couldn't be a nurse. I volunteered as a Pink Lady at Dominican Hospital, thinking they'd let me do some helpful nursing related things. They stuck me at entry reception, pointing out the different wards to visitors — not my idea of being useful. I didn't last long.

"I started to dabble in some alternative medicine, some Eastern, some going back to my Navajo roots, and some, as Olive calls it, 'just out there new agey stuff.'

"I found the different disciplines interesting and often helpful. There are other approaches to healing besides

106

Western medicine, you know. Olive doesn't think so; she thinks I was a scientist, and now I've become a Santa Cruz goof ball and she berates me for it.

"Oh, we make snide comments to one another from time to time, but it's all right. Friends can disagree. Friends can do that.

"Sorry, I'm getting side-tracked here, and you're not interested in any of this, are you?"

Regan's smile was feeble. If only Tika knew just how interested she was in *all* of it.

"Anyway, when we wanted to buy a house, Olive did it for us. She fronted the money and went on title. We set everything up to look like we had a long lease-option with our rental payments going toward the purchase price. But we had a private notarized agreement that the house was ours and that Olive would put it in her will that, should anything happen to both of us or to her, our daughter would inherit the house.

"So can we, because of the lease option, sell the house or does Olive have to do it?"

It took Regan a few seconds to respond to Tika's question; she was lost in mulling over what she had just heard. Fortunately it didn't matter. Tika read her hesitation as thoughtful deliberation.

"It is complicated, isn't it?"

"Um, yes. I'm going to have to do some research about … about the specifics of your recorded contract."

"Take all the time you need. I'm not going to be selling until after the séance and until I find our stash.

"In the meantime, though, what should I do to get the

107

house ready to sell? I figure if it's not too expensive, I can get it started on my own. My bank account doesn't have much in it, but Olive can let me stop paying rent, or maybe she can loan me money or pay for the fix-ups herself. Which do you think would be most appropriate?"

"Does Olive have any money? It would be best if she made the repairs ... but I've heard ..." Regan stopped herself. *Should I go there?*

Regan practically held her breath as she spoke, but she went on, "I've heard she has a big installment payment coming due on her house in Woods Cove. I've heard she's struggling and in danger of losing the house."

"I don't know why you think that. She's already made her second installment payment.

"I told you we've spent some of the money Charlie embezzled. The last big chunk he took out of hiding was for Olive; it's all covered in our private agreement. She fronted us the money for this house, which pretty much took all her savings. In return we give her money, cash, whenever she needs it or wants it, up to what she spent on our house plus interest.

"We gave her four-hundred-thousand dollars in cash in the middle of June."

Regan's drive back to the office felt more like a twenty mile trek than the two miles it was.

Like all realtors, Regan was bound to her clients by a fiduciary responsibility which demanded, among other things, that she owed them loyalty, obedience, and confidentiality. Every four years, for all the years she had been in the business, she had to take a class and pass a test about the meaning of those tenets. She understood her fiduciary duties, at least she did until her meeting with Tika.

She knew fiduciary duties weren't the same thing as attorney-client privilege, even though she intimated that they were to Tika. She knew her duties applied to real estate, but was that where they stopped?

The realtor's loyalty clause said, "To act at all times in the best interest of the principle ..." The confidentiality clause was even more to the point; it read, "To safeguard the principle's secrets ..."

She misled Tika to keep her talking, and Tika had talked, all right. Why hadn't she recalled that wise saying "Be careful what you wish for" when she needed to hear it? Why hadn't it popped into her head when it could have served as a useful warning? P*robably because it would have been inconvenient if it had, and I would have ignored it!*

Next time, Regan.

She berated herself more than Dave would have, had he known what she did.

She lied to her client and as a result Tika had told her about stolen money and the unlawful activities that she, her dead husband, and Olive had engaged in to keep it hidden from the government.

What in good conscience should she do with that information?

She had seen some small-scale pot growing operations, especially in houses owned by long distance parents for their college students. Californians were at odds with the federal government, having voted in favor of allowing medical marijuana which Washington forbade as part of its war on drugs, but she knew the thriving plants she saw weren't being grown for medical use and the student growers weren't engaged in a noble protest.

She had turned a blind eye more than once. She had used the euphemism "make sure to clean the house *really well* before the inspectors and appraisers arrive" to discreetly warn her client's children to get rid of their plants. Inspectors and appraisers owed them no loyalty or confidentiality and were, in fact, required to report illicit horticulture to the authorities.

Fortunately, all the students she advised were smart enough to understand her subtle meanings and her clients never had any problems as a result of their children's hobbies.

Was the Tika-Charlie-Olive scheme of more consequence

than illegal farming?

Charlie stole money from gangsters. She didn't mind that criminals had been fleeced, especially considering the man doing the stealing had turned state's evidence and brought some of them to justice.

She was inclined to remain silent about the missing money.

But if she did, would she be guilty of whatever crime it was to withhold information from the FBI? She might be guilty of tax fraud or evasion, too. *Tax evasion. Wasn't that how Al Capone was finally caught?*

Regan wanted to push the driver in front of her off the road. The woman insisted on driving the posted twenty-five miles per hour on High Street where everyone else went at least thirty-five. They were well past Westlake Elementary School — there seemed to be no risk to going faster — besides, at 1:15 the kindergarteners had gone home and the other children were safely in their classrooms.

Move, please! Regan, wildly frustrated, pounded on her steering wheel with one hand. *I need to talk to Tom.*

It wasn't until she reached Bay Street and turned left — not the most direct way to their office but a way to get out from behind the feather-foot in front of her — that she realized she couldn't tell Tom about what Tika had said, at least not all of it, and definitely not about the part that was most troubling to her.

Tom, her logical, rational husband — her rock — couldn't hear what she knew without being drawn into the same legal conundrum she was in.

If he advised her to tell Dave — which was exactly what

he would do — and she refused, he would either have to go behind her back or become part of her conspiracy of silence. To protect her, he might do the latter. She couldn't make him choose. She couldn't let him get involved.

They had been married for eleven years. In that time, she had learned not to ask if an outfit made her look fat because he would tell her the truth: "Ruffles down the sides; what do you think?" He didn't lie to her. And except for occasionally telling him they needed to be somewhere fifteen minutes earlier than they really did — an acceptable thing to do, she believed, because he was prone to lateness and she was obsessively punctual — she didn't lie to him.

She was only too aware that it was possible to lie by omission; she had learned that from her first husband. And now she made the decision that, by omission, she was going to lie to Tom. She could rationalize all she wanted about it being for his protection, but she was going to lie to him nevertheless. It hurt her heart.

Her next problem was what to do about Dave. She had been pushing Olive on him as a murder suspect primarily because Olive seemed to need money. Now she knew that wasn't true.

When she told him she had been mistaken about Olive murdering husbands to collect money from their widows, Dave would tease her mercilessly and accuse her of doing a flip-flop. She could take that; she could manage a smart comeback if she needed one, but when he finished teasing, he would ask why she changed her mind.

What would she say? What could she say?

Tika had also said something that fascinated Regan even

more during her string of revelations. Tika said Olive told her she had broken her vow to Paul.

Vow was a serious word. It implied much more than a promise or the keeping of a secret and it was often associated with marriage. What vow had Olive broken?

Regan replayed every mention of Paul she could recall Olive making; she had never called him her husband. Was Paul Olive's dead husband, or was he the other man, someone who caused Olive to break her vow to her husband?

She needed to know — that became her first priority — because if Olive had broken her marriage vow, maybe she did more. Maybe she made herself a widow to be free, and the guilt Regan saw in Olive's eyes when they walked together began with her own widowhood.

If that was the case, Dave should know that while Olive might not have a money motive for killing husbands, she might still be a husband killer.

Regan turned into the office parking lot and was relieved to see Tom's BMW was missing — no need to lie to him, at least not yet.

She went to her office without checking in with Amanda, hoping for once that their receptionist's uncanny ability to see backward down the hall would fail her.

I'm being silly; if I want privacy, I should just tell Amanda to hold my calls.

She couldn't speak to Amanda or anyone else right now. She felt anyone who spoke to her or even looked at her would know at once that she was keeping a dark secret and was no longer a law-abiding citizen.

This is how paranoia starts, isn't it?

For all her suspicions about Olive, she still had never bothered to learn the woman's last name. She better start by getting that information.

Regan logged on to her favorite title company site and entered the Rudolph Street address. Her computer screen filled with information about the property. She was interested in only one piece of it: Owner: Olive Gretchell.

Gretchell could have been Olive's maiden name as easily as her married name, but she had to begin her research somewhere, so she made a series of assumptions: the first was that most women past sixty, like Olive was, had taken their husband's name when they married. If Paul was Olive's husband, that would make him Paul Gretchell.

Tika said her daughter had just left for college when Charlie made his witness protection announcement and she complained she hadn't seen her daughter for five years. Regan added eighteen, a typical age for a new college freshman, to five; Tika's daughter must be about twenty three.

She threw in another three years to let Tika get out of the army, start nursing school, meet Charlie, marry him and have his child. Tika probably met Olive about twenty-six years ago.

Tika said Paul was alive when they met at Walter Reed but that Olive stopped working to take care of him before he died. That meant she not only needed to find out if Paul Gretchell was Olive's husband, but if he was, what happened to him.

Regan reviewed her assumptions, trying to think like Tom might. Her next supposition felt more like pure guesswork than anything he might have come up with, but she couldn't think of another way to tackle the problem.

She decided Paul Gretchell had either died within commuting distance of Walter Reed in Washington, D.C., where he and Olive must have been living when Tika knew her, or here in Santa Cruz.

No one had ever mentioned Olive having family ties that drew her back to Santa Cruz after Paul's death. Why had Olive chosen to settle here? Perhaps she had come because of Paul's ties to Santa Cruz. They might have come back to Paul's home as a couple, so he could be with family before he died, and Olive might have chosen to remain here after his death.

There was a Gretchell Street in Santa Cruz; she had sold two houses on the street during her career. Was it possible Paul was a Santa Cruz Gretchell?

Regan's mind worked fancifully.

Maybe Olive was slowly poisoning her husband and he wanted to come home as he grew more and more ill. Olive might have been only too willing to leave her nursing history behind. No. If Paul was her husband, that was wrong.

First I better find out if Olive was married to Paul and then discover how he died. If a bus hit him, there goes my whole theory.

🏠🏠🏠🏠🏠🏠🏠🏠🏠🏠🏠

Regan ducked out the office back door, avoiding Amanda as carefully as she had on her way in, and drove to the Church Street Library which was home base for the Santa

Cruz County Genealogical Society. A friendly female volunteer greeted her as she walked into the genealogical research section.

"Hi, I'm Maggie. I bet I know secrets about your past."

She giggled a bit and added, "I'm not supposed to say that, but it's so much fun, I can't resist sometimes."

"I'm glad to meet you, Maggie. I'm Regan," a*nd I surely hope you don't know secrets about my recent past.* "I'm doing some research on the Gretchell family of Santa Cruz. I'm trying to track down information about one of their members, Paul Gretchell."

"AG or BG?"

"Excuse me?"

"Above ground or below ground."

Regan was the one to chuckle this time. "Below ground, I believe, probably for at least a couple of decades."

"Then you'll want to start with our online cemetery page. Once you know where he is, you can go visit his grave. You can get a death date and maybe some relatives' names from his tombstone.

"Come back once you've done that. We probably have more information here, but it will help me find it if I have some clues. If you'll follow me, I'll show you how to narrow your search for gravesites."

The Santa Cruz Genealogy Cemeteries page, which for some reason featured a picture of the Beach Boardwalk rollercoaster, listed all the local cemeteries and had a "find a grave" icon for each. Maggie scanned the page, talking to herself as she worked. "Evergreen is historical only, Day Family is private," rapidly eliminating some of the graveyards.

Within five minutes, Maggie had located a Paul Gretchell at Santa Cruz Memorial Park, which had its first internment in 1862 and was still accepting new residents.

Regan scribbled the grave coordinates on a piece of paper, thanked Maggie, and headed off to her next stop.

🏠🏠🏠🏠🏠🏠🏠🏠🏠🏠🏠🏠

She turned into the cemetery entrance on Ocean Street Extension ten minutes later and began looking for directions. Within another five minutes, she was parked and walking the last few feet toward Paul Gretchell's gravesite.

She read nearby tombstones as she walked.

"Rachel Gretchell, loving wife of Herbert Gretchell." Herbert's headstone was next to hers and expressed similar sentiments, but in reverse. Samuel Gretchell and Emily Gretchell shared a headstone. Their son, Frederick, who had died a hero in World War II, lay nearby.

She found what she was looking for on a slight rise near a birch tree. Paul Gretchell's grave was in a setting people would describe as "very peaceful" in the hushed tones they used around the dead. She got out paper and pen and copied down the engraving:

"Paul Gretchell, beloved husband of Olive Gretchell.

Born May 2, 1940, died December 17, 1989."

One question was settled. The vow Olive had broken to her husband didn't seem to be the one she made on her wedding day.

🏠🏠🏠🏠🏠🏠🏠🏠🏠🏠🏠🏠

117

Regan returned to the Genealogical Society room and looked for Maggie. The volunteer spotted her first and was already smiling when Regan saw her.

"Oh, Regan, I didn't expect you to come back so soon, but I'm glad you did. After you left, I thought of something about the Gretchell family, something I remember reading about them.

"I thought I could call you, but then I realized I didn't know how to get hold of you. Now you're back so that takes care of that."

Regan gave Maggie the names and dates she collected from Paul Gretchell's headstone and from the other nearby grave markers. Maggie tapped on the Genealogical Society's computer with experienced fingers. She uttered the occasional "Uh-huh" or "Oh yes" as each page came up and she moved through her search. She hit the print icon a couple of times as she mumbled and worked.

"Wait here for a sec while I go to the central printer," she instructed Regan.

Maggie returned carrying several sheets of paper.

"You should find these helpful," she said as she handed the papers to Regan, "And here's a copy of the newspaper story you might be interested in reading. It appeared shortly after Paul Gretchell died.

"It confirms what I remember about the family. They had what Woody Guthrie died of. They had Huntington's disease in their genes.

"Woody's son Arlo didn't get the disease, though, did he? I remember that because I was such a big fan of Arlo Guthrie

— I absolutely loved *Alice's Restaurant* — and I worried for him. I guess Paul Gretchell wasn't as lucky as Arlo was."

Regan thanked Maggie for her help and took the papers to her car to read. The newspaper article, which was fairly long, interested her most. It was an article about Huntington's disease and used the Gretchell family history to illustrate its points.

The piece started with details about when the first of the Gretchells arrived in Santa Cruz and what succeeding generations accomplished during their residency. It stated that overall the family was highly regarded, but in each generation there were always one or two children who, after promising and productive early lives, lost cognitive ability and ultimately fell into what seemed like schizophrenic and sometimes violent behavior and dementia which became so severe they required institutionalization. All eventually died in what should have been the prime of their lives. The article explained that the family was afflicted with what is now recognized as Huntington's disease.

As she read, she imagined the horror each new victim of the disorder must have felt when their symptoms appeared and they realized that they, too, would likely die a horribly debilitating death like other members of their family.

According to the article, Paul and his wife had made the decision to remain childless, and he hoped that he would be the last of the Gretchell cousins to exhibit the genetic malady.

Both his mother and his wife were quoted in the article. Rachel Gretchell said the family privately suspected there had been suicides in prior generations because of the disease, but the deaths had been attributed to other things because suicide held such a stigma.

She praised her daughter-in-law, Olive, who had kept Paul at home and bravely cared for him until his tragic end, an incredibly difficult task given his final year.

There was just a two sentence quote from Olive in the article. It was in response to her mother-in-law's praise. "Caring for Paul was easy. What I could not do was allow him to go when he was beyond all hope and so badly wanted to stop suffering."

Regan finished reading, folded the papers in half and stuffed them in her purse.

What a difference a few hours made. This morning, Regan knew nothing of Charlie Smith's dangerous past or Tika's hidden embezzled money. She had been absolutely certain that Olive was murdering husbands to create cash-flush widows in time to keep her house out of foreclosure.

Now she saw Olive with new eyes and from a new perspective. Olive had become a widow at a young age and had never remarried. She couldn't fall in love again; she was still in love with her husband. Olive certainly hadn't practiced the deadly art of husband-killing on him; that wasn't why she felt guilty.

Olive may have badgered Helen about her Alzheimer's-addled Henry and brutally suggested she abandon him, but she had cared for her own dying husband through a cruel decline, bravely and lovingly it appeared. She understood what that kind of commitment cost. If Olive pressed, it was because she was trying to spare Helen, not trying to rush Henry out of the picture, and certainly not because she was trying to speed up Helen's move into her widow's house.

Regan had planned to press her theory about Olive murdering for money the next time she saw Dave. Now she was going to tell him Olive had no money motive for killing husbands. She was also going to tell him that Olive's past argued against her being capable of murder.

She sighed as she started her car.

Dave's going to have so much fun at my expense. I better get this over with.

Regan parked in the visitor area by the L-shaped two-story Santa Cruz Police Headquarters. A high arch accentuated the entry and gave a faux Spanish flavor to the otherwise architecturally uninspired edifice. She sat in her car and stared at the massive entry doors with blank eyes; there was no need to rush, better to organize her thoughts before going inside.

When she was ready, she gathered her purse and her token gift. As she made her way through the entry arch, she tried once again to decide if the police station was painted a faint flamingo pink or if the reflection off the red tile roof gave it its color.

She was usually in a rush to reach Dave's cubby-hole office. Once she was in such a hurry that she forced her way through the interior security doors into the authorized only section and was chased by an armed policewoman, intent on protecting her fellow officers from a likely deranged woman. Regan behaved sedately on this visit, offering herself up to the reception staff where she presented identification and her gift bag for inspection and waited for a visitor's badge.

She was ready to be admitted past the security doors when she had a change of heart. She was still uncertain of what she was going to say to Dave, but whatever she decided, it wasn't going to be the whole truth. Deception committed in his office, in the very heart of a police station filled with officers sworn to upholding the law, seemed too intimidating for her to pull it off.

She returned to the receptionist. "You know what?" she smiled apologetically. "I've changed my mind about going in. Could you call Officer Everett and let him know I'm here? Please tell him I'll wait outside and that I have coffee and scones for whenever he's ready for a coffee break."

She thanked the receptionist and was just about to exit the main entrance when Dave appeared beside her.

"You got some of that lemon crud in there, too?" He motioned toward the bag.

"You mean lemon curd?"

"Whatever."

He held the door open and followed her to a bench that was shaded by the roof overhang.

"You've never brought me goodies at work before and you didn't flame into the building. That must mean you have a really big problem that needs my help but you don't think anyone is going to die while I eat my scones."

"Not bad sleuthing for a police ombudsman. Maybe I won't have to give you detective lessons after all, like I thought I would." Regan's smile was demure. She had to needle him or he'd wonder why she hadn't, but she wasn't in the right frame of mind to finish her poke with a big grin.

"The thing is …" Regan hesitated for a second, still

123

searching for a last-ditch way of explaining her flip-flop. "The things is, I think I was wrong about Olive …"

Dave clutched his sides and shivered violently, "Brrr! Did you feel that?"

"What," she frowned with concern.

"I think Hell just froze over," he declared with absolute sincerity.

"Dave, I've been wrong before."

"You're wrong all the time, Regan. That's not it. No, no, it's you *admitting* you're wrong — that's what caused the cosmic event."

Regan scowled at him.

"You could listen to me without being so mean about it. I did bring you scones."

"You're right," he offered a seated bow. "Tell me why you changed your mind about Olive," he said with exaggerated and still-mocking thoughtfulness.

"The motive I thought she had — that she needed money to pay the second installment on her house — well, it turns out she doesn't need money after all. In fact, she made the payment before Mike McAllister was killed, so there's no reason to think she was involved in his death."

"And you know this, how?"

There it was. There was the question she didn't want to answer.

"Let's just say I talked to a friend of hers who said she loaned Olive the money …"

Dave pounced.

"This friend of Olive's have a name?"

"Anonymous. She wants to remain anonymous. You really

don't need to know who she is, Dave. It doesn't matter."

If their positions had been reversed, Regan would have fired back and demanded a name, saying, "I'll be the judge of that." She read his expression — that was exactly what he wanted to say, but he refrained and settled for giving her an aggravated squint instead.

"What about all your other little reasons for knowing she offed hubbies, two, three times? Didn't you point out stuff like she could have picked up enough medical knowledge in Vietnam or the Gulf War to know how to cut a renal artery, learned about car transmissions and how to use a weapon in the army, too, and was always missing when a murder was being committed? Oh, and what about my personal favorite: she liked to dress in black to look like Death?"

Regan looked at him quizzically. "Dave, I never said anything about Olive's medical background. You've been investigating her, too, haven't you?"

"Anonymous, huh? No comment, then."

"I found out about what happened to Olive's husband … how he died. She always seems so harsh to her friend Helen about her husband who has Alzheimer's. I thought Olive was being a cruel and unsympathetic woman, the way she spoke to her friend. I don't think that any longer; I understand her better now. Olive's husband died from Huntington's disease. Do you know what that is?"

Dave nodded to indicate he did.

"I found out she cared for him before he died, heroically according to her mother-in-law, even when the disease plunged him into dementia near the end of its course. I think in her own way she's trying to give her friend Helen permission to give up on her husband, to let him go, which Olive said she couldn't do.

"I think she's not a murderer because she doesn't have it in her to be one. If she could kill, she would have helped her husband die."

"Is her friend Helen Mrs. Anonymous?"

Regan was so surprised by Dave's question and how it shifted the tone of their conversation that she startled slightly.

Dave's face hinted at a knowing smile. She didn't correct his impression; if he thought Helen was Olive's financial rescuer that was fine with her.

"I was talking to Tika Smith recently. She thinks her husband's death might have been a professional hit."

Regan sipped her coffee casually; it was Dave's turn to be taken aback.

"I don't know how you manage," he shook his head. "How *do* you get … involved?"

"They've had a while to investigate Charlie Smith's murder. What do the police think? Did a hit man get him?"

His lips disappeared in what Regan recognized as his pondering mode while he considered what to say.

"I should probably say no comment again, although, if your pal already told you …"

"You don't have to say anything. You could just nod your head up and down for yes or side to side for no." Regan arranged her face in an innocent pose.

"Tika Smith wants to know for sure, for reasons of her own safety."

"I bet she does," Dave's whole body rocked forward and backward. His body language said yes, even if he didn't.

"Next time you talk to your buddy, Tika, you should tell her to relax. That's all I have to say."

"Tika says her husband's ghost has been visiting her. She's sure he has been trying to tell her who killed him, but he hasn't been able to speak, so she's planning to hold a séance so he can speak to her through a medium."

Regan watched Dave instantly transform from a glum outmaneuvered cop into a grinning disbeliever.

"A séance? Perfect! I don't know why we don't use séances all the time to solve crimes. Think of all the dead eyewitnesses we don't bother to question. Shocking, isn't it?"

"I'm invited to attend. Should I go?"

"Should you go? Regan, I'll give you a police escort to the event if you want. A séance. What a perfect match for your special skills; sounds like an ideal way for you to play detective. Oh yes, for sure, go. Knock yourself out."

He pulled the last scone from the bag and dunked it in the remains of the lemon curd. A huge smile brightened his face.

"You know I'd go with you myself if the department would let me, but they're kind of stodgy about stuff like that, probably wouldn't give me the time off, speaking of which …" He looked at his watch and stood up abruptly.

"Hey, Regan, coffee break's over. I gotta get back. Thanks for sharing your goodies. And thanks for the coffee and scones, too."

She could hear him laughing softly as he walked back toward the archway.

"A séance," he chuckled as he disappeared inside.

She felt a great sense of relief. She had delivered her message about Olive's innocence without giving up Tika's

127

secret. She also learned something interesting — two things, in fact. The first was that the police had investigated Olive more fully than she thought; the second thing she learned made her smile: Dave, for all his teasing, paid attention to what she said.

"You're a real estate agent so you probably know where the road is even though most people don't. You turn on to Ocean Street Extension and continue past the cemetery and past where the road bends. The house is light green but you can't see it from the street because it's set back a good quarter mile on the property and the driveway curves a couple of times. You'll see the house number out front on your right, though. They used big tiles to spell out 2216. You can't miss it," Tika instructed.

"You're not having the séance at your house?" Regan queried.

"I would have, but that makes it complicated for Helen to come. The medium assures me spirits aren't housebound, so if we have the séance at her house, we can do it when Henry, he's her husband, is taking a nap.

"I want at least six people to be there and Mary Anne — you met her on the walk — has already dropped out of the group. She says it's too dangerous to be a member of the Widow's Walk League given the way husbands are dropping. And Joyce will probably come but she's starting to feel the same way.

"I can understand Mary Anne ... she was divorced for years and has just remarried. They're still in the honeymoon stage and she doesn't want to take any chances with her new man, but Joyce ... she thinks her Robert is so special," Tika snickered. "She's the only one who does. Ah, she's a high-strung thing by nature, maybe that's why she's getting so worked up."

Regan wondered if Olive was invited but didn't want to ask about her by name. "Who else is coming?"

"Linda will be there, but Susan can't come because she's going to be visiting her sister who lives in Carmel Valley; it's her sister's birthday. And Olive," Tika sighed loudly enough Regan could hear her huff over the phone, "Olive says the whole thing is a bunch of hooey and she refuses to come. It's just as well that she doesn't. We'll be better off without her negative energy.

"Anyway, I'm willing to have the séance at Helen's house for the numbers. It will just be Helen, Linda, Joyce, Karen — oh, I forgot to mention Karen is coming. Unlike Joyce, she's a sensible one. Of course, it could be that she thinks since her partner is a woman, there's no danger," Tika laughed, "but Leslie can't make it, she has to work.

"So like I said, Helen, Linda, Joyce, Karen, and you and me. That's six, a good number. I understand it's best to have a number of guests that's divisible by three. If Joyce is a no-show, we'll have the medium to make six. I hope it's OK to count him if we need to.

"The medium will be the only man present; he's someone I know. He's really a psychic reader, but he says he can handle a séance and I thought it might make Charlie feel more comfortable if he has the option of speaking through a man rather than through a woman."

"You said tomorrow at 3:30?" Regan confirmed as she wrote the time in her datebook.

"That's right, but you don't have to be right on time. We'll have some snacks and gossip until everyone gets there. Maybe we'll have some wine, too. I'll have to ask Sebastian if that's all right."

Thursday, séance day, was also broker tour day. Regan held an open house at Linda's. She wore professional attire for the day, which for hosting an open house meant high heels and a skirt and jacket. She wanted to be more comfortable for the séance and Tika had advised her that it was best if all in attendance felt relaxed.

She called it a day early and drove home to change, wondering what exactly constituted the correct outfit to wear to a séance. Should she wear black or would that seem too mournful to the dead? White was the color of mourning in some other cultures; better not wear white either. Would red or yellow seem too bold to the visiting specters?

By the time she left for Helen's house, she was dressed in skinny jeans, low-heeled black boots that reached almost to her knees, and a plain short-sleeved lavender top cinched in by a belt at her waist; she felt ready to greet any apparition that might come her way.

🏠🏠🏠🏠🏠🏠🏠🏠🏠🏠🏠🏠

Helen's house, painted pale green as Tika promised, could have been cast as the ranch house in an old-style western. It was a low-roofed single story wooden house with a deep two-steps-up porch running across the entire front.

The house had been there long enough for a massive wisteria to have coiled around the porch railing and the support columns to the roof. The wisteria had few blooms this late in the year, but the resulting seed pods suggested it must have been breathtaking when it was covered by springtime purple blossoms.

The land along the driveway leading up to the house felt old westy, too. It was dry, flat, and California summer brown dotted with Manzanita and scrub oak until about fifty feet from the house. There the natural landscape gave way to an attempt at lawn, but the area needed water and the rough grass that survived was bald and patchy.

A massive wooden picnic table, rusty swing set, and small swimming pool off to the left of the house hinted that in years past, the property had been home to family gatherings and children playing outdoors.

The pool seemed out of character with the rest of the play area. The clear blue water sparkled as sunlight glinted off its surface; everything else felt worn, tired, and abandoned.

To the right of the house and behind it, the landscape changed. Chaparral gave way to a denser growth of Madrone and Douglas fir and the land began an ascent, gently at first but quickly growing steeper, to Graham Hill Road high above the house.

Regan squeezed her car into the last parking space in a cleared area off to the right of the house where four other vehicles were already parked. She didn't mind being the closest to the trees; given the way the sun should move, she hoped her car would get some shade later in the day.

Regan climbed the wide steps quickly but she slowed to savor crossing the wooden porch. The muffled tapping sound of her boots on the old wood brought back memories. She smiled slightly, recalling days from her early childhood when she visited her paternal grandparents' home in northern California and held her grandfather's hand as they walked along the boardwalks that still lined the main street of their tiny town.

She raised her hand to knock on the front door but noticed it wasn't latched. She grasped the handle and pushed. The living room that opened before her was bright with summer sun.

Tika was seated at the back of the room on a worn rose-colored sofa. She was deep in conversation with a bushy-haired man in his early fifties. He wore dark rimmed glasses and had on tooled boots, jeans, and a blue work shirt with sleeves rolled up to just below his elbows. He was the only man in the room — he must be the medium, she reasoned — but he looked more like a ranch hand than what she expected someone who was about to commune with the dear departed to look and dress like.

Linda was the first to notice Regan. She came over and grabbed her arm, pulled her into the room, and as she had done on the day of the Widow's Walk League hike, mentioned all the women's names.

"You remember Helen, Joyce, and Karen, don't you, Regan?"

"How long do you think this will take?" Joyce twittered in Regan's direction. "I can't stay long."

Regan shrugged and raised her eyebrows, "I have no idea. This is my first séance."

"Mine, too," Karen gushed. "I think it's kind of exciting, don't you?" She took a long swallow and drained her wine glass.

"I think I need a little more fortification," she tapped her empty glass, "and a few more of those yummy little sandwiches." She nodded to the sideboard where diminutive finger sandwiches and wine were set out, as well as an abundant array of cookies, fruit, and iced tea.

"Tika brought everything, and Sebastian, our spirit guide, says we should go into this experience happy, relaxed, and filled with delicious sustenance." Karen giggled mischievously, "I'm giving it my all."

"Joyce, you seem a little tense. Why don't you have a nice glass of wine, too?" Linda suggested.

"I don't drink. And I'll need to be driving soon; I really can't stay long." She checked her watch a second time.

Tika, who was dressed in keeping with Regan's stereotypical expectations of what a medium should wear, fluttered toward them, the silver threads woven throughout her long, gauzy, scarlet-colored dress shimmering as she moved. She grasped the psychic reader by the hand and dragged him toward the group.

"Ladies, this is Sebastian," she proclaimed loudly, and

then cringing, dropped her voice to a whisper. "Helen, I'm so sorry. Do we need to keep it down so we don't disturb poor Henry?"

"He should be fine, Tika. He takes a nap at this time of day and sleeps soundly, better than he does at night. But I did set up the table and candles in the den at the opposite side of the house from his room in case any of our visitors are noisy." Helen smiled weakly at Sebastian, "The only reference I have for spirits is Scrooge's dead partner Jacob Marley and he rattled chains, didn't he?"

"Are we ready, ladies?" Sebastian asked as he folded Tika's hand over his arm and led the way through the doorway on the right side of the living room.

Regan noted a mood change in the women as they crossed the threshold into the den. They grew silent in contemplation of the mission about to be undertaken. Their chatter was replaced by faint new age music — perhaps something by Yanni in his 1980's heyday — Sebastian's contribution to the day, Regan guessed.

The tone of the room changed as well. The den was not oppressively dark, but it was considerably dimmer than the living room. Painted white paneling on the living room walls gave way to dark-stained paneled walls, and the many windows which brought summer light into the living room were replaced by a single window in the den. The window was undraped, but the sheer curtains that normally framed it had been drawn together tightly, not completely eliminating the outside world but diffusing the view and the light.

In the center of the room, Helen had set up a round table that was heavily draped in dark crimson cloth. There were seven chairs evenly spaced around the table. The chairs were far enough apart that the people seated in them wouldn't touch accidentally, but close enough together they could stretch out their arms to hold hands and form a séance circle.

Candles were massed in the center of the table. They were of all colors and sizes and some had telltale black wicks from having been lit and extinguished before.

"These are all the candles I could find, Sebastian," Helen sounded apologetic. "They don't match. Will they do?"

"Perfectly, my dear. The spirits are drawn to the warmth of their flames, you know, but the candles needn't match to create their welcome."

Regan noticed even Sebastian's voice changed once they were in the den: it took on a richer, deeper tone as he invited them to be seated.

He produced a cigarette lighter from his jeans pocket — a wildly incongruous implement, Regan thought, given the care that had gone into giving the den an exotic ceremonial aura — and began lighting the candles.

"We will be calling on the spirits today, especially on the spirit of our recently departed friend Charlie Smith, and asking that they may enter our circle of love …"

As Sebastian spoke in increasingly soothing and almost hypnotic tones, Regan snuck a peek at Tika. Sebastian called on Charlie Smith to join them; shouldn't he have called Charlie by his real name, Konstantin Kola?

Since Tika gave no indication of concern, she decided it would be inappropriate for her to suggest the spirit's correct name. Perhaps Charlie had become as comfortable in his new name as he was in his new identity and didn't use Konstantin

Kola in the spirit world.

The idea struck her as humorous; she could feel a chuckle rising in her throat. She sucked in a cheek and bit it hard enough to stifle her impending snigger with discomfort.

She returned to Sebastian's words just as he was stressing the importance that there be no doubters at the table. Skepticism, he said, caused the spirits to take flight even as the warming glow of candles drew them closer.

Uh-oh.

She repeated her cheek-biting and wondered if any of the other women were doing the same thing.

Regan didn't expect Charlie to commune with them, but she wasn't a bit skeptical about the séance outcome. Tika would get answers to her questions thanks to Sebastian's showmanship and her own desires.

Sebastian was a physic reader. To be successful in that calling, he had to have learned to be a careful listener and a subtle questioner. When Tika first contacted him, he would have asked a few sympathetic questions and discovered she wanted to know who was responsible for her husband's death.

If he needed details, Sebastian might have probed a bit until Tika said it looked like her husband had died at the hands of a professional hit man. She was quick to speculate with Regan; Tika would have told Sebastian, too, that she needed to know if that was true. It was what likely happened to him; both the police and Tika thought so. The police based their theory on hard evidence; Tika probably did, as well, but she needed additional assurance before she could take up her life again. By the end of the séance, Sebastian would have

137

Charlie provide her with that assurance.

Tika also wanted to find Charlie's hidden treasure. She probably told Sebastian — cleverly she may have thought, and without mentioning what it was — that Charlie hid something of value to the two of them. Sebastian, as Charlie's conduit, would offer vague hints as to where Tika should search for the embezzled money.

The psychic reader turned medium, skilled as he must be in picking up cues from his clients — a skill Regan understood because she also had learned it — would lead Tika to remember something Charlie said, a suspicious move he made, a clue he inadvertently dropped, which Sebastian could seize on and incorporate into Charlie's message to her. In that way, the medium would create an illusion that Charlie had revealed the money's hiding place.

If the secreted money was uncovered, it would be because Tika recalled something she already knew without realizing it and not because Charlie's spirit offered her a revelation.

Regan might know the tricks; nevertheless, the show promised to be entertaining.

"Now let us all join hands and as a loving united body call upon our Charlie to come to us." Sebastian closed his eyes and slowly swiveled his upper body in small circles.

Tika's eyes were closed, as were Karen's and Helen's, but Linda, a fellow closeted skeptic, Regan guessed, was, like her, watching the performance.

Joyce's eyes remained open, too, though probably because she was afraid Sebastian might actually raise the spirit of Charlie Smith.

"Come, Charlie, we are waiting for a sign from you."

Sebastian issued the invitation in a stage-worthy slightly wavering voice.

Joyce, who was holding Regan's left hand, suddenly tightened her grip until Regan's wedding ring became an instrument of torture. Sebastian's polished invocation was interrupted by her chilling shriek. "Death!" Joyce screeched. "Death is here. He's looking in at us!"

Regan followed Joyce's terrified gaze, spinning her head toward the window. Death was indeed there, his bony face peering at them from its shroud through a haze of gauzy curtains, and though he dissolved a second later, she was certain she had seen him.

For an instant everyone at the table remained frozen in place, unable to speak or even release hands. Regan was the first to break their stupefaction. She bolted toward the living room and cleared the doorway before Sebastian, Linda, and Karen, all quick to their feet, collided there and jostled one another through the narrow opening. Tika, hoisting her skirt to move more quickly, came next. Even timid Joyce, still pale after her fright, and Helen, the last of the women to reach her feet, joined the rush.

Regan was out the front door and leaping off the porch by the time Helen reached the living room. The others followed Regan, but Helen hesitated at the front door and then turned back toward her sleeping husband's room.

As Regan rounded the front corner of the house, she caught sight of a dark figure climbing the hill and disappearing into the dense woods to the right of the house. She sprinted across the open area, ran past the parked cars, and raced up the slope after the fleeing specter.

Sebastian had reached the upslope and was within a couple of strides of her when the wailing near the house began. She couldn't tell who was screaming; the cries sounded more like the shrieks of a wounded animal than a human voice, but gradually words became recognizable.

"No! No, my God, please, no, Henry, no!"

The other women, arrayed from the house to the bottom of the upslope, stopped as had Regan and Sebastian when they heard the first scream. They turned as of one mind and rushed back to the house.

"I'm going back," Sebastian shouted.

Regan looked up the hill to where she last saw the escaping figure. She saw nothing. She turned back to Sebastian. "I'm not. I'm going to try …" She stopped; Sebastian was already back down to the parked cars; she was wasting time.

As she climbed, the hill grew steeper and more densely covered with brush and trees. She needed to watch her feet and chart her path forward frequently — she was spending as much time looking down as she was looking up the hill in search of the fleeing apparition.

She spotted the silhouette as it crested a hill high above her. From her vantage point it was impossible to tell if Death turned left or right or continued up another ridge. She was not going to catch him.

"Damn!" Regan swore with frustration. She scanned the hilltop a final time, hoping to pick up his form again even though she knew her search was futile. Finally she gave up and retraced her steps back down the hill toward the house.

As she returned to flat ground, she pinpointed the agitated

voices as coming from the far side of the house. She cut behind the house to the play area and came upon a scene bordering on existential despair.

Tika had her arms around Helen. She was holding her tightly and slowly easing her away from the pool and toward the house.

"Come inside. You need to sit down. Help is on the way. See? Linda is calling for help." She spoke in a slow singsong, but loudly, as if she were trying to make herself heard to someone who had fallen into a deep well.

Linda held a door open at the side of the house while the pitiful Tika-Helen-being moved toward her little by little. She pressed her cell phone tightly against her ear and nodded rhythmically, speaking so softly that Regan couldn't hear what she was saying.

A soaking wet Sebastian stood dripping over a prostrate body; Karen pushed repeatedly on its chest. She counted rapidly and bent over periodically to press her lips against the body's face. Joyce grasped the body's flaccid arm and squeezed it where its limp hand joined the arm.

"No. Nothing. Nothing yet. Nothing," she repeated over and over until her words became a ridiculous mantra.

Regan rushed to the pool-side. She knew the supine figure was Helen's husband before she got close enough to judge the body's age or gender. She could see that Karen's efforts were pointless. The man beside the pool was pale; he looked at the sky with unblinking and unseeing eyes.

Sebastian stooped and put a wet hand on Karen's shoulder. "You did everything you could, my dear. He's gone. He has already spoken to me from the spirit word. His head is clear;

141

he doesn't want to come back. I'm going to reassure his wife that he has crossed over and is in a place of serenity."

Sebastian delivered his words with such compassion, Regan could feel that, though she doubted his ability to speak to the dead, his intensions where kind and genuine.

Karen rose haltingly and Joyce bent Henry's arm and laid his hand on his chest before she backed away from his lifeless body.

🏠 🏠 🏠 🏠 🏠 🏠 🏠 🏠 🏠 🏠 🏠

The siren grew closer and then abruptly stopped. Within moments a fire truck cleared the curve in the driveway and came into full view. It lumbered toward the house silently, the crew having turned off the blaring siren once they were on private property.

Two firefighters in complete fire-ready uniform jumped off the rig and hurried to Henry's still form even before the vehicle came to a full stop.

"How long was he in the water?" the lead firefighter asked.

"We don't know," Sebastian spoke for the group. "I went in after him shortly after his wife discovered him and this young woman has been administering CPR with the utmost efficiency since we got him out of the pool, but no one saw him fall in. We have no idea how long he was in the water."

The second medic-fireman took off a glove and dipped his fingers into the pool. "It's really warm water. Not good."

The lead firefighter completed his evaluation by checking for a pulse and looking at Henry's eyes. "Fixed and dilated,"

142

he said softly to his fellow fireman.

"Yes," Sebastian spoke again. "I've been in touch with him … in the spirit world."

The lead firefighter's eyebrows shot up so high they disappeared under the brim of his helmet. "That so? Jason, you may as well tell the ambulance no rush, no sirens."

🐜🐜🐜🐜🐜🐜🐜🐜🐜🐜🐜🐜

Within minutes, the scene by the pool became one of composed and respectful quiet. Henry's body was covered with a drape. The firefighters spoke in the hushed voices they used in the presence of the dead while they filled out forms and waited for the ambulance to arrive.

The bedlam inside the house, where everyone else congregated, was in marked contrast to the scene by the pool. Linda was huddled in a rocking chair in a corner of the living room, vigorously rocking forward and back while tears cascaded down her cheeks. "Please don't worry about me," she pleaded insistently with Karen, who had pulled another chair over to face her. Linda's words were delivered too wildly to be convincing. "I'm perfectly fine … really … it's just … the water … and the fire truck and the firefighters … it brought back such memories of Mike … but I'm OK."

Helen was seated in the center of the rose-colored sofa with Tika on her right and Sebastian on her left. The sofa had darkened around Sebastian as water wicked from his clothing into the fabric. It created an odd picture; he seemed to be a true medium surrounded by dark otherworldly shadows.

He held Helen's hand and spoke comfortingly to her, "It's

not your fault, Helen. Henry doesn't blame you; you mustn't blame yourself."

She was inconsolable. "I should never have left him alone. Even when he naps, I sit with him. Susan and Olive do the same. Susan said he shouldn't be left alone — he might rouse himself and wander. He liked to sit by the pool with his feet in the water. If he awoke and was warm ... if he fell in, he wouldn't have remembered how to swim. Oh, Henry, I'm so sorry.

"Even Olive ... and you know how she can say such cruel things, things I know she doesn't mean ... even Olive takes such good care of him. She sits with him when he has his feet in the water and she sits with him when he sleeps. Olive would never have left him alone, either."

Tika grasped Helen's other hand. "You couldn't have known, Helen. The kitchen door has that childproof gadget on it. How long has it been since he opened that door? You couldn't possibly have known he would get it open today."

"I don't think he did," Regan interjected. "I think he had help."

"But we were all ..." Tika frowned.

"I don't think this was an accident. We need to notify the police."

Helen cried out hysterically, "No, no police, Regan, please, they'll do an autopsy; they'll cut up my poor Henry!"

"There, there, Helen, Regan isn't going to call the police," Tika spoke reassuringly to Helen but shot an eyes-wide what-are-you-thinking look at Regan.

"I'm sorry, Helen," Regan apologized, "I'm so sorry to cause you more distress, but Joyce saw someone in the window …"

"No I didn't!" Joyce swamped Regan's words. "I didn't see anything. It was my imagination. I was just frightened by all that's been happening. First Susan's husband, and then Linda's husband, and then Tika's husband … and then the séance. I didn't see anything."

"I saw it, too, Joyce," Regan tried to sound as emotionless as she could. "I saw Death, too. That's why we ran outside. That's who we were chasing."

"I didn't see anyone," Karen said. "I was running because you and Sebastian were."

"I was running after you for the same reason," Linda added.

"Sebastian, you saw the dark figure climbing up the hill, didn't you?"

"I'm afraid I didn't, Regan. We all followed your lead …"

"… like sheep," Tika finished Sebastian's sentence with words he probably wouldn't have chosen. "Like hysterical sheep.

"Sebastian, you said you've spoken to Henry. Did he say anything to you about how he died?"

Sebastian shook his head. "He may not know. He's clear headed now, but he wasn't at the time of his death, of course, given his disease. Even without Henry's former affliction, it often takes the recently departed some time to settle into their new situation.

"No. No he didn't mention anything about his death except the feeling of pressure on his back, which I assume might be a common experience as one leaves this plane and moves to the next.

"I must admit, though, I haven't done this before … haven't spoken with such a newly departed. Well, I haven't really tried to speak with any departed person before … so this is all new to me, too. I may not fully understand his communication."

"Henry's physician is on his way. No police, Regan, at least until his doctor gets here." Tika's directive was presented with force, rather than as a request.

"If his doctor feels comfortable declaring Henry's death accidental as the result of his Alzheimer's disease, let him, won't you? If he feels the police need to be brought in, let him make that call … after he has made Helen more comfortable." Tika drew the fingers of her free hand into a fist with her index figure extended. She touched her finger to her arm and flexed her thumb like a child pretending to shoot a gun. Her meaning was clear; she wasn't telling Regan to not contact the police, but only to wait until Henry's physician had injected Helen with a sedative.

"I want to go home now," Joyce squeaked like a little child. "Will someone tell the fire engine to move? It's blocking the driveway and I want to go home."

Helen had Tika, Linda had Karen; Regan left Sebastian to minister to Joyce. She needed to get some fresh air — and to poke around a bit.

She walked around the house to the den window. She knew better than to disturb anything right at the window, but she could get answers to some of her questions without touching anything.

The ground immediately below the window had once been a flowerbed. The area hadn't been tended recently, it certainly

146

hadn't been watered recently, but the dirt wasn't packed hard like it was a few feet out from the window. As she bent to look at the dirt, she had a fleeting image of Sherlock Holmes, a magnifying glass held up to his eye, searching for footprints.

She didn't have a magnifying glass, but she thought she saw two rounded depressions inches from the wall and exactly in the middle of the window. She moved until she stood next to the window off to the side and clear of the flowerbed. Regan put her hand next to the bottom of the windowsill and moved it toward herself in a level motion. Her hand came to her lips; she calculated the window sill was a little more than five feet high on the outside of the house. If someone looking in the window leaned forward trying to peer through the gauzy curtains and put his full weight forward on his toes, would his feet have made marks like those? She thought they might.

If Death had found something to stand on and had returned it to where he found it — unlikely, given how far he had run when she gave chase — the weight of a person on a box or a footstool would have left marks in the dirt. There would have been evidence of either a regular rectangular or square outline, or if the device had legs, three or four deep depressions left in the dirt. But, except for the two pointed depressions, the flowerbed was undisturbed. The pointed depressions had to be footprints; Death had to be tall enough to peer in without standing on anything.

She moved as close to the window as she could without disturbing the flowerbed and looked in. She was tall enough to see in but she couldn't position herself as Death had. The

147

person who looked in the window during the séance was likely taller than her five-feet-nine-inch frame by at least a couple of inches, maybe more.

Regan walked back around to the front of the house. Two new vehicles made Joyce's departure even more impossible. An ambulance had arrived, quietly as instructed, and behind it was a blue Cadillac.

She walked between the fire engine and the ambulance toward the pool. A man and a woman, the medics from the ambulance, were engaged in conversation with the firefighters by Henry's body. She avoided them. Instead she walked around the pool past the picnic table and the swing-set on the other side until she reached the far end of the pool.

Regan noticed the pool leaf rake — a net scoop on a long tubular handle — was not lined up with the other maintenance tools that paralleled the pool a few feet from the firefighters and medics.

The leaf rake jutted toward the pool at a sharp angle. The back of the handle was almost touching the other pieces of equipment while the net scoop was at the edge of the pool.

It would have been easy for someone, especially someone as unsteady on his feet as Henry must have been, given his advanced Alzheimer's, to have tripped on the tool. Perhaps the pool rake had caused Henry to fall into the pool.

Regan squatted down next to the basket and touched it. The basket was wet. Had the women held the basket out to Sebastian as he swam one-armed while holding Henry with his other arm?

Another idea crept into her mind, a disturbing and sinister idea. The pool rake could have been used to hold Henry underwater until he drowned.

Regan reached into her pocket and pulled out her cell phone. She had no moral dilemma here as she had with telling anyone about Tika's ill-gotten cash. Enough dawdling. She hit speed-dial to Dave's office phone.

"Dave Everett." His tone was clipped and all business.

"Dave, it's Regan. I think there's been another Widow's Walk League murder."

"What makes you think so? Did some spook tell you that at your little séance?"

She could tell he was smiling even though she couldn't see his face.

"Another husband's dead, Dave. It happened during the séance. One of the women called 9-1-1. Firemen are here and the paramedics came. Someone called the dead man's physician. He's here, too. I don't know if anyone called the police yet …"

"That crew sounds like natural causes or maybe an accident," he interrupted.

"It wasn't natural causes or an accident."

"Little drum roll here. It wasn't natural causes or an accident because …" He drew out the final word and then paused for her.

"Because I saw Death. Someone dressed like Death looked in the window before we found the body."

"OK. I gotta admit that wasn't the punch line I expected."

Regan heard a siren. The police car came down the driveway with its bubble-gum lights whirling and its siren splitting eardrums.

"I guess someone did call it in," Regan said. "A patrol car just arrived. You can probably hear it, can't you?"

"Loud and clear."

"Dave, the thing is, I'm hoping you can come, too. I don't want to interfere with the investigation, but there are some things I need to talk to you about privately … things I don't want to say to a uniformed officer who will think I'm nuts."

"As compared to me who knows you are," he chuckled but cut it off immediately. "Sorry, this isn't a joke is it? Where are you?"

"I'm on Ocean Street Extension at number 2216."

🏠 🏠 🏠 🏠 🏠 🏠 🏠 🏠 🏠 🏠 🏠

By the time Dave arrived, the police were finished talking to Regan, Linda, and Karen and the coroner was removing Henry's body. Fortunately Helen was asleep. The family doctor had given her a sedative as Tika hoped, so the new widow didn't need to see her dear husband taken away for the autopsy she dreaded.

During her interview, Regan told the policeman who questioned her that Joyce screamed Death was looking at them and that she, too, had seen someone looking in the den window. She couldn't tell the voyeur's sex, age, or coloring, though, she said, because their face was obscured by the curtains and the mask and dark hood they were wearing.

The policeman questioned Joyce next and was having a hard time with her interview. Initially she told the officer she had her eyes closed during the séance when everyone started screaming. Her story didn't jive with Regan's. When the policeman pointed that out to her, Joyce did a 180 degree change in her story. She described staring at Death for several seconds before she started screaming. She insisted what she saw was Death, not a death-like figure, but Death in the flesh, as it were, come to collect Henry.

When she noted the police officer's reaction to that idea, she changed her story again and insisted she had seen nothing. The police would not release her and she was sobbing.

A policewoman was having an even more eventful interview with Sebastian. He began by explaining they were having a séance before Henry's body was discovered. He told the officer in excruciating detail how he was trying to reach the departed spirit of Charlie Smith, a name the policewoman recognized instantly, when everything went wrong. Sebastian went on about his retrieval of Henry's body, and about Henry's recent communication with him from beyond the veil.

Regan thought she heard the phrase "psych evaluation" whispered between officers, although she couldn't be sure, and if she had, she certainly didn't know if it had come up in reference to Joyce or Sebastian … or both.

She was clear about what Sebastian said about getting Henry out of the pool, however. The police tried to separate the witnesses so there would be no sharing or influencing of their answers, but Sebastian was near her during his interview and used his booming stage-trained voice to describe the afternoon.

Sebastian was clear about jumping into the pool feet-first without taking time to remove his shoes and pulling Henry, who was just out of reach for a dry grab, to the pool side in one quick motion. Karen and Tika had knelt down on the pool apron and pulled while he pushed from the water. They had the frail Henry out of the water in seconds.

There was absolutely no mention by him, and Regan doubted by any of the others, of moving or using the leaf rake as part of the rescue.

🏠🏠🏠🏠🏠🏠🏠🏠🏠🏠🏠

"I'm not here for moral support, am I?" Dave asked when he saw her.

"No, you're not. I call Tom when I need a hug."

Regan motioned for Dave to follow her and took him outside to the porch.

"I'm sure the officers are good at their job, but I need your professional opinion. I've been doing a little looking around and think I know what happened here. I have an idea, one that I don't like, one that I don't want to share with just any cop. My conclusions might be ridiculous … but if I tell the police about them … well, suppose I'm wrong but they run with my inferences? They might make an arrest, and I might make a mess of an innocent person's life."

Dave beamed, "You can always count on me to tell you your conclusions are ridiculous."

"Don't start; just listen and tell me what you think."

"OK. Shoot."

Regan dropped her voice until it was close to a whisper.

"I did see Death. There was someone looking in the den window where the séance was being held. It was impossible to see him clearly because there was a filmy curtain over the window and I think the person wore some sort of mask, too.

"I've been looking around and I've figured out a couple of things. Let me show you."

Regan led Dave to the den window. "I don't see any evidence that the person looking in stood on anything so he had to be tall enough to see in on his own. I could barely see in even standing away from the window where the weeds make the ground higher. I could see about this much of him," she drew her hand across her body just below her neck, "The person looking in had to be at least my height and probably a little taller for me to see all of his head and a bit of his shoulders from inside the house."

Dave nodded. "Seems reasonable; so far you're not ridiculous."

"The person I saw escaped up that hill." Regan pointed toward the chase route. "I was pumped on adrenalin and am in reasonably good shape but I couldn't catch him. I think our Death is athletic or at least fit to be able to run up that slope. What do you think?"

Dave tilted his head back and rubbed his chin as he studied the hill. "Probably, although he may have had as much adrenalin pumping through his system as you did. What else you got?"

"I think he had to be familiar with this house, with who lived here and their situation. He must have known about the séance, too, not only that there was going to be one, but when it was being held, where it was being held, and where it was in relation to Henry's room. I think he knew the hill, too, and that's the way he got to the house."

"Now you've lost me."

"It makes sense if you think about it. Death could have come down the hill and stayed behind the house and out of sight until the party moved to the den. Then he could have let himself in through the kitchen on the opposite side of the house from where we all were, gone to Henry's room behind the kitchen, and taken him out to the pool, again using the kitchen door.

"When he finished," Regan swallowed hard, "when Henry was dead, he put on the mask and looked in through the window. And then when Joyce screamed, he ran away up the hill."

"You were doing OK till you got to the part about the mask. Why would he have a mask with him and why would he look in the window after he killed the old man?"

"I've been asking myself that." Regan reviewed her reasoning silently one last time. "I can't come up with a great answer but I do have an idea. I think if he was caught outside he planned to say he'd changed his mind about coming to the séance and had hiked down the hill to join the group. The mask may have fit in with that somehow, especially if the person had a reputation for … an unusual … sense of humor."

"Why do I get the idea you think you know someone who fits your idea of the Perp … you know, somebody tall, and physical with all this specialized knowledge you think he had

155

to have, who had an invite to the big ghost get-together?"

"Because you're right, I do think I know someone who fills the bill. But I don't like who that is."

"You going to share voluntarily, or do I have to say pretty please?"

"Olive."

"Olive? Your mushroom lady? The same Olive you thought killed a bunch of husbands to get their wives' money and had designs on Tom until you decided she didn't have it in her to hurt anybody and as it turns out didn't need any money?" He spoke so rapidly he didn't breathe and was gasping for air by the time he finished.

"Uh-huh."

"I … ahh … ahh," he sputtered.

"Can I at least tell you why I think it was Olive before you get any redder in the face?"

"You mean your reason for why you're undoing your other reason?"

"If you want to put it that way, OK."

Dave's level of exasperation was off the chart. "There's no other way to put it, Regan."

"At least hear me out. Olive is the right height; she's over six feet tall. She's an avid hiker. I bet she's used to powering up inclines. I think her house isn't even too far from here, Dave — I looked at it on Google Earth on my cell phone. The road at the top of the hill," Regan pointed up the slope, "is Graham Hill Road. Her house is a little over two miles from here if you cut through some open land; it's in the general direction where the person I tried to follow was heading."

"That doesn't prove anything. Any old murderer could

have parked his car up there. He could be anywhere in the county by now."

"Olive knows this house and its occupants well. She spells Helen in caring for Henry often. Helen says she sits with him in his room when he naps, which he does at a regular time — that's why the séance was held when it was — and she takes him out to the pool to let him put his feet in the water."

Regan inhaled sharply as she realized what that might mean, "He probably would have gone with her to the pool without a fuss."

"I don't want to derail your thrilling train of thought here, but wouldn't the Vic have put up a big noisy fuss if she pushed him in?"

"That's one of the worst discoveries I made. The pool leaf rake was out of place and wet. I think she used it to hold him underwater until he drowned."

The fleeting expression that flashed across Dave's face belied his tough cop exterior.

"Olive was invited to the séance. She was told when and where it was going to be and maybe even enticed to come, by being told everyone would have snacks and a little party before getting started.

"She refused to come because she said the whole thing was silly, but if she was discovered near the house, she could have said she decided to come at the last minute and hiked in.

"I know everything is circumstantial, and I know I'm changing my mind again."

"As near as I can tell, it's what you do best. Before you go getting all overwrought, could we calm you down and have you think about this? For starters, you've got no motive for your mushroom-lady killer, have you? Why would she kill a sick old man she helped take care of? Don't tell me it was to get his wife's money. You yourself told me she no longer needs cash — you can't have it both ways."

"I think she may have killed Henry in a misguided act of kindness. She may have thought he was suffering and that his wife was suffering trying to take care of him and having to watch him slip away a little more every day."

"You think she killed the other hubbies with kindness, too? You are back to thinking the death costume ties them all together, aren't you?"

"I don't know."

"Another thing. For all you know, your Olive may have been having a cuddle with some Popeye in front of about a hundred witnesses. She may have a perfect alibi for today."

"Could we at least go talk to her, Dave? Could we just stop by her house and casually ask her where she was today? I so want to be wrong about her this time and I'm so afraid I'm not. Please, I need to know one way or the other.

"I could introduce you as my friend and not say there's anything official about your visit, because there wouldn't be.

"Olive is very house-proud. I could say I told you she had this great house and I wanted you to see it. Better yet, I could say you and Sandy are considering buying in Woods Cove and I was just out showing you around and thought of her.

"Please, Dave. I want you to talk to her and tell me what you think."

Dave took in a loud deep breath and released it slowly, not in a protracted sigh, but in an attempt to be calm, as if he were counting to ten in his head.

"You said she lives nearby? I'm at the back of the line and your car is still pinned. I'll drive."

Regan was the only one to speak as they drove the short distance back down Ocean Street Extension, turned left at the cemetery on to Graham Hill Road, and went uphill toward Woods Cove; and she only spoke to issue driving directions.

She knew the gate code — real estate agents had access to private information like gate codes so they could show property — but she didn't need it; Dave followed a resident's car through the open Woods Cove gate before it had a chance to swing closed.

It was close to 7:30 by the time they reached Olive's house and the summer daylight was fading into dusk.

"Now remember, you and Sandy are thinking of buying here so we were driving around Woods Cove to see the nice amenities," Regan coached while they walked up the stairs to Olive's front door.

Dave nodded silently. He was listening to her, but surveying his surroundings at the same time. He was working.

Regan rang the doorbell and waited. When no one came, she tried again.

"Do you think she's not home?"

Dave shook his head. "Lights are on at the back. You've been here before? Is the kitchen back there?"

"I think so."

"Looks like your Olive's here with a clear conscience making herself some nice dinner. She gonna freak out if we turn up at her back door?"

Dave didn't wait for an answer. He loped down the front stairs and walked briskly toward the back of the house.

Regan scurried after him, trying to get into the lead. She called Olive's name repeatedly as she hurried along the side of the house. She pulled even with Dave as they got their first glimpse of the back patio.

Linda's improvement money was in the midst of being spent. A large flat concrete pad was in place and work was in progress to tile it with patterned Italian pavers. Lantern-style lights on tall posts were in place around the perimeter and apparently hooked up because several were lit. Their glow was soft and moody. On the far side of the patio were counters, the beginnings of an outdoor kitchen.

Neither of them was prepared for what they saw next. Regan froze; Dave sprinted toward Olive.

She was near the not-yet-a-kitchen using the countertops to hold her grill tools and a plate with the remains of her dinner. A distinctive red Webber dome barbeque rested on the countertop as well, but rather than the expected dying charcoal embers, it contained a blazing fire.

Olive held her hands high over her head and shook out a long black garment with an attached hood that flopped limply forward.

"You've gotten me in enough trouble already, you sorry thing," she chastised the shroud. "In you go."

She dropped the mantle into the fire just as Dave reached her.

Olive shrieked in surprise as Dave bolted past her. He grabbed the grill tongs and pulled the flaming shroud from the fire. He dropped it onto the patio and stomped on it wildly to put out the consuming flames.

"Who are you? What are you doing on my property?" Olive demanded as she picked up a long-handled grill fork and pointed the sharp end menacingly at Dave.

He did a quick sidestep and knocked the fork out of her hand so fast she startled backward, threw her hands up to the sky, and squealed.

Olive spotted Regan. "Run for your life, Regan! Call the police! This crazy man is trying to murder me!" she screamed.

Regan held up her hands, "No. No, Olive. He *is* the police. He's with me. We … I … I was showing him property … I was showing him Woods Cove," she stammered.

Dave grabbed the still smoking shroud. He slapped the smoldering edges until the hot residue fell away.

"What are you doing? Give me that!" Olive commanded.

"You want to tell me why you were trying to destroy potential evidence?" Dave countered.

"Evidence? Evidence of what? That's my Halloween costume. I'm getting rid of it."

"Why are you burning it?"

"Why not burn it? I can burn my Halloween costume if I like."

"Are you sure you're not trying to destroy blood traces on it?"

"Regan, whatever is the matter with your policeman? What are you talking about, sir?"

Dave spoke evenly, "A murder was committed on Pacific Avenue on Halloween night by someone who witnesses say was dressed in a costume like this."

"What does that have to do with me?"

"I believe this could be the costume worn by a murderer."

"Don't be ridiculous. It's my costume. I wore it on Halloween, and I didn't kill anyone," Olive had changed from startled to outraged.

"Ma'am, I am preserving this costume as evidence."

"Next you'll be telling me my Miranda Rights. Regan, did you hear that? Are you arresting me for burning my costume?" Olive was, if not incredulous, certainly doing a fine acting job of seeming so.

"I am not placing you under arrest, ma'am, therefore I am not advising you of your Miranda Rights. Were you on Pacific Avenue this past Halloween night?"

"Of course I was. I go every year. It's lots of fun."

"And were you wearing this on Pacific Avenue last year?"

"Yes, I was."

"Were you handing out notes to people on Halloween, notes with future dates and times on them, ma'am?"

"Future dates on them, yes." Olive's habitually broad smile began to creep back onto her face. "It was great fun. You wouldn't believe the way some people reacted. That's not against the law is it, the notes I mean?"

"Did you give a note to Walter Henshaw that night?"

163

Olive chuckled, "I did. He was such a pain about it, though. He started shouting at me and making a scene. He upset me so much I stopped handing out notes and left. He ruined Halloween for me."

Olive looked down at her feet, "Oh my. That sounds bad, doesn't it? I shouldn't have been so touchy, should I? He was the one with the truly ruined Halloween, wasn't he? He and Susan, poor dear."

Regan looked at Dave, her eyes wide, expecting a little conspiratorial eyebrow raising from him. He was so focused and serious, she might not even have been there.

"Where were you between three-thirty and four-thirty today, ma'am?" a consummately professional Dave asked.

Regan could see Olive's face flush even in the soft light.

"I'm busted, aren't I? What I did seemed like it would be funny, but when I saw how people at the séance reacted ... I am so sorry ... clearly no one was amused.

"In fact, that's why I was burning my costume. I've often been told I have a ... well ... a different sense of humor. I didn't want to be tempted to do something like that again and that darn thing just seemed to encourage me to behave so outrageously.

"I really put a lot of effort into making that costume. Watching it burn was going to be my punishment for the upset I caused today. I already burned the mask part ... the wonderful mask," she spoke wistfully, "with such a perfect skull painted on the same kind of scrim I used for the face-piece.

"I do hope I didn't upset dear Helen too much. The last thing she needs is having to take care of Henry after she's had a shock. Oh, but I must have upset her or you and your policeman wouldn't have come by, would you? Perhaps I should apologize for what I did and offer to sit with Henry tonight so she can get to bed early. What do you think, Regan?"

Regan was open-mouthed and unsure what to say. Dave spoke in her place.

"Henry Sprokly drowned under suspicious circumstances today during the time you admit to being at the Sprokly residence."

"What?" Olive asked breathlessly. No trace of a smile remained on her face.

"I am not placing you under arrest, ma'am, and you do not have to accompany me to the police station, but I am requesting you come with me and answer a few more questions."

"If you think it's important, I'll come, of course, sir."

"Would it be all right with you if some of my fellow officers took a look around your house while we are in town talking?"

Dave's expression softened and he sounded friendly and like his question was offhanded, but Regan knew he was choosing his words and his tone carefully.

He chuckled a bit. Regan recognized it as a carefully produced little guffaw, but he made it sound completely natural and casual.

"I'll tell them not to make a mess. I can tell from here you keep your home very tidy."

Regan had never seen Dave working a suspect before; he was good, she noted with a new sense of appreciation. He had saved evidence, gotten his quarry to admit to being in two places at or near the time of a murder, and to having given one victim a damning note essentially telling him he was going to die. And even more amazingly, he had convinced his suspect to come with him and to let her house be searched in her absence.

He had done all that without needing to arrest Olive or convince a judge to issue a search warrant. Without an arrest, he had no need to advise his suspect of her rights. Since he wasn't arresting her, he could be relaxed and friendly. He could get Olive smiling again and talking freely to him. And he could keep asking her questions — questions she might answer without realizing she was incriminating herself.

"Regan? I've never been to a police station before," Olive reached out and took her hand. "Would you come with me, please? That would be all right, wouldn't it?"

"Of course it would, Olive. It is OK for me to call you Olive, isn't it? Regan and I are old friends."

Dave's smile was full of warmth and almost as big as Olive's usually was, but his eyes didn't match his smile: they were still coolly professional.

Regan rode to the police station in the back seat of Dave's car while Olive sat in front, not like someone being taken into custody or even under suspicion, but like a friend who had called shotgun. Regan had never seen Dave be so charming. She had watched enough police shows on TV to know that if he was involved in Olive's interrogation, he would play the role of the good cop, the friendly one who seemed to be on the suspect's side.

By the time they reached the police station on Center

Street, Dave had Olive laughing, and more importantly, trusting him. If Olive had any sort of protective inhibitions, Dave had breached them.

He had her joking about the members of the Widow's Walk League who always started their walks for exercise but were quick to find a widow's walk so they could stop walking and go eat lunch.

He effortlessly moved from Olive's love of walking, which he said he bet came from her spending some time in the military, and within a few minutes, had her raucously telling him about the time she had so much to drink at a party during the Gulf War that she, as a volunteer who had no threat of court-martial and knew all about the mechanics of cars, hot-wired an officer's Jeep and drove a bunch of junior officers back to their post.

Under the influence of Dave's skillful camaraderie, she even told her new friend about her husband's Huntington's disease, and her broken promise to him.

"My darling Paul always said he planned to commit suicide if it became apparent he had inherited his family's curse. When his symptoms began, I begged him not to. I promised him I would give him an overdose of morphine to help him out of his body when the time came, if only he would stay with me a little longer." Olive's eyes held tears.

"But as much as I loved him, I couldn't do it. I broke my promise. He was a brilliant and accomplished man. I watched him die as dementia took everything from him. I watched him suffer so."

Regan wanted to tell Olive to be quiet and ask for a lawyer. She could imagine what a good prosecuting attorney could have Dave say on the witness stand.

"Yes, the defendant did admit to having mechanical knowledge of cars."

"Would you explain the basis for your statement?"

"She told me she had occasion to start a car by hot-wiring it."

"And did the defendant tell you how she felt about victims of dementia?"

"She said she wished she had helped her husband die before he fell into severe dementia."

"Do you think she might have felt she was acting in the best interest of her friends Helen and Henry Sprokly by killing Mr. Sprokly to end his suffering caused by advanced Alzheimer's disease?"

Even though the attorney for the defense might leap to his feet and yell, "Objection, Your Honor, speculation," the seed would have been planted. The jury would speculate on their own.

She could even imagine the prosecutor's final question to Dave and his answer.

"Did anyone witness the defendant telling you she had mechanical knowledge and about wishing she had ended her husband's life?"

"Yes. Regan McHenry did."

16

"I'm out ... sprung ... free as a bird," Olive sang out. "This is all thrilling, don't you think? What an adventure!" Olive sounded even livelier on the phone than she usually did in person.

"I'm sorry they wouldn't let you come into the interrogation room with me last night, Regan, but you didn't really miss much. Being interrogated wasn't as exciting as I thought it would be. No harsh lights, no rubber hoses," she laughed loudly. "They even let me use the bathroom when I needed to. I always thought they made you hold it; that the threat of peed pants was a tactic they used to get you to confess," she whooped.

"They did make a mess of my house, though, even after your friend promised they wouldn't. He's a lovely man, by the way. I like him almost as well as I like Tom. Dave's married, isn't he? You know his wife, don't you?"

"Sandy? Yes I know ..."

"Is she nice, too? I wonder if she would care to join us on our walks."

"I don't think she could. She works over the hill, for one

169

of the tech companies in Silicon Valley."

"That's too bad. We do need some new members, some fresh blood, now that Mary Anne and Joyce have dropped out."

Olive spewed her thoughts so manically that they sounded less like her zestful manner of speaking and more like something alarming … something closer to raving than to enthusiasm.

"Oh, Regan, I haven't told you the best part yet. The police suspect me of murder! Just think, before last night I had never even been in a police station. Now, I've been interrogated and am a suspect — I think they call it being a person of interest, but that's just politically correct for being a suspect, isn't it?"

"Olive, when were you released? Did you get any sleep last night?"

"Who needs to sleep when all this excitement is swirling around?"

"Have you spoken to an attorney yet? It might be a good idea."

"You know, I considered it when the police told me they made some significant discoveries at my house."

"What kind of discoveries?"

"The police found a scalpel. They think it may have Walter's blood on it. They're running some tests. I'm certain the blood will turn out to be dried red corn syrup or whatever it is they use for blood in the movies. Someone put it in my house; I think someone is playing a grand joke on me!"

"A joke, Olive?" Regan frowned, "Who would do something like that? Planting a scalpel and making it look like a murder weapon isn't funny. It sounds diabolical."

Olive chuffed, "Nonsense. I might do something like that. I have been known to look in windows to try to scare people, haven't I? It's the same thing."

"It's not the same thing at all; besides, you regret what you did."

"Well, yes." Olive paused to consider, "I do regret it because it turned out not to be funny — but at the time it seemed like it would be. I'm sure the person who planted the scalpel thought it would be funny," Olive chuckled, "and it has gotten the police in a dither. If this little joke starts to truly upset people ... my prankster will reconsider, too, like I did.

"The point is someone has been hiding a macabre sense of humor much like my own. I can't wait to offer my congratulations and share a good laugh."

"There's no possibility it really is the murder weapon is there, Olive?"

"Don't be silly. I didn't kill Walter. I wasn't anywhere near Pacific Avenue when he was getting skewered. I was with Tika and Charlie. It's too late for Charlie to speak up, of course, but Tika confirmed my alibi — Oh, doesn't that sound marvelous, this is my first alibi, as well — as soon as I told them I was at her house when Walter was being murdered — Think of it — I was probably still complaining to Tika and Charlie about Walter being such a spoil-sport over the death date card I gave him when he was being stabbed.

"Since I didn't kill Walter, what they found at my house can't possibly be a hidden murder weapon.

"My friend the prankster left an old manual about car transmissions and a target-card from some old rod and gun club, too. Looks like I know all about cars and am a crack shot," her statement ended in laughter.

"The police got all excited about circumstantial evidence, wondering if those things tied me to Linda's husband's murder in his Woodie and to Tika's husband's shooting. Isn't that a hoot?"

"No, Olive …"

"Well, you're right, I don't like guns, but still!"

"Who would put things like that in your house, Olive? You have to think. You have to remember who's been in your house recently, because if the scalpel does have Walter's blood on it …"

Olive roared. "Almost everyone I know, except you and Tom, have been in my house. All the members of the Widow's Walk League have come by to see how the backyard is progressing. Oh, and then I had that Tea for the Dominican Hospital Pink Ladies two weeks ago. It was a marvelous event. We honored several volunteers."

"Olive, please talk to a lawyer before this goes any further. I don't know any criminal attorneys, but I can call the real estate attorney that Tom and I know and ask him for a recommendation."

"Regan, you don't seem to understand. I don't need an attorney. I didn't do anything wrong except look in on Tika's séance — I've already confessed to that and apologized for it — and I've been assured that, while that joke may have been tasteless, it wasn't criminal. People only need attorneys when they are guilty of something criminal."

"But the police … doesn't it seem like they might be trying to build a case that you …"

"Regan, you sound overexcited," Olive interrupted. "I have great faith in our local police department, especially if your friend Dave is representative of them. They would never make a mistake about something as serious as murder.

"They'll solve these nasty crimes. And if they don't, my fellow prankster will come forward and explain it's all just a joke. In the meantime," her voice took on a dramatic tenor, "I'm going to wear sunglasses everywhere I go and try to look," she breathed a melodramatic, "dangerous."

When Regan and Tom arrived at their office the next day, Amanda didn't greet them with her perfunctory, "How are you today?" Instead, her question was filled with excited expectancy, "What do you think of the news? I've spoken with her — she seemed nice — and now she's been arrested for murder. I guess you just can't tell about murderers, especially not serial killers, which is what it sounds like she is.

"Have you ever seen a picture of Ted Bundy? He was cute. I would have gone out with him. It gives me goose bumps thinking about it."

"Who are we talking about here?" Tom asked, as he peeled the safety lid off his coffee and tossed it like a Frisbee into the recycle bin behind the reception desk.

Regan didn't need to ask; she knew Amanda was talking about Olive.

"I'm signed up for local news alerts on my phone. One of the agents likes me to keep her up to date about what's happening locally. It's not like she's an ambulance chaser, but she says she might know someone in the news and need to offer her services or sympathy," Amanda's voice trailed off and she squirmed until one of her shoulders almost touched her cheek.

"It was broadcast as breaking news this morning. The police have arrested Olive Gretchell for the Halloween murder on Pacific Avenue. They found the murder weapon at her house."

"This is wrong, all wrong. I was afraid of this," Regan said more to herself than to either Amanda or Tom. "Olive couldn't have killed Walter Henshaw."

"People-reading again, are you, sweetheart?" Tom asked offhandedly as he put his arm around her shoulder and walked her to his office.

His tone changed as soon as they were inside and he had closed the door. "I didn't want to say so in front of Amanda, but I'm not surprised Olive's been arrested. After what she said when she called you, and then what she told Dave on the way to the police station. Wow! Someone playing a joke on her? Fake blood on a scalpel? Come on. And then the car stuff and the target practice card she kept; you read about killers keeping souvenirs. Olive even placed herself at the Sprokly house when Henry was drowned. She did everything but confess outright.

"It looks like you were spot on dragging Dave up to her house. I only wonder why it took the police so long to arrest her and why she hasn't been charged with more murders."

"I know what I said to Dave about her, and I understand how bad it looks for her, but I don't think she killed anyone — not after I watched Dave questioning her."

Tom was perplexed. He held his palms face up in a gesture

175

of questioning, "But why, sweetheart?"

"She was so open and genuine about everything she said. She happily placed herself at the murder scenes. She had an air of childlike innocence about her when she described what fun it was to be on Pacific Avenue handing out death notes. It seems to me a murderer would deny being at the crime scene, not gleefully admit they were.

"She regrets peering in the window at the Sprokly's because she upset people. How could peeping in windows trouble her so much and murder not at all?" Regan sounded more like she was pleading for Olive's innocence than assuredly stating a case for it.

"She was so believable when she said she didn't kill anyone; I don't think she was lying, Tom. I don't think she could carry off that kind of deceit. You've spent time with her. I thought you liked her. You can't really believe she killed all those men."

"Like Amanda said, think of Ted Bundy. As I recall," he shook his finger at her, "you wouldn't let me eat some mushrooms Olive gave me. Thank you. You may have saved my life. I don't see her as a common killer, though. She's probably not greedy or jealous; she probably doesn't have any of the usual motives you associate with murder. It may be that she's a disturbed, lonely woman — childlike as you said — who doesn't fully understand what she's doing.

"Given the way Olive blurts out inappropriate things, I'm not sure she fully grasps reality. If I were her attorney, I might argue diminished capacity or something like that as a defense."

Regan frowned, "Olive is completely in touch with reality.

She just calls life as she sees it. Most people aren't as candid as she is because they're afraid of seeming insensitive, but she enjoys being outspoken and she delights in saying shocking things, sometimes with such force it's like she's almost hoping to offend others. It's her way of hiding how softhearted and caring she really is. And deep down, I think she feels she deserves scorn.

"The murders of all these husbands ... they were all so violent. Olive isn't a violent person. Every time I've seen her with a widow, she's been so kind and gentle, nurturing them like the children she never had.

"I can't imagine her stabbing Walter. And poor Henry. To hold him under water and watch him struggle until he drowned? No." What started as a small head shake grew into a fervent denial. "No. If she had given him a drug overdose, like she promised she would do for her husband, and then held his hand and watched him fall asleep, I might ... No. I don't believe she could kill Henry like that. And you should have seen her reaction when Dave told her about him ... I watched her when she heard the news ... she was shocked speechless ..."

Tom cut her off, "Or shocked at being caught."

Regan only took a moment to consider. "No. Olive tells the truth as she sees it even when it's a brash thing to do. If she had killed Henry, when Dave asked her if she had, I think she would have said yes.

"If she were troubled, as you suggest, she would have assumed she could make people understand what she had done. She would have admitted to killing Henry and explained her actions. I think she would have stood up

177

straight and said she understood the burden Helen was facing because she watched her own husband go through a similar agony. She would have confessed — or more likely proudly announced — that she killed Henry because she thought it was best for Helen … and for him, too."

"She ran away when you all saw her, sweetheart. She didn't stay put and explain anything. She acted the way you would expect a woman to act who was trying to get away from the scene of her crime."

"If you just killed a man, would you call attention to yourself and *then* run away?" Regan fired her question back at Tom.

"I wouldn't, no," Tom shrugged. "But clearly, I don't think like Olive does. She did call attention to herself — and then she ran away. Those are the facts. She admits it.

"Don't you think it's possible," he asked gently, "and please consider for a moment before you say no again, that the enormity of what she had done finally hit her and knocked her back to her senses, as it were? When she realized she'd just murdered Henry, she decided to run. I think that's what happened, sweetheart. Running became reasonable behavior to her like it would to anyone else. I'd be trying to get as far away as I could as quickly as I could if I just killed someone."

"So would I. That's my point. I wouldn't stop to peer through a window where seven people could look back at me … and I wouldn't admit to being at the house at the time of a murder. I'd be getting away fast, and being stealthy, too. And I don't think people can be knocked back to their senses like you said," Regan was close to sputtering.

"Olive was telling the truth about what she did even though it was likely to make her look guilty, even though it wasn't in her best interest.

"I think her explanation about wearing her death costume to the séance and looking in the window to scare us makes sense — she did it because she thought the séance was ridiculous, more so because it was organized by Tika, a former nurse, a scientist like herself, and that it would be funny to shake people up and disrupt Tika's plans. Olive did what she did to demonstrate her disapproval of the séance.

"I know it's not what most people would do and it's not something she should have admitted doing, but it's consistent with the way Olive's sense of humor works. Besides, if she were lying, wouldn't she come up with a better story?" Regan questioned stubbornly.

"Maybe she said what she did because it was the first story that popped into her mind. You and Dave did surprise her by turning up when she was trying to burn her costume. She may not have been facile enough to come up with a better explanation."

Tom spoke quietly; he wasn't being accusatory. "You're not being rational, sweetheart; you're basing your belief in Olive's innocence on your feelings and on speculation rather than facts."

"I pay attention to people when they're under stress, when they're distracted — I read them. That's what I do, Tom, and you know I do it well. Olive is such an open person; she's an easy read.

"Olive didn't kill Henry. She didn't kill anyone else, either, although trying to burn her shroud did make it seem

179

like she was trying to cover up evidence," Regan admitted. "I did tell you she was talking to it as she burned it, didn't I, saying it had gotten her into trouble?"

"Talking to it? Like it was a sentient being?"

"Possibly," Regan said hesitantly.

"Awh, here we go again," Tom sounded as exasperated with her as Dave so often did. "Forget diminished capacity. It sounds to me like Olive should go for a full-on insanity plea."

Regan had moved past being defensive; she was thinking about the shroud. "Remind me to ask Dave if the police found Walter Henshaw's blood on Olive's costume."

Regan pulled her chair toward Tom's desk and leaned forward until she could put her elbows on his desk and prop up her chin with her hands. "Remember all the effort the police went through looking for a discarded costume with blood on it? They thought it would have been impossible for the murderer to inflict the kind of damage done to Walter Henshaw without getting blood on himself ..."

"Or herself," Tom recommended.

"Or herself," Regan acquiesced.

"If it turns out there wasn't any blood on the costume, wouldn't that prove she wasn't the person who stabbed Walter?"

"Not necessarily. Remember that there's more than her costume linking her to Walter's murder. Susan had the card Olive admits giving him with the date and time of his murder on it, and now the murder weapon has been found at her house."

"Yes," Regan agreed, "but if you want to consider all the evidence, you can't overlook Tika saying Olive was at her house when Walter was murdered. That kind of alibi trumps a note and a murder weapon, doesn't it?"

"If Tika's telling the truth, it does, but you have to wonder how truthful Tika is or how accurately she remembers the night. I'm sure the District Attorney will be wondering those things."

Regan barely heard Tom's answer; she was only partially listening. "Let me be as logical as you usually are," Regan challenged her husband. "Assuming the shroud didn't have blood on it, does it make sense that she would destroy a costume she liked and used more than once while keeping other items that might link her to murder?"

"She may have intended to get rid of the other evidence after she burned the costume. You and Dave might have stopped her from finishing her clean-up."

The pace of their dueling points of view as to Olive's guilt or innocence picked up speed once again.

"Olive is eccentric; she's not dim-witted. Wouldn't she have realized that giving the police the OK to search her house would mean they'd find the other evidence?"

"That kind of confused reckless behavior argues my point: Olive's thinking is disturbed."

"How did Olive slip away undetected on Halloween when everyone was looking for Death?"

"How do you explain the transmission manual and the target card linking her to the other murders?" Tom fired back. "Those are pretty damning pieces of evidence, as well, circumstantial certainly, but when taken as a whole ..."

Regan interrupted him, "When taken as a whole ..." She leaned back in her chair. "That's what's wrong. There's so much evidence." She bit her lip, "and you don't know all of it."

Regan looked into her husband's eyes. It was time for her to tell him the truth. "I did something I shouldn't have. I didn't tell you about it because," she took a deep breath, "because I didn't want to involve you in what I'd done, and because I knew you wouldn't approve of my behavior or my decision to keep the information private."

She watched the expression on Tom's face change from bemused curiosity to concern as she spoke.

"What did you do?"

"I told you Tika wanted to have a séance because of a disclosure question, because Charlie was appearing to her as a ghost."

At the mention of Charlie's ghost, Tom's apprehension lessened. His eyes began to dance and his grin threatened to burst into laughter.

"You did."

"There was another reason Tika wanted to have a séance that I didn't mention," Regan winced. "When Tika had me come by to talk about listing her house, the house that, as it turned out, Olive owns, she told me quite a story about her husband, Charlie."

"Go on," Tom said slowly, his concern growing once more.

"Charlie Smith wasn't really his name. His real name was Konstantin Kola and he and Tika were in the Federal Witness Protection Program because he had turned state's evidence against Albanian mobsters."

Tom looked as surprised as she must have when Tika told

her about Charlie's past.

"Tika said Charlie, or Konstantin — even she didn't seem to know what to call him at that point — had been coming to her in ghostly form, trying to tell her where he had hidden the money he embezzled from his underworld connections. That was one of the reasons she wanted to have a séance — she thought he could better communicate with her through a medium.

"The problem is he was supposed to have given all the money he stole to the FBI when he and Tika went into witness protection, but he didn't. Olive bought the house the Smiths live in with her own money, but they were paying her back in cash. She was in effect laundering their money for them."

Regan saw a sea-change wash across her husband's face.

"Tika told you all this?" he frowned.

Regan nodded. She had a hard time meeting her husband's gaze as she continued, "I implied realtors have something very much like attorney-client privilege with their clients to keep her talking. When she told me what was going on, I was relieved to know Olive didn't need to kill husbands so their wives would move in and pay the next installment on her house ... but I didn't know what to do about Olive's money laundering."

"You didn't tell me any of this," Tom's voice was soft but sharp.

"I didn't want you to be guilty of anything."

"Let me get this straight," his blue eyes narrowed and blazed with anger she hardly ever saw and even more rarely saw directed at her. "You unethically misrepresented yourself to a client, withheld information of some sort of criminal behavior from the authorities, and left me in the dark about what you were doing?"

"For your own protection," she implored him to understand.

"You went too far this time, Regan."

She had been prepared for anger; his calm words hurt her more than any outburst would have.

"I need some time alone to think about this or I'm going to say something I'll regret."

He was out of his chair, out of his office, and out the back door of the building in what seemed like a mere heartbeat.

She leaned against his outside window and watched him drive past her toward the street. He kept his eyes straight ahead, not once glancing in her direction, though he surely knew she was watching him. He turned down Swift Street toward the ocean, gunned his engine, and drove away through the commercial section recklessly, at close to freeway speed.

Regan would have gladly sat in her office and cried, raged, and felt sorry for herself, not necessarily in that order and not necessarily serially. Tom's reaction to her confession was about what she expected — it still hurt.

It filled her with anger, too, mostly at herself. Her mess-up strained their relationship. Not telling him what she had done made everything worse. But even though he was right, he walked out; he shouldn't have done that. If she owed him the truth, he owed her staying in the room and letting her finish what she had to say.

Amanda's voice on Tom's intercom interrupted her plunge into self-pity. "Yoo-hoo, Regan, are you still in Tom's office? Tika Smith is here to see you."

"Amanda, yes, I'm here. Could you show her into the seller's conference room and give me a minute? Thank you."

Regan could hear herself speak. She sounded cool and together, like the consummate businesswoman, ready to meet with her client. The show must go on.

Sometimes I wonder about you, she sighed loudly, *you're either close to multiple personality disorder or you missed your real calling in life: you should have taken up the stage.*

By the time she joined Tika a few minutes later, Regan had forced her clash with Tom into her mental to-deal-with-later file. Since there wasn't any way to repair what just happened until Tom came back, she hid her emotions under a business-like image and embraced work. She even managed a genuine, if low-key, smile as she greeted Tika.

"I probably should have called first to arrange an appointment, but I've just been to see Olive. She called me, not an attorney or anyone else, with the phone call the police had to let her make. You do know she has been arrested for Walter Henshaw's murder, don't you?"

"Yes, I just heard."

"I don't understand why she was arrested. She couldn't possibly have killed that man; she was at my house when he was being murdered. I told the police that. I don't understand why they don't believe me."

"I've heard there was other evidence tying her to the ... to Walter's death. Olive must consider you a very close friend since she called you first. Maybe the police think you are ... not exactly covering for her ... but confused about the time she got to your house. Could it have been later than you remember?"

"Not a chance. Leave it to Olive," Tika issued a bemused chuckle, "she caused quite a disturbance when she came to my house on Halloween night.

"This father was at my door with a passel of kids he was ushering around the neighborhood trick-or-treating. Some of them were pretty little, they probably shouldn't have been out so late, and they were getting tired and whiny and wanted to go home. The older kids wanted to keep going; they didn't want to miss out on any candy collecting while they took their little brothers and sisters home, and they were whining, too.

"I think the guy was at the end of his rope anyway, but when Olive turned up, she was in full death costume and she came running up my walkway with arms raised yelling at them, 'I'm going to get you all.'"

Tika rolled her eyes at Regan. "You should have seen the commotion that caused. He screamed at her that she shouldn't be out scaring little children … I think he thought she was a teenager or a young punk having fun.

"She ripped off her headpiece, which caused another round of screams from some of the littlest children, and yelled at him that he was an irresponsible parent who shouldn't take such little kids out so late at night.

"He looked at his watch and hollered right back that it wasn't even nine yet and how dare she accuse him of bad parenting.

"That's when Charlie came rushing to the door ready to defend Olive. I was afraid he and the man were going to come to blows. I had to drag Charlie and her inside and give all the kids an extra piece of candy to settle them down.

"Olive was mortified once the door was closed. She said she didn't realize there would be little kids out after dark and she felt terrible about scaring them, but Olive being Olive, she still had her dander up at the father.

"She made it a point of looking at the clock in my kitchen when she went in there to have a calm-down drink with Charlie and me, and pointed out it was five minutes after

187

nine, not nearly nine like the man said, and that the little ones should have been home and in bed by eight.

"I told all that to the police. I don't get it; they're still holding her. Olive's bail has been set at a million dollars. I guess such a high number is kind of mandatory in a murder case, but she has to come up with ten percent of that before a bail bondsman will consider putting up the rest so she can come home.

"She may have called me hoping I'd found Charlie's stash by now, but I haven't, so I don't have that kind of money to give her. I'll talk to some of the other widows and some of her Pink Lady friends and her husband's relatives and see if they can chip in some money, but for now, Olive's stuck in jail."

"I don't think I can help, Tika …"

"Oh no, I didn't come here to ask you for money. I have this note Olive wanted me to give you. She wants to hold off listing my house for the time being. When I told her I still hadn't found the money, we decided she better not risk putting the house up for sale. Suppose she got an offer for it? She'd have to sell it, wouldn't she?"

"It's not that simple. If it was a perfect all-cash offer with no contingencies, she might owe the buyer's agent a commission, but she couldn't be forced to accept an offer and sell if she didn't want to."

"Even so," Tika said, "better safe than sorry."

Tika clasped her hands together in her lap, raised her shoulders, and puffed out her breath. "I called my daughter. She didn't get married during the five years I couldn't talk to her and I don't have any grandchildren yet. It was so wonderful to hear her voice. She's going to fly out and stay with me for a while; in fact, I have to go to the San Jose airport later today to pick her up.

"We have a lot of catching up to do, and I have some explaining to do. I haven't told her about her father yet — not the witness protection part, she already knew about that — but about him being killed. I couldn't tell her that over the phone.

"I'm going to keep her close for as long as she's willing to stay; I hope it's a long time. Since I won't be moving in with Olive any time soon, you can see there's no point in having the house up for sale right now, anyway."

Tika handed Regan an unsealed envelope. "Olive wrote this note to you explaining that she doesn't want to cancel the listing but she doesn't want you to tell other real estate agents about it until she authorizes you to move ahead."

Regan read over the note. Olive's dramatic signature began with an oversized O.

"I'll take down the information, right now," she said as she turned to the conference room computer.

"You haven't heard anything from Linda or Susan, have you?" Tika asked while Regan typed.

"Um-umm," Regan murmured, not raising her eyes from the computer screen. "There. The listing is down. I'll order the street sign with the 'coming soon' rider to be removed. It may take a couple of days, though, because the sign man has a route and doesn't go everywhere every day.

"Why do you ask about Linda and Susan? Do you think they will be taking their houses off the market, too?"

"Probably not. I just wondered. Linda and Susan are tight

with Olive — they'll probably still move in. Linda is so involved with her charities — did you know she's setting Olive's house up to host parties? I think she and Olive had a big luncheon for the Dominican Hospital volunteers, the Pink Ladies, a couple of weeks ago; they're both very involved in volunteering there and the luncheon was sort of a trial run for Linda's playing host out of Olive's house."

"Susan volunteers there, too, doesn't she? Is that how Susan met Olive, through that group?"

"Susan does some volunteer work at the hospital, but that's not how she knows Olive. Susan and Olive go back many years, at least all the way to the Gulf War and I think they knew each other longer than that because of Santa Cruz connections, but I couldn't say for sure. Susan was a nurse in the military then and they wound up in the same field hospital.

"Olive volunteered as a nurse for a while during the Gulf War. It started not too long after Olive's husband died. She wasn't getting over his death well at all and she may have thought serving again would be a good way of coping, although I halfway think she volunteered hoping she'd be in a dangerous place like she had been in Vietnam and that she might get killed.

"Our guys getting shot in the Gulf War ended quickly and Olive came home, but Susan was stationed in the area for a while. I've heard her tease Olive and say that the danger was gone but the gore continued for a few months and that she would have been in her element had she stayed.

"I guess Susan spent most of her time there treating a lot of the other side's soldiers who had some pretty hairy wounds.

"Susan was an operating room nurse and a good one, I've heard. She said she got to do a lot of procedures by herself if they had a rush of casualties. She wouldn't have been allowed to do work like that on our guys by herself, but with enemy soldiers, well the standards might not have been as high; and if she didn't at least try, some of the poor fellows would have died before a doctor got to them."

"Susan did cardiac procedures?"

"No, nothing like that. She wasn't a cardiac nurse then. She did more basic stuff, emergency room kind of stuff. She'd see soldiers with all kinds of bleeding out wounds and would be trying to sew-up arteries and veins. Susan and Olive may seem like an odd couple, but they've been friends since then.

"I sure hope Linda and Susan are able to free up some money for my Olive fund or that my daughter and I find Charlie's stash quickly, because things could get worse in the bail department if Helen changes her mind and tells anyone about the card."

Tika grimaced and put a hand over her mouth. "Never mind. Pretend I didn't say that. No client privacy thing here. What I started to say isn't related to real estate in any way."

Regan made an impulsive decision. She could at least tell Tom she had cleaned up part of her mess if she told Tika the truth about what her fiduciary duties were — and what they were not. It might get her into license–losing trouble if Tika complained to the California Department of Real Estate, but she spoke up anyway.

"What I told you about privileged information between a

real estate agent and a client … I may have suggested it was closer to what happens between an attorney and their client than it really is. If my exaggeration caused you to believe …"

"That we had established attorney-client privilege?" Tika grinned. "I know it's not the same thing with real estate agents as it is with counsel, even if you implied it is. I'm not a naive woman, Regan, especially when it comes to the workings of the law.

"If anyone was doing any game playing, it was me. Charlie and I knew we could have created problems for Olive with our house buying scheme. We explained it to her, but she said she didn't care if she got into trouble."

Tika put a hand on each side of her face, shook her head from side to side, and blew out loudly. "That woman really should see a professional to work through her guilt complex; she feels so guilty about her husband that sometimes she doesn't seem to care what happens to her.

"You were going to have to know about Olive owning our house if you were going to sell it. I didn't want you thinking too hard about why Olive suddenly had enough money to make her installment payment when she had been talking poor to so many people, and by so many people I do mean Linda and Susan who can both be such gossips, or wondering why she didn't sell our house if she needed to raise money.

"I figured if I explained to you what we did in my own terms, you wouldn't have to start asking awkward questions. I knew I was taking a chance with you, but when you answered me the way you did about privacy, I thought I could count on you."

Tika's face lit up with a bright smile. "I was right, wasn't

I, because you didn't give us up, did you?"

"No. I didn't." *Not even to my husband.*

"Regan, I need to tell you something else. I know I can trust you not to share information that doesn't help anyone by spreading it around. There's a problem. Maybe you can figure out what to do.

"When I called Helen to ask for help with Olive's bail, she told me when she went to check on Henry while we were all running after Olive at the séance, she found a card in his room next to his bed. It was like the one Olive gave Walter on Halloween. It had the date and it had a time, 3:45, on it. That's when Henry was drowned.

"Helen put the card in her pocket when she ran to look for Henry and was so upset after what happened, she forgot about it until after she talked to the police.

"Helen says even if Olive complained about Henry and made her oh-so-public pronouncements about how she should put him away, she knew Olive didn't really mean it.

"Olive was absolutely wonderful to Henry; I don't think I'd be exaggerating if I said she loved him and she is closer to Helen than she is to anyone else, even me. She would never do anything to cause Helen pain. Olive understands only too well what it's like to lose the love of your life to dementia; she would never have taken even one little hand squeeze or smile that Henry might still give Helen away from her.

"Of course Helen doesn't believe Olive drowned Henry, but that card is starting to gnaw at her. She doesn't want to give it to the police because she thinks they'll use it to strengthen their case against Olive. But she feels like she's withholding evidence, or even worse, a clue.

193

"Helen's right on two counts. The card is a clue. But law enforcement people can be so rigid in their procedures and bulldoggish when they think they have the bad guy, that they'll only see it as incriminating Olive; they *will* use it against her.

"Olive told me about that policeman who came to her house with you the night of Henry's murder. She says he's a friend of yours. She raved about what a great guy he was. Maybe he'd be more open-minded than most policemen. Could you figure out how to let your friend know about the card ... privately?"

Regan slumped onto her chair, crossed her arms on her desk and crumpled forward onto them. She rolled her head from side to side on her folded arms. *Swell.*

Her potential ethics problem had gone away but now she was being asked to get Dave involved in hiding evidence from his peers, and it was supposed to be a given that she wouldn't say anything about Tika's latest info dump to anyone else, not even Tom.

Regan felt she was being sucked into a maelstrom of swirling secrets with dangerous implications. She needed a branch, or better yet a strong hand, to grab if she was going to keep from sliding into the depths of the whirlpool, but neither was in sight.

She closed her eyes and tried to figure out what to do.

She didn't hear Tom come into her office. He announced his presence with his hands on her shoulders and a softly spoken, "I'm sorry."

She was on her feet with her arms around his neck before he could say another word. "I'm the one who should be apologizing. I didn't tell you what I was doing. I wanted to protect you; that really was part of it." Tom raised his eyebrows in an indictment of her explanation. "But, you're right, it was mostly that once I made up my mind to keep quiet about Olive and Tika's money scheme, I didn't want you to go all logical and tell me I was making a mistake."

He leaned over and kissed her gently. "Apology accepted. I think about eleven years ago I promised to stand by you. I knew what I was getting into," he smiled. "You've always had a bit of a Don Quixote complex, wanting to right wrongs that aren't any of your concern. I just want to know I'm more your partner than your Sancho Ponza."

"You're much too tall to be my Sancho. Besides, I tend to think of us as more glamorous, a couple more like Dorothy Sayers' Lord Peter Wimsey and Harriet Vane than as Don Quixote and his faithful sidekick.

"There's been another," Regan made a face, "... development ... while you were away forgiving me."

"Another one? I wasn't gone very long."

"Long enough. Tika came by with a note from Olive instructing me not to put Tika's house on the market as planned. She told me she always knew I was exaggerating our fiduciary duties, and told me another piece of information I shouldn't know.

"You've come back in time to keep me from getting in deeper — or for me to drag you into more trouble. Which it will be, remains to be seen."

Tom sat down on one of Regan's chairs, tilted it back, and put his feet up on her desk. "All set. Talk to me. I'm ready for anything. What's the latest thing you shouldn't know?"

"I shouldn't know that Helen found a note in Henry's

room with the date and time of his death on it." Tom's feet thudded to the floor and his chair flew to full upright position.

"What? A note like Walter got?"

"Exactly. Tika swears Olive was at her house when Walter was killed; she's told the police that, but Olive was still arrested. That must mean they don't believe her. If I tell them Olive was essentially laundering stolen money for the Smiths, they'll be convinced Tika's inclined to play games with the law; they'll be convinced she's lying.

"Another card at another murder with Olive admitting to being at both crime scenes ..." Regan fell silent and looked distraught.

"There's more if you want to hear it."

"More?"

"According to Tika, Helen doesn't believe Olive is a husband killer any more than I do. She doesn't want to give the note to the police. She understands how it will look for Olive, but she does think it could be valuable as a clue. Maybe she thinks there will be fingerprints on it; I don't know.

"Tika says Helen wants me to somehow tell Dave about the second card and convince him to investigate it but not tell his fellow officers what he's doing."

Regan took a deep breath and blew it out slowly. Her cheeks puffed up and deflated in concert with her breathing.

"I think that's everything." She offered a weak smile. "Aren't you glad I decided to be completely forthright with you?"

"Sweetheart, I know how badly you don't want her to be, but Olive may well be guilty of murder. Maybe your first instincts about her were right after all. Why are you so willing to trust what you feel about her now and ignore your initial impression of her?"

Regan tried to put her intuitive sense into words that didn't sound silly even to her. "When I thought she was a husband killer it was because there was something about her. I felt it at Walter's memorial service but couldn't figure out what it was for the longest time. Will you laugh at me if I say I was suspicious of Olive because she gave off a guilty vibe?"

"I may chuckle a bit, but you know I wouldn't laugh at you."

"When Susan told me Olive needed money for her second mortgage installment, Olive's guilt made sense. I read Olive's pressing need as her motive for killing, and the fact that she killed explained her guilt to me. The circle was complete, but it surrounded something that wasn't real.

"Olive does feel guilty, probably every day, but not because of something she did. She feels guilty because of what she couldn't bring herself to do. She broke her word to her husband and because of that he had to die a miserable death. That's the guilt Olive carries, the guilt I was sensing from her.

"The Smiths were always going to make Olive's installment payment for her. Olive had no motive for making widows; she never did."

"Olive may not have had a monetary reason for creating widows, and she may feel guilty about her husband, too, but she may have had another reason for creating widows; she could still be a widow maker."

Tom chose his words carefully; he didn't want to push his

wife. She was as capable of storming out of the room as he was. "For the sake of argument ... suppose I'm right about her wanting widows in her house for some other reason.

"Suppose Olive was lonely, rattling around her big house, and wanted widows to keep her company? She's clearly unconventional ... maybe she's more than a little eccentric ... maybe she's mentally unbalanced ... and maybe Tika is lying to the police to protect her ... and lying to you, too."

Regan was about to protest that Tika hadn't lied to her when she realized Tom was right. She found out about the money laundering scheme, not because she manipulated Tika into saying more than she should have, but because Tika played gullible and let Regan think that's what happened. In reality, it was Tika who was the manipulator, and she hadn't seen it.

"Tika did play me, didn't she? And she's trying to do it again with the card, isn't she? I only have her word about what Helen wants me to do with the note. It is incriminating. If Tika can get me to keep it away from the police or somehow limit its exposure to Dave ..."

Tom was nodding his head. "That's how it looks to me."

"I have to call Dave, don't I? I have to tell him everything."

Amanda's tense voice crackled over the office intercom, interrupting them. "Regan, Linda McAllister is here. I put her in the seller's conference room and closed the door. I know you and Tom are talking but I don't know what to do with her. She's pacing. I can see her through the conference room window. She's really wound-up and says she needs to speak with you immediately."

"I'll be right there, Amanda. Thank you. You did the right thing.

"I don't think I can make a hasty two-minute call to Dave. I need to meet with him in person and explain everything carefully. What I knew about the Rudolph house and withheld may make me guilty of committing a felony. I don't know. You wanted in, now I'm asking you what I should do. Is it reasonable to wait and set up a proper meeting with him somewhere away from his office, or am I going to make it worse if I don't call him right now?"

Tom thought over Regan's question.

"With Olive in jail, it seems OK to wait until you can talk to Dave on your terms. Even if she's a killer, she can't do any more harm from a jail cell. And since you've already knowingly withheld information from the police for quite some time, I don't see how a few more hours can make it worse.

"Go see what Linda's problem is … then call Dave and tell him everything you know."

20

"Please Regan, take my house off the market immediately," Linda wheezed.

She was so agitated she was out of breath; she sounded like she had run all the way to their office from her house on the other side of town. She went from hand wringing to an almost prayerful hand clasp as she spoke, "Have you heard about Olive? Isn't it awful?"

Regan put her hands on Linda's shoulders and used enough force to steer her to a seat and press her into it. "I'll do whatever you want me to do about your house, but please calm down. I'll ask Amanda to bring us some tea."

Given the way details were unfolding today, Regan wasn't about to assume she knew what anyone meant or what they were really asking. "Now, have I heard what about Olive?"

"She's been arrested for Walter Henshaw's murder. Tika asked me for money to try to bail her out of jail. Can you imagine? I gave Olive money for home improvements; I was getting ready to move in with the woman who killed my husband!"

"You said she was arrested for Walter's murder. Why do

you think she was involved in your husband's murder?"

"My God, Regan, isn't it obvious? Susan saw her at the wharf. Olive must have been the one who reversed Mike's transmission."

"Susan said she saw Olive at the wharf?"

"Not Olive per se, but a person dressed as Death. Olive has a death costume. It's clear that person was Olive."

"Linda, I was with Susan on the wharf. She did say she saw Death, but I don't think she meant it literally."

Linda was disgruntled, "You sound just like the police. They said if Susan saw a death figure she was hallucinating or that she was having something like post traumatic stress that made her see things or made her think she was back on Pacific Avenue when Walter was killed."

Linda's mood, which had been overwrought moments before, swerved into wrath aimed at the doubting authorities.

"Other people on the wharf saw Olive, too, you know. What do you think the police excuse is for them? Were they hallucinating as well?"

Regan was having a difficult time recalling why she thought Linda was the most sensible and rational of all the Widow's Walk Leaguers.

Amanda opened the conference room door with one hand while she held a cup of tea in her other hand and balanced a second cup and saucer on her wrist. Regan had seen well-trained waitpersons carry dishes like that, but Amanda was far from an experienced waitress.

Regan jumped up to rescue the cup and saucer that was about to part company with Amanda's wrist. Her timing wasn't perfect — some tea sloshed onto the underlying saucer

— but she did save the teacup from a full-fledged crash.

She put her rescued tea on the table in front of her seat and let Amanda present the intact cup and saucer to Linda.

"I chose Good Earth Original tea. It's already sweet tasting; I don't think you'll need sugar. Do either of you want milk?" Amanda asked. "Oh, and it's caffeine free."

"Nothing for me." Linda was too angry thinking of how callous police could be to add a thank you.

Regan made up for her oversight. "Thank you, Amanda. We're both fine. Excellent choice of tea," she winked discretely at her receptionist.

"Tika said she was taking her house off the market. So am I. I wish Susan would do the same. I wish she wasn't so set on selling; she doesn't need to any more than I do.

"I could sell my place and move into her house; we are best friends, you know. It's a spectacular house and it would be perfect for my charity entertaining." Linda twisted her mouth into an expression of disapproval, "but she doesn't want to do that.

"If she sells her house, I hope she at least has the good sense to move in with her boyfriend instead of into Olive's house. She may not, though, because she says his house is too small and rustic for her taste."

"Susan met someone? How nice for her."

"Yes. He seems like a nice guy. I'm so afraid that when Olive goes to prison, Susan will still buy into her house and wind up living there all by herself. Olive would turn it over to her, I'm sure she would, given all their connections.

"Being alone in that place wouldn't be a healthy environment for Susan. That house will have such negative energy because of all the murder relics it's held. She shouldn't live there, at least not alone. She's far too sensitive to do well there by herself."

"Do you think she's serious with her boyfriend? Perhaps he might move into Olive's house with her," Regan suggested.

"That's not going to happen. Susan says Byron needs a barn or a big separate structure for doing his metal sculptures. Woods Cove has restrictions about things like outbuildings.

"Besides, I'm sure the residents wouldn't approve of the noise and scrap metal he needs for his creations." Linda harrumphed, "Why, I heard they were unhappy when his old truck was parked there for a few hours when he helped Susan move some of her things. No, unfortunately it wouldn't work out for him to live in Olive's house."

"You wouldn't consider keeping her company?" Regan realized the folly of her question the moment the words left her mouth.

"Are you kidding? Live in a murderess' house? There might be ghosts. Mike might walk her halls at night!"

Regan was definitely having a hard time thinking of Linda as the most level headed of the widows.

"I didn't know Susan had met someone ... that she had a boyfriend." Regan smiled cheerfully, determined to move Linda away from talk of ghosts; having one client at a time who believed her husband had assumed a spectral form was enough.

"She hasn't said anything to me about him, but then, I'm not a close friend like you are so she might not, and I haven't talked to her recently, either. She's Tom's client so he calls her regularly, but I don't. Of course, if he's a new boyfriend, she might not have had time to mention him to me, yet."

"The boyfriend part is recent but she's known him for a long time. They were friends in college. Susan says she really liked him, that he was lots of fun, but he always wanted to be much more, and she wasn't interested in him in that way at the time. They reconnected about a year ago, shortly after he moved to Ben Lomond.

"Susan's not in the habit of talking about him to anyone, though. I ran into her having lunch with Byron last summer. It was just lunch, totally public and aboveboard, but she asked me not to mention their lunch in front of Walter. I shouldn't speak ill of the dead, especially since I know how much Susan loved him, but Walter could be so jealous that Susan thought it would be easier for all concerned, Walter included, if he didn't know about her friend.

"Walter was one of those men who simply didn't approve of male-female friendships. I think he didn't like it that my husband and Susan remained friends, even though they'd known each other since high school, way before Walter came into the picture. The fact that they had once been a couple troubled him, which was so absurd because Mike was happily married to me and not in the least interested in Susan in that way; and Susan, well, she was married to Walter."

Tika was right, at least about Linda being a gossip, it seemed. Once she began about Susan's men, there was no stopping her.

"It wasn't his fault, I guess. His first marriage ended when his wife left him for another man. As if that wasn't bad enough, she soaked him financially and then worked their kids until they didn't even want to see him anymore."

Gossiping worked like a calming salve for Linda, soothing her distress as she indulged. A talkative Linda was much easier to work with than an agitated Linda. Regan let her ramble.

"You can kind of understand why he didn't exactly feel women were trustworthy, but he should have realized he didn't need to be so controlling of Susan. She was mad about him. He should have realized he didn't need to worry about her."

Linda had temporarily forgotten about Olive and ghosts.

"I remember when Susan met him. She went absolutely gaga over him. Walter was a respected physician and she was a cardiac nurse. The first time she assisted him with surgery, she said she had met the man for her.

"She just flung herself at him. They became a couple right away but he wouldn't marry her for the longest time and marriage was what she wanted. She said she was ready to give up her moving around and just make babies with him. Can you imagine Susan, the career woman, being willing to change her life so completely for him? I guess she thought better of it once they were married, though, because she kept working and didn't have children.

"Walter was so wary of marriage, he said he'd never take the plunge again. Susan tried everything she could to land him. She finally suggested they do a bulletproof prenuptial agreement that pretty much put her on the street if she ended their marriage or if he ever caught her fooling around.

"Even with that offer, Walter thought about it for a couple of years before they did get married," Linda sniggered. "The funny thing is that by the time they married, Walter said he didn't care about a prenup. She's the one who insisted they have one like she proposed just to put his mind at ease.

"She called it her wedding present to him. He put her on title to his house as a wedding present; she gave him a prenup. Isn't that the strangest wedding present you've ever heard of?"

Regan was a good one-eared listener and multitasker. She used Linda's narration as a time to type listing withdrawal information on the conference room computer. She occasionally nodded as she typed, and smiled whenever it seemed appropriate. Her typing was finished by the time Linda needed an answer.

"It does seem unusual," Regan agreed.

"There, your house is off the market. I hope you don't mind, I made it a temporary withdrawal. That way if you change your mind, I won't have to re-enter all the information we have about the house's historical past."

"That sounds like a good plan, Regan. I'm sure I will want to sell as soon as I figure out where I'm going to live. I'm still enjoying how much my mother-in-law doesn't want me to let the house leave the family. She's scurrying around trying to get Mike's sister and her husband to buy the house from me, but they live in Santa Fe and built a gorgeous custom house there. They don't want to move back here and live in a drafty old house any more than I do."

Linda patted Regan's arm and leaned toward her conspiratorially. "Pretend you didn't hear that. We'll make the old house part a plus when there's a buyer, won't we? It is on the National Registry of Historic Homes, after all. We can make the draftiness become something positive like natural air conditioning, and we'll advertise how many traditional June weddings and successful marriages have begun with the house as a backdrop, won't we? We'll emphasize what a great place the house is for parties, too.

"Oh, Regan, that reminds me, you and Tom are coming to my fundraising event on Thursday night, aren't you? It was going to be my final sendoff for the house, but now it may be just another of my many events at the old place. This thing with Olive being a murderess is just so inconvenient," Linda huffed.

21

As soon as Linda left and Regan was back in her office, she retrieved her cell phone to make the dreaded Dave call. She wanted to use her private line; it would be a nightmare if she was accidently overheard by any of her office mates.

You're a good person. You didn't mean any harm. Dave will understand, she told herself as she speed-dialed his number. *You're not going to tell him anything over the phone. You're just going to arrange ...*

"You've reached Dave Everett. I will be out of the office attending a seminar in San Diego until Thursday afternoon. Please leave a message, or if you need immediate assistance press 9 and someone will be right with you."

She smiled. "Yes!" she said as she did a mini-fist pump. She was not only a good person but one who, once she made a promise to do something, kept her word. She promised Tom she would call Dave as soon as she finished with Linda. She had. And now she was being rewarded for her good behavior by two days of Dave's unavailability. Karma wasn't always a bitch.

Dave's message ended and his phone beeped. "Dave, it's

Regan. No rush, but I need to buy you a quid pro quo cup of coffee when you get back in town. Please give me a call when you have a chance."

Her office phone rang seconds after she ended her cell phone call.

"So soon, Dave?" she whimpered as she reached for the phone.

"Regan, it's Susan Henshaw. I tried Tom's number but it says he's away from his desk. I'm in the neighborhood and need to talk with someone about my house. It should only take a minute. Can I see you about it instead of Tom?"

"Yes, Susan, of course."

"Terrific. I'll be there in five."

Regan went to Tom's office and took Susan Henshaw's document file from his desk before she walked down the hall toward the conference rooms. She saw Susan, elbows propped on the reception counter, leaning over talking to Amanda as she got to the front of the office.

Regan smiled pleasantly and motioned Susan to the seller's conference room.

"Susan, that was fast. Let's go in here." *Here we go again — another house off the market, no doubt.* Once Susan was in front of her, Regan turned back toward Amanda and mouthed, "What a day."

Susan didn't seem anxious but her words belied her composed appearance. "I can't take all the loose ends any longer. I want an offer on my house by the end of the week. I have obligations to meet. I want everything over with by the end of the month so I can move forward with my life.

"Tom has explained to me how a house in such a high price range like mine has few buyers and told me patience will be financially beneficial to me."

She slapped both palms on the table to signal the finality of her decision. "But the bottom line, Regan, is I don't care what it takes to make it happen. If it costs me a million dollars, I don't care anymore. I want to be happy. I want out now."

"We can do another price reduction if you want."

Susan sat motionlessly and silently looking down at her hands without answering for so long it made Regan uncomfortable. When Susan finally raised her eyes to meet Regan's, it didn't take her people-reading skills to know there was more troubling Susan than how long her house was taking to sell.

"Walter's children are threatening legal action; they want to get his will overturned. The irony is I didn't have to give them anything, but because I knew he loved them, I agreed to give them a generous settlement after the house sells.

"What's that adage, Regan? No good deed goes unpunished? Now they're behaving like impatient little brats." She used an angry fist to punish the table.

"Someone has been putting a bug in their ear, probably their mother, Walter's ex. They think they have a case because he didn't provide for them. They don't. An excellent attorney drew up our wills and trust. Our documents are in perfect order, everything is ironclad.

"Nevertheless, they want to look at all of Walter's and my

private papers — everything — even from before we were married. There are documents that pre-date our marriage that aren't any of their business.

"My darling stepchildren are claiming I exerted undue influence on their father to get him to cut them out of his will. They are mistaken; I didn't do any such thing. They only have their mother and their own behavior to thank for being disinherited.

"I think they're having me watched. I wouldn't put it past them to have a private investigator following me around to see what I do and who I see. My banker is a long-time friend; he intimated in the strictest confidence that a request had been made to look at my finances. He wouldn't say where the request had come from, only that he thought I should be aware of it. I'm certain they're behind it.

"I want to make them go away and they're not going to until the estate settlement is finalized and they get paid off. The house is holding that up."

"Susan, I'm so sorry for what you're going through and for the way you're being treated."

Susan produced a wan smile. "I'm glad Tom wasn't here. He's a dear man and I'm sure he has my best interests at heart, but I don't think he would understand … not like you do.

"I don't want to lower the price again and hope a buyer comes along. Tom showed me an offer that was made a couple of months ago. It was a terrible offer; I think the buyer was a bottom-fisher who was hoping I was about to lose my house and was desperate. I turned the offer down and instructed Tom to yell at the agent who wrote it.

"Could you ask him if he still has it? Could he tell the agent that I apologize and am ready to accept it now?"

"Susan, I'm sure you've given this serious thought … but before you do something as drastic as that, maybe you need to get away for a while, back off and get some perspective. You could take a short vacation, get away from your stepchildren and let things settle down. When you come back, things may look different to you. Better."

"Now you sound like Tom; I thought you understood." Susan's voice broke and tears swam in her eyes, "I don't need a vacation. I need to get my house sold."

Regan patted Susan's hand. "I'll tell Tom what your wishes are. He'll handle everything. Don't worry.

"Tom and I discussed the offer when he got it. I remember it was a lowball offer, but the agent presenting it said his client could close in a week, maybe less. I think you're right about the buyer chasing about-to-be-foreclosed homes. He considered his client's ability to close so quickly a big plus and emphasized that aspect of the offer.

"Given what's been happening in your life, he might be right. Would that kind of closing timetable be helpful to you? If things come together rapidly, would you want to move that quickly?

"I know you moved some of your possessions to Olive's house already …" Regan trailed off ambiguously.

"I can have the rest of my things out the day after tomorrow, if that's what's needed."

Regan hadn't planned to say anything about Olive's arrest unless Susan brought it up. The urgency of Susan's instructions changed her plan. "You have heard about Olive, haven't you?"

"Tika called asking for bail money. She said both she and Linda were backing out of the Widow's Walk League house."

"Olive must appreciate that you're standing by her — that you're being such a good friend and will be going forward with your move."

"What gave you the idea I was?" Susan's tone turned strident.

Regan was flustered. "I assumed … since you said you could move out so quickly … since you've already moved some of your furniture … that you'd move to her house."

"I'm not moving in there. I don't want anything to do with her or her house. Olive is a murderer!" Susan screwed up her face in horror. "The police found evidence she killed four men; she's a monster."

"Are you going to move in with Linda, then?"

"My best friend?" Susan filled the phrase with dripping sarcasm. "I've met someone, Regan. He's a wonderful man. I didn't think I would ever fall in love again after Walter, but I did.

"I'm not about to move in with Linda and have him come see me at her house. Oh no. She's already proven how good she is at stealing boyfriends. Mike McAllister and I were high school sweethearts until Linda decided she wanted him. Losing out to Linda once was painful enough. I'm not giving her a shot at doing it again, although she'd have a harder time now that I know her tricks, and unlike Mike, Byron knows his own mind.

"Still, the less time he spends around Linda the better. No. He won't be coming over to a house shared with that floozy any time soon.

"I'll put most of my things in storage and quietly move into Byron's house. For my darling stepchildren's benefit, though, my permanent address will be my sister's house in Carmel Valley.

"I'd have made the move already and very publicly if it weren't for Walter's children. I don't want to give them any reason to question my devotion to their father. If I moved in with Byron, they might decide six months after their father's murder wasn't a decent interval for their widowed stepmother to mourn before she started dating, and I'm sure they'd be horrified that I chose a man like Byron; he's so different from their father."

The change that swept across Susan's face when she talked about Byron was stunning. The corners of her mouth turned up, all hurt and anger disappeared from her eyes, to be replaced by what Regan could only describe as pure joy.

"I haven't told you about Byron, have I?"

"Linda was in earlier today to take her house off the market. She mentioned that you were seeing someone ..."

"How I love today's technology." A warm smile spread across Susan's face. "First it aided the Arab Spring and then it helped little 'ole me find happiness.

"I've known Bryon for years. He was a poor starving college student I met when I was getting my B.S. He fell hard for me but I was still carrying the torch for Mike and didn't appreciate him. I couldn't come back to Santa Cruz after I got my nursing degree; I couldn't watch my best friend with Mike. I joined the military for a while, and moved around a lot. We lost touch. When I finally was over Mike enough to move home, I met Walter and the rest, as they say, is history.

"I had no idea Byron moved to Ben Lomond a couple of years ago. He was from Florida and I assumed he was living there, and he had no idea I lived in Santa Cruz.

"When Walter was killed … his murder was so dramatic … like most people in the county, Byron followed the story about Walter's death. He recognized me from a photo in the newspaper. After all these years," she giggled, "he recognized me because he said I hadn't changed at all.

"Once he had my name, he got on Facebook and looked me up. I had set up a page shortly before Walter's death. When I couldn't sleep at night I'd look up old friends and play games. His timing was perfect. He contacted me and we started talking online. Before long he asked to see me, and again, the rest is history."

Regan may have presented herself to the world as a no-nonsense businesswoman, but she loved nothing better than a romantic tale with a happy ending.

"What a fantastic story, Susan; it's like a modern day fairytale. I'm delighted for you."

"He's such a talented man," Susan beamed, "although at the moment he's still starving. He creates the most exciting metal sculptures, and even though his work is underappreciated right now, I'm sure that will change in the future. He just needs to get his pieces in front of the right eyes. He hasn't had the drive or the money to do that; I'm going to make it my mission to correct that state of affairs."

Susan's smile grew impish, "Why, Regan, when my house sells, maybe you and Tom would like to use some of your commission to purchase one of his pieces for your office entry."

"We'll have to seriously consider that, especially since he's going to become famous," Regan responded with her own giggle.

"Byron lives in a little house that's barely on the grid. His rent is cheap and the house comes with a huge outbuilding where he works. Because of Walter's children's little games, I've become stealthy, almost like a secret agent sneaking out to see him and spend time with him. Sometimes I make it seem like I'm off somewhere, like to my sister's in Carmel, and then I double back to his place.

"Let me give you his phone number. If I don't answer at home, that's probably where I am. My cell phone's performance at his house is sketchy at best; it's better if you use his landline to reach me."

Regan wrote down the number. "I'll let Tom know what you want to do as soon as he gets back to the office. This number may come in handy in the not too distant future; let's hope so.

"Susan, I really am happy for you. You've had such a difficult past few months. You deserve a brighter future."

🏠 🏠 🏠 🏠 🏠 🏠 🏠 🏠 🏠 🏠 🏠 🏠

Tom checked back in from his appointment in time to say goodnight to Amanda. He ducked into his wife's office with a smile on his face and a bouquet of flowers behind his back.

"I come with tokens of my affection," he said as he dramatically swept the flowers into view. "In case I still have a paw in the doghouse, these are for you. I thought they might help.

"I'm also willing to buy you dinner at some little Thai place that doesn't have a romantic atmosphere. That's my way of expressing my displeasure with you for keeping secrets from me — food, but no tender surroundings."

"Have I told you lately how much I love you? You are absolutely the goofiest, most wonderful man I know."

"I am pretty darn adorable, aren't I?" he grinned.

"As tempting as your offer is, I'm afraid I'm too tired to accept it; I'm too exhausted to eat. It has been quite a day. I just want to go home and flop into bed — I can probably stay awake long enough for a cup of tea, but that's about it."

"I know about Tika and our little tiff, and I know you were about to call Dave and confess and that an overexcited Linda McAllister was waiting for you. That doesn't sound so bad," Tom grinned, "and you're a tough lady and not known to be meal skipper. Suppose I listen now, like I should have earlier, while you tell me which of the day's events did you in. Maybe I can share your tribulations and unburden you enough that you'll change your mind about dinner."

Regan took a deep breath. "I met with Linda before I called Dave. She, like Tika, took her house off the market because of a ghost."

"Two clients with ghost issues?" Tom started to laugh. "My poor wife. Isn't there a rule somewhere that says you can't have more than one haunted client at a time?"

Regan almost smiled. "Only one of the ghosts is a problem. Tika's specter is haunting her to be helpful; he's trying to tell her where he hid the money. Linda's ghost, her husband Mike's ghost to be specific, is the only negative one.

"Linda is worried that if she sells her house and moves in with Olive, she'll run into him walking Olive's halls. She doesn't want to risk living with him now that he's dead. She couldn't take having him go bump in the night or whatever it is ghosts do.

"Linda votes with you, by the way. She thinks Olive is a husband killer."

"Well, then," Tom applied his best ghostly logic, "I guess technically Mike would be haunting Olive, since she's the one Linda thinks killed him."

Regan did smile. "After Linda, I tried Dave, I really did. He's out of town until Thursday. His unavailability was the high point of my day, except for your apology and these flowers, of course.

"Next up was Susan. You had gone off to an appointment and she did a drop-in. She asked me to help her."

"We lost three listings in one day?"

"No, Susan's house is still listed; she just wants it sold yesterday. She wants you to contact the agent who brought that insulting offer a couple of months ago and make it work."

"I can try." Tom looked at her suspiciously. "You're not planning to tell me Susan is seeing ghosts, too, are you? Did a ghost tell her to accept that rotten offer?"

"No," Regan chuckled. "It seems your golfing buddy's widow is being influenced by happy little cupids. She has a new love in her life. She wants the house sold so she can tie up loose ends and make a new life with him."

"Susan? Susan has replaced Walter so quickly? Wow. That makes me wonder how long it would take you to replace me."

"You're irreplaceable; you know that, although I might have fun …"

He wrinkled his nose and finished her sentence before she could, "… you might have fun trying. Just as I thought."

Regan's laugh was genuine and wholehearted; Tom's mission was accomplished.

"I would like to change my mind about dinner. Being with you — and the nice flowers — has revived me. I think I can manage dinner after all. And I keep thinking there was something I was going to talk to you about, but I can't remember what it was. Maybe food will raise my blood sugar level enough that my mind will start working again and I'll remember.

"If not, it mustn't be that important."

Tom tried to resurrect the offer for Susan's house without success. The buyer's agent gloated that his buyer didn't stick around pining for houses. He struck like a shark, and like a shark, kept moving when he didn't get the response he wanted. He and his offer were long gone.

Susan was distraught when Tom told her the news and Regan was glad he made the call rather than asking her to do it.

Thursday morning an unexpected offer arrived from a high profile Chicago businessman who wanted to buy a beach house situated within an easy limo drive to San Francisco and Silicon Valley. His was a perfect offer and it needed a prompt response. But Susan, off feeling sorry for herself, Tom presumed, was nowhere to be found.

"She may be at Byron's," Regan suggested. "Susan said she's gotten good at hiding out there. I'll pick up that trail; we'll track her down."

Regan tried Byron's phone number. After six rings it went into answer mode. The masculine voice directing her to leave a message had a sexy resonance not unlike actor Sean Connery's voice, although it lacked his accent. He played on the similarity, consciously or unconsciously, by opening with, "You've reached James, Byron James."

For a woman like her, who might forget a face but never a voice, hearing him conjured up the final clinch scene in every James Bond movie she had ever seen. Her heart beat double time for a few seconds. She decided Byron James knew exactly what he was doing.

"Byron, this is Regan McHenry. I'm trying to reach Susan Henshaw. She gave me your number …"

"Yes. I'm here." He picked up, sounding a bit breathless. She hoped she hadn't interrupted a romantic interlude. "I missed the beginning of your message. I was using a blowtorch."

"My name is Regan McHenry. I'm trying to reach Susan. She gave me your number; is she there?"

"Who did you say you were?"

"Regan. My husband, Tom Kiley, is Susan's real estate broker. He just received an exciting offer for her house and needs to reach her as soon as possible."

Byron fell silent — thinking, she guessed. Susan had trained him well.

"You've nothing to do with her stepchildren, have you?"

"No, Byron. She told me about the difficulty she's been having with them."

Regan tried to recall positives that Susan had shared with her that Bryon would know about, but a representative of the dreaded stepchildren would not. She hit on their college past and their Facebook connection.

"Susan told me the two of you were old college friends who lost track of one another. She credited Facebook for your reconnect. Isn't it astounding what's happened because of social networking these past few years? I mean, old friends finding one another like the two of you did and becoming more than friends. You read about it, but I've never met anyone it's happened to before; I believe you and Susan are members of the romantic vanguard."

He laughed, but guardedly. "Believe what you like. Susan and I are both on Facebook, but neither of us would use it to further a romantic connection. Neither of us are what you'd call avant-garde when it comes to courtship."

Regan made it a point to smile as she spoke, hoping her voice would reflect her expression. "That's too bad. Here I was looking forward to telling people it's all true about Facebook bringing lost loves together."

He laughed again, more easily this time. "Sorry to disappoint, but it was just happenstance that I decided to move to Santa Cruz, Ben Lomond specifically, a couple of years ago. Facebook had nothing to do with my decision.

"Honestly, neither did Susan. I had no idea she had moved home — unless you think we had some sort of psychic connection that drew me here. The reality is I'm not even sure I remembered her saying she was from the Santa Cruz area.

"I do admit to trying to look her up on Facebook once, though — right before I moved here, as a matter of fact — so maybe there was a psychic connection or a memory hidden away so deeply I didn't recall it. Hey, you could tell people about that, couldn't you? It would make for a great story,

223

especially in Santa Cruz."

Byron laughed freely and rolled on with his saga of lost love recovered. He had clearly decided Regan was who she said she was and his talking to her posed no threat to Susan.

"It was right after a bad breakup. I was a newly single man who maybe still had a crush on her, but I didn't know she had married or what her married name was, so I didn't find her on Facebook.

"I discovered her on Pacific Avenue on Valentine's Day — perfect date for the beginning of a romantic reconnection story, isn't it? It was love at first re-sight, at least for me."

"I'm beginning to like this much better than a Facebook meeting." It was Regan's turn for good-spirited laughter. "Old friends share Valentine's Day meeting ... love ensues."

"Well, not quite. It was last Valentine's Day and Susan was a married woman. I had to settle for friendly lunches for a long time. But they were clandestine lunches." His warm laughter came again and his emphasis on clandestine made the lunches he described sound vaguely wicked.

"I'm an imaginative man. I liked to believe that if Susan didn't secretly have some feelings for me, too, she wouldn't have insisted our meetings be so hush-hush.

"I remember one of her friends spotted us one afternoon. Susan turned bright pink and fumbled around trying to explain how we were old friends with nothing going on between us, but that, even so, it was better if her husband didn't know about us.

"After her friend left, Susan said her husband was extremely jealous, which was probably why she didn't want to take me home and introduce me to him. But, like I said,

I'm the creative type; so again, in my fanciful mind, I imagined she did return my feelings and figured he knew her so well, he'd be able to see how she felt just by looking at her.

"It was a great fantasy, and at the time, I didn't have anything better to do with what I felt for her than to play make-believe.

"Hey, am I ruining the story for you by letting you know I occasionally think like a hyper-romantic teenage girl?" he whooped abruptly.

"A bit, maybe," Regan chuckled. Even without meeting him, she understood Susan's attraction for Byron. He was charming, funny, and easy to talk to … and then there was his deep baritone voice.

"Funny how things work out, isn't it? Before the year was out, she was a widow."

A sharp frown crossed Regan's forehead.

"Enough with my storytelling. I may try novel-writing if I don't start making a respectable living as a sculptor pretty soon. I understand writing is easy and all writers make pots of money."

He was back on track as a charming wit, but Regan had lost her sense of easy rapport with him. She switched back to being all about business.

"I take it Susan isn't there right now and I really do need to reach her about the offer. Do you have any idea where she might be?"

"You've tried her cell phone? Of course you have. If she doesn't answer and she's not here, that means she's probably still at her sister's. Casey lives in Carmel Valley. Cell service is as bad there as it is here; you're probably not getting through to her.

"Susan said she had some errands to run and was going to see Casey when she finished. She promised to be home … here, in time for dinner, so if you don't catch her before then, I'll tell her to give you a call. You want to give me your number just in case she misplaced it?"

Regan read it off to him.

"Could I have Casey's number? I don't have it. I'd like to try reaching Susan there like you suggested."

23

"She was here but she left about ten, twenty minutes ago. I'm sorry. Give her a couple of hours or so and try Byron. As usual, she was in a rush to get back to him.

"It's so funny," Casey twittered. "I used to have a sister I couldn't get rid of; once she stopped working she'd stay a week at a time if I let her. Then along came Byron and it was all, 'Hi Sis, Bye Sis, gotta go.' Even on my birthday, she barely finished lunch before she wanted to leave."

Regan promised to do as Casey suggested, thanked her for her time, and hung up, frowning once more. Something was wrong.

She knew the sensation she was feeling. It was the same one everybody had from time to time, that awareness of knowing something, but not knowing what it was, and not being able to retrieve it from the brain's complex information storage system.

That frustrating sensation happened to her occasionally with song lyrics but most often with names. I met him at the escrow company party; what was his name? Julie introduced us; what did she say his name was? He works for a mortgage company; who is he?

Regan was still trying to make her mind connect dots when she noticed Dave leaning against her office door jam with his arms folded casually across his midsection and an amused smile on his face.

"You're pretty fun to watch when you don't know anyone's looking. You do this kind of frowny thing and your eyebrows take turns going up and down."

He startled her, but by the time she spoke, her voice was flat. "I thought you were in San Diego until later today."

"Yeah, that's what I've been telling people. I left the seminar and caught a flight back early. I figured I could use a couple of hours to catch up on some work before anyone realized I was back in Santa Cruz.

"That was my plan, but then I got your offer of a cup of quid pro quo coffee and I couldn't pass it up. I love that stuff."

Her answer to his growing grin was a smirk, "Let me tell Tom I haven't found his client, and then let's make it lunch."

"Ask him to come along."

"Not this time, Dave. I need to talk to you alone." She took a deep breath. "I've been bad."

Dave rolled his eyes heavenward. "Oh, thank you," he said. "The seminar was so boring and now I'm gonna have so much fun."

🏠🏠🏠🏠🏠🏠🏠🏠🏠🏠🏠

They walked in silence the short distance from her office to The Cellar Door Café on Ingalls Street, but Regan's mind clamored the entire way as she tried to organize her thoughts. Should she confess first that she withheld information about money laundering? Should she start by telling Dave about the death note Helen found and was hiding? Should she ask about Olive?

When they reached the building shared by the café and the Bonny Doon Winery tasting room, they walked in the back door to the restaurant. The ten-foot-long flying cigar, the signature icon from Bonny Doon Winery's Le Cigare Volant wine, hung from the structure's lofty ceiling. It caught her eye every time she came here.

The cigar had pointy navigational fins and was festooned in elaborate metalwork that made it look like an 1895 escapee from H.G. Wells' *The Time Machine*. A flying cigar would be out of place anywhere, but given its adornments, it seemed doubly incongruous in the modern concrete and rough-hewn wooden structure. Anxious as she was about what she was going to tell Dave, Regan almost smiled at the sight of it.

The walls of the restaurant stopped her. They were painted in what she always considered the bold colors of Bordeaux and Zinfandel; today the colors reminded her of blood: Walter's spilled on Halloween night and Henry's, older and less vivid, spilled in the broader sense as he was drowned while seven members of a séance conjured the dead.

She shivered so noticeably that Dave picked up on it, but he misread the cause.

"I like this place because it's cool even on a hot summer day like today," he said. "A lot of people must like it here for the same reason. I don't see an empty table anywhere. Let's try the other side."

They walked past falling water that fed a small fish pond into the tasting room. During the summer, any time after noon was prime wine tasting time. The bar was packed three people deep with convivial men and women well along in the tasting process. Their voices shrilled and their laughter was boisterous.

Dave tugged Regan's arm and pulled her into a newly vacated booth. The enclosure had high walls, and together with two other similar booths, served as a divider between the tasting room and the restaurant. The private tasting pods, so named by the idiosyncratic owner who considered them part of his Dooniverse, were elongated and highly stylized barrels with oval tables in their centers and curved banquet seating for ten or more along their bowed walls. They were meant for large groups doing private wine tasting; their shape dampened the noise from the bustling tasting room.

When a conscientious wine pourer poked his head in to tell them the barrels were reserved, Dave flashed his badge and in his best stern voice said, "Police business." The pourer backed out wide-eyed while mumbling an apology.

"I'll be scratching this restaurant off my list of places where I'm welcome," Regan scowled, "now that I've been seen being officially interrogated by a cop."

"I should come back with some great wisecrack, but I keep replaying you saying you've been bad. It's distracting me from my usual humorousness. Time to fess up, Regan. What did you do?"

"I think I'm an accessory after the fact in a money laundering scheme."

Dave's noncommittal "Really" worried her. She would

have felt better if he had a clever comeback. His seriousness meant he was in cop mode, looking at her as he might a suspect rather than as a friend he was free to torment.

"The police know about Charlie and Tika Smith being in witness protection?"

"We do."

"Tika said, as the Kolas, they were supposed to turn over any mob money Charlie embezzled to the authorities before they went into witness protection."

"I assume you have a point you're getting to."

"Tika told me Charlie didn't. He turned in most of the money but held on to around two million dollars. They had Olive buy the house that Tika lives in a couple of years ago, and in exchange, they gave her money — cash — whenever she needed it. That's how she was able to make her second installment payment when she had been complaining to everyone that she was broke.

"Tika told me they explained to Olive that the government would consider what they were doing money laundering, but she didn't care. I should have told you or the police what was going on when Tika told me. I didn't. That makes me guilty of a crime, doesn't it? Am I guilty of covering up some sort of tax evasion, too?"

Much as she had been dreading her talk with Dave, Regan felt a lightness of spirit as she finished her confession. It lasted for less than fifteen seconds.

"You want to turn around and put your hands behind your back, ma'am?" Dave said as he produced handcuffs from his belt where they had been hidden under his Hawaiian shirt.

"Dave!" Regan's voice broke and her heart raced. "You're

arresting me?" she squeaked.

He stared at her coldly and unblinkingly until his stomach began contracting and the breath he had been holding to keep from laughing began escaping in small puffs.

"Not really," Dave snorted, "but you should see the look on your face. I think this is the best I ever got you."

Regan closed her eyes, unsure what she was feeling more: rage or relief.

"Give us a little credit, Regan. We knew about Olive getting money from the Kolas, or Smiths. Remember how I told you we like to pay attention to widow's finances whenever a hubby dies unnaturally? We've been watching where money comes from and where it goes to with all our recent local widows, and since your buddy Olive seems connected to all of them, her financial situation found its way on to our radar, too."

He rolled his head off to one side. "If I recall, you even suggested Olive needed watching … 'course that was back in the day, before you decided she was a nice old nut."

"But it wouldn't have mattered if the police were looking at bank accounts and money transfers from institutions. Tika said Charlie had hidden embezzled cash that never made it to a bank. How would you know about the Smiths giving Olive cash?"

"Olive told me. Or I should say Olive confirmed what we thought. It seemed funny that if Olive was strapped for cash, she didn't put the house the Smiths rented up for sale or at least take money out of it since she owned it free and clear.

"Yet, somehow her cash flow problem went away, anyway. The widows Henshaw, McAllister, and Sprokly didn't make any noticeable cash transfers recently — well, except for Linda McAllister giving Olive money for landscaping, but it seems that money really was being spent as Mrs. McAllister wanted and for her future benefit. Anyway, what the widow McAllister gave her wasn't anywhere near enough for Olive's second installment.

"That left the widow Smith who conveniently lived in the house that Olive owned but didn't mortgage.

"We thought about the Smiths and good old Charlie's background and wondered if maybe he did a little fancy footwork with the Feds. He may have, but it seems Charlie salted away about eight hundred grand that he made in legit investments through the stock firm where he worked before he went rogue — legit, that is, if you think the money that brokerage houses produce is legit.

"The money disappeared from his private savings account right before he flipped on his criminal buddies. The Feds figured he was planning ahead but they never figured out what he did with the money. Kinda looks like we know now, don't we?

"Olive and I are best of friends since we spent time together the other night, you know, so I asked her if Tika and Charlie Smith were responsible for her in-the-nick-of-time windfall. You know Olive; no matter what, she tells the truth."

"If Charlie earned the money and paid taxes on it, the money wasn't dirty," Regan said hopefully, "was it?"

"That's what we figure."

Regan brightened. "Then neither Olive nor I did anything wrong, right?"

Dave shrugged. "Maybe not, at least not this time. The way I figure it, if the Feds have a beef with the Smiths, let them work it out. The FBI is full of special agent hotshots. Little old Santa Cruz PD," he exhaled loudly, "phiff — what do we know.

"And if we're second rate investigators, what would the FBI boys and gals have to say about the discoveries of a real estate agent who thinks she's a detective?"

Dave, who to Regan's never-ending amusement used an imperial we when he spoke of police investigations, had said "I figure." His turn of phrase wasn't lost on her. She grabbed his hand and squeezed it.

"Thank you."

He bobbed his head from side to side, embarrassed by her gesture.

"You said quid pro quo. What you got for me?"

"I have an important piece of information for you. Helen Sprokly found a death card in her husband's room like the one Walter Henshaw received. It had the date and time of his murder on it."

Dave leaned back against the booth wall. "Mrs. Sprokly didn't mention that little detail."

"I know. Tika told me about it. Evidently, Helen found the card and put it in her pocket and then forgot about it after the trauma of finding Henry. She didn't think about it until after the police left.

"Tika said Helen doesn't believe Olive killed her husband, but she realizes a death note in his room, like the note Walter Henshaw got, would make it seem like Olive did, so she decided to keep quiet about it. Tika thinks there might be clues on the card. Helen does, too. They want to get the card into police hands without making things worse for Olive. Do you have any ideas about what they should do with the card?"

"Yeah, Regan, I do, but you won't like my suggestion. The card has to be turned in and the chips have to fall where they will, even if they fall on your buddy Olive."

"Did Olive say anything about Henry's death note during her official interrogation?"

"Nope. She said she put on her death costume and looked in at the séance as a joke. She didn't say anything about delivering a note."

"Wouldn't she have mentioned the card if she left it?"

"Might have slipped her mind. She's weird about death cards, anyway. She freely admits giving one to all those people on Halloween and even to having a special one that she saved for Walter, but she insists the notes only had dates on them.

"The card that the widow Henshaw saved is in evidence. It had a time on it like the one you're talking about the widow Sprokly finding, and it had Doc Henshaw's blood on it, so we know Olive is at least, shall we say, mistaken about what was on the note.

"I'm not saying she's lying about that, just that I think she's closer to being a real nut case than most people think and that sometimes she's not one-hundred percent sure of her facts."

"Dave? Quid pro quo. I have a question for you."

"I've probably said more than I should already."

"Just one simple question. Did Olive's costume have Walter Henshaw's blood on it?"

235

Dave sighed loudly, "Not a drop."

"How do you explain that? You said the police were convinced whoever murdered Doctor Henshaw would have been covered in his blood. If Olive stabbed him, how did she keep from getting blood on her shroud? You know Tika swears Olive was with her at the time of the murder and if there was no blood on Olive's costume, doesn't that make her story believable? Doesn't that mean Olive couldn't have killed Henshaw?"

Dave studied his hands and didn't answer.

"You don't believe she did, do you? You believe she was at the Smiths when the murder was happening, just like Tika says she was."

"It's hard to argue with evidence, and the murder weapon is heavy-duty evidence. The widow Smith could figure she owes your buddy Olive because she helped her with her little money problem. It seems pretty clear your friend Tika doesn't always play by the rules. She may have supplied an alibi for Olive as a nice little thank you gift.

"Maybe Olive did manage to do the deed without getting blood on her." Dave almost winced as he speculated about avoiding a blood trail.

The look Regan gave him made it clear she didn't buy a word of his explanation.

"Olive said she didn't kill anyone. You just said she tells the truth …"

"I was being ironic when I said that. You must be slipping, Regan. Didn't you get that?"

"I'm not slipping and you weren't being ironic. Admit it, Mr. Tough Cop, you don't believe she's guilty."

"What I may or may not believe," he made *believe* a pejorative, "doesn't enter into it. I don't go by my gut like you do. I go by facts and evidence, and there's a lot of evidence that points at your pal Olive as the one who's been making widows, a lot of it is straight out of her own mouth.

"Come on, Regan, she admits to being at two murder scenes. She says the first Vic was a pain in the patushka and she loudmouthed it up about how it would be a better world if the Alzheimer's guy was out of his wife's hair. She says she knows how to mess with cars. She has a medical background, probably enough of one to know where to stab a guy to do the kind of damage Vic number one had."

"That's all just circumstantial evidence, isn't it?"

"Lots of criminals are sitting in jail because of a bunch of circumstantial evidence. But don't forget a nasty knife with Henshaw's blood on it was found at her place. That's more than circumstantial — you've got the murder weapon found in her house, the knife the killer used to do the deed.

"Look, I know you like her and you figure you've got a real talent for knowing who's telling it like it is … I like her, too … I admit it. But just because she's a likable old kook and you think she isn't a killer, doesn't mean she's innocent. Real life doesn't work like that."

Dave gave his head a frustrated shake.

"There's just so much evidence, Regan, murder-one evidence, and it all points to her."

"What's going to happen to her?"

"She's only been charged with Walter Henshaw's murder so far, but Henry Sprokly's murder is a lock, too, even without your death note making Olive look guilty for sure.

It's not gonna take more than those two crimes to put her away for the rest of her days. You gotta accept the fact that your pal's gonna see the world from behind bars from now on."

24

Regan handed the parcel to Tom. "I brought you some deep fried brussel sprouts. I'm sorry they're cold."

He reached into the bag, produced one of The Cellar Door Café specialties, and bit it in half. "Cold isn't as good as hot, but it's still good," he smiled. "The best part is you're delivering them. You had your talk with Dave, didn't you? I thought by now I might be visiting you in the hoosegow in a cell adjoining Olive's."

"It looks like I'm off the hook. The police already suspected the Smiths were giving Olive money. She confirmed it as soon as Dave asked her if it was true. He said, since they already knew what was going on, my not coming forward didn't hinder their investigation. Your wife isn't a felon after all."

Regan exhaled in shoulder-dropping relief. "Olive isn't as fortunate as I am, though. Dave told me not to feel guilty about incriminating her in Henry's murder by telling him about Helen's note — that the note would just be icing on the cake; there's plenty of evidence to convict her without it.

"If that's true, why do I feel like such a snitch?"

Tom tried to come up with a helpful answer, but he couldn't. "You can't let yourself think that way."

"I'm going to be useless for the rest of the day, so unless you need me to do something for you about Susan's offer, I'm going home to mope."

"You go ahead and do that. I can't raise Susan. Her boyfriend Byron promises to have her call when she gets to his place. Given how long ago she left her sister's, that should be any minute now. I'll take the offer to her and swing home from there. We can go to Linda McAllister's shindig in one car."

"That's tonight," Regan moaned, "I forgot all about it. We paid for our tickets — I'm really not in the mood — can't we skip it?"

"It's for Shakespeare Santa Cruz, your favorite local theater company. There's supposed to be a surprise guest from the Royal Shakespeare Company who's come all the way from London to make an appearance and maybe give a short performance. You'll have fun. And, sweetheart, you seem to me like a woman who could use a little fun right now."

🏠 🏠 🏠 🏠 🏠 🏠 🏠 🏠 🏠 🏠 🏠

Regan was determined to think about anything other than Olive and the weight of evidence against her as she drove home. Her younger son, Alex — her almost rock star son — had given her a new CD, his band's latest release, before he left with the group on their summer tour to promote it. She hadn't taken it out of its wrapper yet. It promised to be loud and exuberant like their other releases, and thoroughly distracting. She opened it and put it in her car's CD player.

The music started many decibels above her comfort level. She reached for the volume control but hesitated and then impulsively pressed the button to open the sun roof instead. When she reached the stop light at the top of Swift Street, the driver in the car next to her swiveled his head and glared at her. She stared back brazenly and left the volume untouched.

Her behavior matched her mood. She was on edge and troubled, and like an angst-filled adolescent looking for answers without enough life experience behind her, she couldn't quite figure out why.

Regan remembered that was what being fifteen felt like. Thank goodness that was a temporary condition; she wouldn't want to go back through the ordeal of that age. But for the moment, being past forty didn't mean her thoughts were any more settled than they had been when she was a teenager.

She let her music blare so loudly the world had to listen to it. She felt the wind whip her hair as she tackled the first twists of her climb up Empire Grade Road toward home. But her self-imposed distractions failed to engross or soothe her.

She couldn't control where her mind went any better today than she had when she was a girl. The only difference was that it wasn't worries about boys or what someone had said to her in class that propelled her present thoughts — it was the disquieting image, on this gorgeous summer day, of Olive sitting captive and motionless in a tiny jail cell, unable to escape its confines to take one of her long hikes. It was the possibility that all of Olive's future days might be like today that drove her thoughts. And it was the certainty that Olive was no more a murderer than she was that fed her past-forty anguish.

The music, the wind, and the road's twists became mere background noise; she was as oblivious to her surroundings as she was to the music pouring out of her car or the wind tugging at her hair.

There was so much evidence. Olive, dressed as stalking Death, had given Walter a card telling him he was about to die. There were witnesses and she admitted it. The bloody knife used to kill him was found at her house.

Mike's transmission had been tampered with by someone who knew how to do things to cars. Olive admitted she had learned such things while she was a nurse in Vietnam. A manual about transmissions, a refresher course as it were, had been discovered at her home.

Olive had been cruelly outspoken about Henry; even Regan had heard her say Helen would be better off without him. Olive placed herself at his house when Henry was being drowned. Another murder card had been found in his room and Olive had been Death once more, looking in the window for seven witnesses to see.

Olive, dressed in black, arrived late for the Widow's Walk League walk the morning Charlie had two bullets put in his chest by a long distance shooter, and a target scorecard had been found at her house indicating she was a good shot from a distance …

It hit her with such force she thought for the slightest of instants that she had hit an animal: an unlucky deer crossing the road at midday or a coyote nose-down following its prey's scent.

Why hadn't it been clear to her before now? There was so much evidence. Everything pointed at Olive. Everything.

She was about to say it to Tom before he stormed out of their office; it was what she kept forgetting to tell him. It was what Dave said as he spoke of following facts instead of his gut. There was so much evidence.

There was *too* much evidence.

Olive was right, she was having a grand joke played on her, except it wasn't a laughing matter. She was being set up to look like a murderer by someone who overdid it.

Who was trying so hard to make Olive look guilty; more importantly, why? Did the framer have a reason to hurt her, or was she just a convenient suspect to divert attention away from her crimes?

Crimes. That was the right word. It wasn't a coincidence that several husbands were killed whose wives were connected to Olive. The same person was responsible for three dead husbands and for setting Olive up to look guilty for all the murders.

If she had settled for three murders, she would have pulled it off; but she threw Charlie Smith into the mix, Charlie, a fourth husband who probably didn't belong there.

The police were investigating his murder as mob-related. Tika, the woman with the most to lose if she misjudged who killed her husband, had come out of hiding and called her daughter. She wouldn't have done that unless she believed Charlie's death was the mob's final retribution against her turncoat husband. The police must have confirmed it was.

Setting Olive up for killing three husbands had been done

243

so well, but if Charlie's death was a mob hit instead of an outside job, the target score card was a mistake. The murderer had put evidence in Olive's house that didn't belong there.

Why would she do that? If she hadn't killed him, why make it seem as if she had? Because she thought his murder *was* random. She didn't know about Charlie's past.

She was tying up loose ends. It wouldn't do to have two murderers working the Widow's Walk League. The police would start asking questions again, and she had committed murder and framed Olive to stop them from asking questions. Better to have Charlie's murderer go free than to have the police poking around her real crimes.

Regan was parking her car in the garage when it occurred to her that she thought of the killer as female: *she* framed Olive, *she* overdid, and *she* didn't know about Charlie.

A female murderer did make sense. Whoever planted evidence in Olive's house had to have access and know it well enough to place the incriminating items where Olive wouldn't come across them prematurely but the police would find them easily. She also would need to be in the house without causing alarm; she would need to move freely without attracting attention.

Who fit that profile? Attendees at Olive's Pink Ladies event would have access to the house. Realistically, though, most might not know the house well and none would have known they would be invited to a party there when the murders started last Halloween. Those facts ruled out most of the volunteers.

The facts didn't rule out all the women, however. Linda and Susan were at the event and knew Olive's house well —

they intended to live in it. They both also had access to it on many other occasions and they knew what Olive intended to do with her house before husbands started dying. Either one of them could have planted evidence to frame Olive.

Proximity made Tika another possibility, but a more remote one. Since she knew about her husband's past and suspected who killed him, she wouldn't have put the wrong evidence in Olive's house, would she? Tika had tricked her, used her, and she was the one who told her she suspected a mob hit. Tika was also the one who let her know about the death card Helen found. Was Tika trying to use her again? Did Tika have another agenda that she was missing this time as well? Tika was a trained nurse. Could she have enough medical knowledge to dispatch Walter Henshaw?

Regan's reasoning hit a snag: Tika was Olive's alibi for the time of Walter's murder, which meant Olive also provided an alibi for her. Regan couldn't place Tika at Walter's murder without making it possible for Olive to be there, too.

What about Linda, the Grande Dame of charitable events? She didn't know about Charlie. It was impossible to know how people mourned, and there was certainly no right way to do so, but of the widows, Linda was the only one who was taking advantage of her husband's death to do what she had wanted to do for a long time.

Linda was getting rid of the family home, a residence she didn't like anyway, to get even with her mother-in-law for twenty-three years of criticism and unkindness, and she was loving the payback.

Linda admitted to stealing her dead husband from Susan,

her best friend, but she had never mentioned anything about doing so because she loved him. Linda was a goal setter and a goal getter. She wanted a particular lifestyle. Once she realized Mike McAllister, with his wealth, connections, and Santa Cruz history, could provide it for her, she had gone after him, never mind the pain her actions caused her best friend.

Linda demonstrated ruthlessness when it came to following her plans. Was it possible, now that she was confident in her place in the community and no longer needed Mike to have the life she wanted, she decided to get rid of him?

She was at the wharf the day he was killed and she did know about car transmissions. She also had the perfect alibi for Henry's murder: she was with Regan and five other people while it was happening.

Then there was Susan. She didn't know about Charlie's history. She was with her husband on Pacific Avenue when he was murdered and she was at the wharf when Mike died. According to Linda, she had taken a mechanics class in high school to be near Mike, yet she down-played her knowledge of cars. Was she a poor student or did she know more about them than she admitted?

Susan had medical training like Tika, maybe even more because of her wartime experience. She had ample opportunity and access to plant evidence in Olive's house. She could have moved all the incriminating items in with her furniture.

Regan's mind began to race. Wasn't it Susan who suggested that Olive needed money, the initial motive for

Olive making widows, the motive that she herself had been so quick to accept and pass along to Dave? Since Susan didn't know about Olive's arrangements with the Smiths any more than she knew about Charlie's connection with the mob …

Regan's theories unraveled before she could weave them into a convincing cloak of guilt. Susan, like others, heard about Olive's money woes from Olive herself, she was just the first to mention them. And Susan wasn't anywhere near the Sprokly house when Henry was murdered. She was at her sister's in Carmel Valley that day, helping her celebrate her birthday.

Regan's mind was pulled from swirling conjecture back to the solidity of Bonny Doon the moment she opened the garage door into the house. The insistent ringing of their home phone demanded her attention. Caller ID indicated Tom was on the line.

"Susan's not back yet," Tom sounded frustrated. "I just checked with Byron; he thought she was running errands before she went to her sister's; now he thinks he got everything backward, that she went to her sister's first. I'm going to have to wait until she shows up, present the offer, and get a counter-offer or an acceptance off to the buyer's agent before I can come to Linda's party.

"Even assuming some fast turnaround, I'm at least two to three hours out. I may get to Linda's in time for some entertainment but well after the festivities begin. You better go without me. I'll catch up when I can."

The thought that she might yet be able to skip Linda's fundraiser made Regan the happiest she'd been all day.

"We can both skip going. Business or duty or whatever

calls."

"No you don't," Tom shot back. "I need you to go and save me some dinner, carnivore fare please; don't bother with salads and precious little nibbles."

"Tom, did Walter Henshaw love his wife?"

"Where did that come from?" Tom sounded more startled than curious.

"I've been thinking about who could have put evidence in Olive's house. I think it had to be Tika, Linda, or Susan. I can't make any of them fit, though, because I think the same person killed all the dead husbands and I can't place any of them at all the murder scenes, so I'm trying to think about it from a different direction."

"You do remember I told Dave the Henshaw marriage seemed solid to me."

"I remember. I'm just trying … I'm playing with ideas. Linda says Susan was crazy about him, too. You said something about him being controlling. Linda says he was wildly jealous of Susan, that she couldn't even let him know she had the occasional lunch with her old friend Byron. I was wondering …"

"The same Byron who is now the boyfriend?"

"Uh-huh. But the boyfriend part came later. They were just friends until after Walter was killed. Their relationship became a romance when Byron consoled her after Walter's death."

Regan finished her statement slowly. Although Tom didn't pick up on it, Regan's thoughts shifted and the memory of Byron's words played in her head and mixed with Tom's.

"We ran into one another on Valentine's Day."

"Walter liked to be in control ... it was obvious in his golf game ..."

"... it was last Valentine's Day ..."

"... go nuts if he missed ..."

"... and Susan was a married woman."

Regan momentarily lost track of what Tom was saying.

Susan said she and Byron reconnected on Facebook after Walter's death. Byron said they ran into one another face-to-face after he moved to the area and that it happened well before Walter's murder.

Regan caught the end of Tom's opinion as plots and schemes filled her head.

"He ran his operating room in the same way, and his practice. It probably carried over to Susan as well. But I still believe that Walter, for all his cardiologist's ego and controlling nature, loved his wife.

"Yes, Amanda," Tom's voice echoed on the phone. Regan couldn't hear what their receptionist was saying over the office intercom, she only picked up Tom's responses. "Put him through, please.

"The buyer's agent for Susan's house is calling for an update. I've got to go. I'll see you tonight," Tom signed off hastily.

Regan held the phone to her ear for a minute after the line went dead. She was frozen in thought, replaying what she knew about Susan and Byron.

Linda said Susan was crazy about her husband. She said Susan and Byron were friends in college; Susan liked him, but he wanted to be more than friends and Susan didn't. Byron said he still had a crush on Susan when he moved to

Ben Lomond and felt the same way he had in college about her as soon as he saw her again. He even spoke of imagining that Susan secretly returned his feelings.

For Susan's part, however, it seemed she didn't. She probably met him for lunch, like she might any old college friend new to the area, and enjoyed his company as she had in college, and in the same way.

Byron might fantasize that Susan secretly returned his feelings and was keeping their lunch get-togethers undercover, but there was another explanation for Susan's circumspection. According to Linda, Walter was unreasonably jealous of even the most innocent male-female friendships.

What about the discrepancy between Susan's and Byron's stories about when they reconnected? Byron was telling the truth about that — Linda said she saw them together last summer — but given Walter's children's intrusive look into her affairs, Susan may have decided to concoct a more innocuous story line, one which couldn't possibly raise any eyebrows even among the most aggressively disbelieving offspring.

As Regan considered Byron, a sinister idea pushed its way into her thoughts. She began to replace her image of Byron as the charming old college friend whose comforting attention after Susan was widowed grew into love, with a darker, dangerous being: Byron the stalker — a man who kept track of a disinterested Susan for years, fantasizing all the while that she secretly returned his feelings — Byron who came to Santa Cruz in pursuit of her.

Stalkers were known for occasionally killing the object of

their misguided affection; some were known for eliminating their rivals.

Suppose Byron was the fleeing death figure Susan pointed out as Walter lay dying. Susan said she saw Death at the wharf when Mike died. Had she seen a darkly clad Byron that day, too?

Regan could even potentially place Byron at the Sprokly house — Susan could well have innocently told him about the séance — he was alone that day because she went to her sister's for a birthday celebration.

She had questions. Byron as widow maker was by no means a perfect fit, but then, real murder was never as tidy as framed-for murder. How had he planted evidence at Olive's house? Why try to incriminate her at all?

Regan quickly came up with possible answers to her questions. Linda said the residents of Woods Cove complained when his truck was parked in front of Olive's and they saw him moving furniture into the house. If he helped Susan move some of her furniture to Olive's, he could have planted his murder castoffs and circumstantial evidence while he was being a helpful friend.

That might explain why he targeted Olive, too. It may not have been a let's-set-up Olive decision so much as a why-not-set-up Olive situation. Mere opportunity could have dictated who Byron decided to frame.

Regan tripped over a stumbling block in her theory. There were multiple killings. Byron might have wanted to make Susan a widow, but why would he add Mike McAllister and Henry Sprokly to his victim list?

The answer she came up with was chilling in its cruelty. It

could be that two uninvolved and innocent men had to die so the authorities wouldn't look at Walter's murder as a singular event. Olive may have been set up as part of a bigger plan, too; her link to all the victims through the Widow's Walk League was a perfect connection for the police to discover.

Byron as the murderer worked. Regan saw the murder of Walter Henshaw to eliminate his rival and the murders of Mike McAllister and Henry Sprokly and the framing of Olive to cover it as an artistically executed scheme, a work of art in many ways. It was a very neat, very tidy, and very creative solution to Byron's problem, and as Byron said, he was a creative man.

As long as Olive was jailed, husbands weren't at risk; Olive's frame-up would be blown if more were killed. Even so, Dave needed to know about Byron's artistry and this time she wasn't going to wait to tell him.

25

Regan was dressed for Linda's fundraiser in a current and stylish outfit that topped a white lace summer blouse and short linen skirt with a khaki-colored long-sleeve safari jacket with its cuffs turned up to three-quarter length. Her sandals, which began as three-inch wedges, were mostly red straw straps that wrapped over her feet and up her legs past her ankles, gladiator fashion. They weren't her style or at all sensible and they would probably fall apart after being worn a couple of times, but with a ten-dollar price tag dangling from them, they had been an irresistible find.

She bought her bargain impulsively, crowing inwardly and with a big smile on her face, but without a plan for where she'd wear them — not to work, certainly — and put them unworn into her closet. They remained there through late spring and most of the summer until it occurred to her they would be perfect party-ware for mingling with the theatrical crowd and patrons at Linda's fundraiser.

When she got dressed, she hadn't considered how outlandish she'd feel wearing them to the police station to see Dave, her first stop before dinner at Linda's, but then, when

253

she planned her Shakespeare Santa Cruz getup, she didn't know her first stop would be a trip to the police station to explain why Byron James was a cold blooded killer.

Regan had been to Dave's office so many times before she knew how to find his ground-floor cubbyhole without trying — in fact her sometimes excited bursts into his office had on occasion caused a commotion or gotten him into trouble. She recognized several of the officers she passed in the hallway; some recognized her as a familiar if not everyday face. Those who did may have wondered what a, thanks to her foot-ware, six foot tall Regan was going to do to Dave this time.

A young female officer who saw Regan remembered her clearly, and reflexively touched her holstered weapon as they passed one another. Once she realized that today, unlike the first time they crossed paths, Regan had a proper visitor's pass pinned to her jacket, she offered a tepid smile instead of drawing her weapon.

Dave was on the phone when Regan stuck her head into his office. He acknowledged her with a finger held up and then turned his hand and pointed to one of the folding chairs leaning against his side wall. She understood his meaning, unfolded a chair, and set it up opposite his desk.

"Yes, you can quote me on that, Marc. Use it for tonight's news," Dave said before he hung up the phone.

He produced what could only be described as a cat-that-just-swallowed-the-canary smile: satisfied, happy, and unabashed.

"You're seeing me twice in one day, Regan? This is going to be good, isn't it?"

"That's right. I'm pretty sure I've figured out — no — I

have figured out who's really been killing husbands." Her features remained poker faced straight as she spoke.

"Did you, now?" he asked quizzically as his smile faded away, "I can hardly wait for you to tell me."

He leaned forward and rubbed his hands together, "And I'm sure you're going to."

Regan blurted out her news just as Dave expected. "Byron James, Susan Henshaw's struggling artist boyfriend is the killer."

He pursed his lips, a hint of a smile twitched at the sides of his mouth, but he immediately rearranged his face into a sober pose.

"Hummm," he nodded. "I'm sure you've worked out all the details about motive and opportunity, all the important fine points like that or you wouldn't be here."

He continued nodding, involving more and more of his body until he was bobbing up and down.

"I'm kinda busy here, you know how it is when you get back to work after being away for a couple of days, so could you skip the minutiae for now and just hit the high level stuff for me? In a dozen words or less, how do you know what you know?"

"He's the only one with motive who could be at all the murder scenes."

"That's fourteen words." Regan started to protest as he held up his hand in a stop gesture, "But who's counting when there are crimes needing solving and that root'n-toot'n amateur sleuth'n Regan McHenry has everything worked out."

Dave turned to his computer and tapped in a few key

words. "Here we are. Walter Henshaw, murder investigation, status, open." He tapped away again, "Byron James."

Dave read silently and then said, "Good-looking guy, romantic, like his name. You gals like that, don't you?"

Regan was surprised that the police had Byron James on their radar and even had a photo of him. "May I see …?"

"No you may not. This file is not for general perusing," he snapped as he threw his hands in front of the screen.

"FYI, Regan, next time before you come running down here with your ducks swimming every which way, you might want to spend a couple of minutes doing a little serious investigating like we real detectives do. It's harder work than running ideas around in your head to see if they feel right, but you'll get better results.

"Or if that's too much trouble, you might want to take thirty seconds to find your pal's website and see him getting a big hug from, uh … let's see … Abigail Evanston, the charming wife of Jud Evanston at last night's opening of their new restaurant *Epic*," he read off the computer article.

Dave's voice rose to a falsetto as he quoted Mrs. Evanston: "'We are delighted to feature a Byron James sculpture welcoming you to an epic,'" he twittered and touched his fingers to his cheeks for added effect, "'dining experience. We are especially delighted to feature the work of one of our own Sarasota native sons.'

"From the way she's looking at him, I bet they either have some history or she wishes they did."

Dave shook his head, his eyebrows raised innocently, "See, if you had just done that much, you would have seen the article is datelined October 31, last year. Your pal was being ogled in Sarasota when Walter Henshaw was being done to death by Death in Santa Cruz.

"Oops — didn't you say your bottom line reason why he's the killer is he could have been present at all the murder scenes?" Dave held up his index fingers and pointed them to the left. "But how could he have been here when …?" Dave switched his fingers to the right and didn't bother to finish his question.

"How did you, the police, know about Byron James?" Regan was as curious as she was crestfallen.

"You were there when I interviewed Tom. You remember me asking him about the Henshaw's marriage and telling you we always look at the dead guy's wife as suspect numero uno?" He opened his eyes wide, "Duh, Regan."

"Tom said he thought their marriage was a good one," Regan sounded defensive.

"Yeah, he did. Tom was on my list because I know him, but we asked other people that question, too. I got some useful information from Tom's perspective, but he didn't know Susan Henshaw was spending time with a good-looking old college buddy of the male persuasion. One of her friends whose name was on another list did, though."

"Linda McAlister?"

"Doesn't matter who. The official verdict was things were innocent at that time and he didn't have anything in his background that said he could have done the kind of wound damage Henshaw had, but in the process we took a look at him. We also kinda squinted extra hard at Susan Henshaw, what with widows always being suspects anyway, but what with most innocent widows not having single good-looking extra-curricular guys in their lives that they only see on the down-low.

"I gotta say, for a while there little Susie was sitting right on the top of our list — military hospital background where she might have been able to pick up a few surgical skills, a hook-up with a guy who's aging well, coupled with that nasty prenup agreement that said her lifestyle would change dramatically if she divorced her husband or got caught fooling around on him, and a husband who was maybe beginning to feel more like a python than a life partner."

Regan detected a hint of apprehension sweep across Dave's face; he was wondering if he had told her too much. She resisted the urge to let him worry. "You haven't told me anything new; I knew about all of it, including the prenup. Linda McAllister is a chatty woman — and so are several other members of Olive's Widow's Walk League."

"So I gather," Dave chuffed.

"Then Mike McAllister went swimming with the fishes and other husbands started dropping one by one and Olive looked so good as the widow maker, that she knocked Susie Q off her prominent spot."

The sound Dave's hands made as he brushed them across one another, palms together, sounded like what he was saying: Susan's name was wiped off the police suspect list.

"Like I said at your lunch confessional earlier, it doesn't look good for your old buddy Olive."

"There is one thing I'm still not absolutely sure of, Dave, and I want to know. Do the authorities think Charlie Smith's murder was a mob hit?"

Regan was glad she reassured him that he hadn't given out

258

too much information; he only weighed whether or not answering her question was OK for a second. "If I tell you, are you going to go away and let me get some work done?"

"Yes, I promise."

"More than think. The FBI guys have been all over it. They even figure they know which Albanian mobster did it. They think he's done some other nasty stuff, too. It was the same style hit with Smith as it was with a few other people the FBI guys think he offed. But so far they can't prove anything because it seems their favorite gangster always has a bunch of buddies who swear he was hanging out with them being the life of the party when bad stuff was happening. Charlie Smith's murder is one the whole department is glad is off our books."

"But if Olive didn't kill Charlie, then why was a target score card part of the evidence found at her house? It doesn't make sense. She wouldn't save a souvenir of a murder she didn't commit."

Dave looked left and right like he was looking for eavesdroppers, a farcical thing to do given the size of his office, and then leaned toward Regan. She waited skeptically for the punch line of a Dave-joke as he began with a muted voice. "The thinking is your Olive is a nut case. Look at the things we know she did for sure: the death cards, the dressing up, the looking in windows," he shrugged. "Some of the team think Charlie was on her list, but a pro got to him first. She kept the score card to make it clear she could have killed him if she wanted to."

Regan liked Dave's explanation less than anything he said before; it wasn't perfect, not like the setup of Olive as a

259

murderess. That's why it was troubling. It was just a messy enough idea that it made sense in the real world and she could imagine a prosecuting attorney presenting it in his closing arguments. She could imagine a jury believing it, too.

"Sorry, Regan. This one isn't going to work out the way you want."

She nodded slowly, an admission of defeat to him and to herself as well.

"I made cookies for Olive. I was going to tell her to keep the faith a little longer when I gave them to her, that after what I discovered about Byron, she'd be getting out soon. I'll have to rethink what I say now."

"You're going to have to rethink the cookies, too, I'm afraid. Inmates can't get cookies. Radios, books, stuff like that is OK, but no food."

"Why not? Do the authorities think visitors might bake a tiny file or a lethal weapon like a pair of nail clippers into a cookie?"

"Those are the rules at County." He rubbed his chin thoughtfully. "Course things may be easier at Blaine Street. Your pal Olive is charged with murder and the Blaine Street Facility is minimum and medium security, mostly for women who do forgeries and stupid non-violent stuff, but it's possible, given her age and background and how crowded County is, she got moved there. Let me see."

He returned to tapping on his computer. "You're in luck. Looks like you can take your baked goods to her at home. She made bail right around lunch time. She still shows as being processed out, but these things," he tilted his head in the direction of his computer screen, "can be a little behind

260

the time. She's probably out, home, and barbequing any evidence we missed by now."

"Tika Smith was trying to raise bail for Olive; I guess she came through. I'm on my way to a party, but I have time to swing by Olive's house first. Thanks, Dave."

He gave her a dismissive wave and picked up his phone. She folded her chair, returned it to its leaning spot, and was halfway through the doorway when Dave finished dialing and caught her eye.

"Nice shoes by the way. Sexy. I bet Tom likes 'em."

🏠 🏠 🏠 🏠 🏠 🏠 🏠 🏠 🏠 🏠 🏠

The enticing aroma of dark chocolate greeted her when she opened her car door. The chocolate chips cookies she made for Olive were melted and oozy after spending the past half hour sitting in her August-heated Prius, but she was sure Olive wouldn't mind eating gooey cookies since she would be doing so at home.

Regan started her car and cranked up the air conditioning, pressed the number for Tika on her cell, and put the phone in her car's hands-free device. Tika answered before Regan was out of the parking lot.

"Hi, Tika, it's Regan. Great job. I'm going to swing by for a quick hello unless you think Olive is too tired."

"Regan? What are you talking about?"

"My friend on the police force told me Olive made bail. I thought since you were working so hard to get it for her, you might have been the one to give her a ride home."

"Olive made bail?"

261

"Yes."

"It wasn't my doing. I couldn't get commitments from anyone but Helen and a couple of Olive's poorer relatives. I could only come up with about thirteen thousand dollars, not nearly enough for her bail."

"How did she get released?"

"Not a clue, Regan, but it wasn't me. It's good she's out, though. I'll go by and see her tomorrow morning."

🏠 🏠 🏠 🏠 🏠 🏠 🏠 🏠 🏠 🏠 🏠

Regan pulled into Olive's driveway and parked next to an unfamiliar car. She tossed her purse over her shoulder and collected the bag of cookies. She held the bag up to inspect its bottom as she walked to the front door and was pleased to see there were no signs of melted chocolate coming through the bag's bottom.

Regan rang the doorbell and waited. She rocked back and forth in her elevated sandals. She wondered if, with her footware added height, she'd still be shorter than Olive or look her directly in the eye when the door opened.

She stood facing an unopened door for what seemed like a long time before she made a fist and knocked. There was still no response. Maybe Olive was resting; she could be tired after her jail ordeal.

If Olive wasn't available, she wondered why the car's owner didn't open the door. Could Olive be out on a hike, dragging her visitor with her? Perhaps they were on the back patio enjoying the sun … that was a possibility.

Regan took the side path and headed toward Olive's

backyard, but when she reached it, no one was there. She walked to the French doors that opened out from the breakfast room and peered in as she tried the handle. The door was locked. She rapped on it, "Olive? Olive, it's Regan. Are you there?"

The afternoon sun glared against the glass doors. She shaded her eyes with her free hand and leaned close for a better look. She could see in past the open-plan kitchen all the way to the family room. There was sudden movement deep within the house. A woman's figure dropped low and disappeared behind one of the high-backed seats in the family room.

The figure was too small to be Olive; Regan's best guess was that she might have seen Linda or Susan. Linda was elsewhere of course, opening her house to Shakespeare Santa Cruz supporters, so Regan quickly ruled her out.

She rapped again, "Susan? Olive? Susan, I'm out back."

The figure rose slowly and stared back at her unmoving, and then suddenly rushed toward her. The woman was indeed Susan. The expression on her face was one of horror.

Susan struggled with the French door, seeming to do everything wrong in her attempt to open it. When it finally swung out in Regan's direction, it was almost a weapon, Susan pushed it open with such force.

"Oh Regan! Oh, it's Olive. She's committed suicide," Susan sobbed as she flung herself against Regan and into her arms.

Regan shifted Susan from a full hug to slightly off-center as she dropped the cookie bag and thrust her hand into her purse to retrieve her cell phone. She had never used the

263

emergency 9-1-1 function before — she had never needed to — that was about to change.

Susan gave out a sudden despairing howl at being dislodged and seemed to lose her balance. She flailed wildly and then clung to Regan more tightly than she had before. In the commotion, Regan's phone crashed onto the patio tile, shattering as it hit.

The noise of the splintering phone elicited a distressed wail from Susan. "I'm so sorry. I'm so upset. Now I've broken your phone."

"I was calling 9-1-1 but I don't think it went through."

"I've already called for help," Susan said as she released Regan, "but it's too late."

Susan was a trained nurse; she would have been able to check Olive's vital signs before making her pronouncement. The last thing Regan wanted to do was see Olive's body. Her reaction to dead bodies went well beyond what could be considered a slight phobia. Her natural inclination was to stay where she was and wait until responders came and attended to Olive, and she intended to obey that impulse …

Why hadn't Susan opened the door when she knocked?

Regan's brow furrowed with the thought. Susan had called 9-1-1 … why wouldn't she rush to let the first responders in as soon as she heard someone at the door? She had done the opposite — worse — she tried to hide.

It wasn't like Susan hadn't seen death before. It seemed unlikely that finding a friend's body would send her into such a tailspin that she would lose all sense of medically trained detachment and be unable to react reasonably to a knock on the door.

"Susan, are you sure there isn't anything we can do?" Regan asked in a steady voice as troubling questions began playing in her mind. Regan pushed past Susan and moved with determination toward the family room.

Olive was in a wing chair like the one Susan had tried to hide behind when Regan was rapping on the French doors. She was slumped to one side; her head had fallen forward onto her chest. Her left arm dangled limply over the arm of the chair and her right arm was crooked so her hand rested in her lap, not in a graceful position, but bent up sharply, possibly left that way after Susan had checked her for a pulse. To Regan's great relief, she couldn't see Olive's eyes; looking into the unseeing eyes of the dead was what she dreaded most.

She had seen the aftermath of death before, but in those instances it had been days or weeks since the life force departed — all that remained was on its way to becoming dust — but Olive's body still seemed robust, as if life, though gone, still hovered nearby.

Everything judicious in Regan begged her to turn away from Olive's remains, but given how oddly Susan behaved … some blend of appalled fascination and overriding uncertainty pulled her closer to the woman.

Regan slowly lowered herself to her knees next to the chair. Her hand trembled with reluctance as she pressed her fingers against Olive's neck and bent her head forward so her ear was close to Olive's mouth.

"Ahhh," a soft sound carried by Olive's exhaled breath reached Regan's ear.

"Ehhh!" Regan screamed. Her hands flew up and away

265

from the slumped woman and she fell back onto her heels. *Is that what a death rattle sounds like?*

She had heard that corpses on occasion seem to moan. A short, shallow, raspy breath struggled to reach Olive's lungs. She had inhaled. Corpses did not do that.

"Susan! She's breathing! How long ago did you call for help?"

"I ... I don't know. Right before you got here, I guess.

"Regan, let her be. She may not be clinically dead yet, but her body is shutting down. There's nothing we can do for her. Even if she survived ... she hasn't been getting enough oxygen. I'm sure there's been such brain damage by now that the Olive we know is gone. We have to accept that. It's what she would want us to do."

Susan was a nurse; more than that, she had combat experience. She had no doubt seen people who, though not yet dead, were moving inevitably toward the conclusion of their lives. Susan may have learned how to wait coolly until the end came, but Regan couldn't. "We have to try. I'm going to call 9-1-1 again and ask if they have any ideas, things we can do until help arrives."

Regan spotted an empty phone cradle on a kitchen counter. "Susan, where's the handset? What did you do with the phone after you called?"

"I found a note, Regan."

Susan grabbed a piece of paper from a nearby table and brandished it in front of her, but she waved it so quickly Regan couldn't read it.

"It's hand written. Olive confesses to killing all four men. Let her go. I found her after she had taken pills." Susan spoke rapidly. "She feels so much guilt ... she told me before she lost consciousness. It goes all the way back to breaking her promise to her husband. He had Huntington's disease. Do you know what that is? Do you know what happens to people who inherit that malady? Olive promised him she would help him end his life and then she didn't. She made him die slowly because she couldn't bring herself to give him an injection. She couldn't let him go peacefully with an overdose of morphine like she promised.

"Leave her alone, Regan. We mustn't make the same mistake. Let her go gently. Think about what her life will be like if she survives. Can you imagine her spending the rest of her life in a jail cell — Olive, who loves the out-of-doors, who loves her hikes?"

"You didn't call for help, did you? Where's the phone?" Regan demanded as calmly as she could, "Susan, call 9-1-1."

"I won't. You can't make me," she pouted and stamped her foot. There was something suddenly quite wrong about her, about the way she was behaving. She wasn't acting like a mature woman; she certainly wasn't acting like a medical professional pleading her case. She seemed more like a small child who didn't understand the difference between what was real and what was fancy.

Susan had held her husband as he died. She had been present when her first love and life-long friend drowned. Was finding Olive and reading her suicide note the proverbial final straw that pushed her over the brink?

"Where's the phone, Susan?" Regan yelled, trying to use words like a slap across the face to bring her back to reality.

Susan burst into gulping sobs. "I don't know. Please don't

267

be angry with me. I forget," she cried and ran from the room.

Olive took in another breath, louder this time, but it seemed shallower and less productive than her last breath. Regan scanned the room frantically but didn't see the handset. She fought her own panic; she had to buy time for Olive and she had to get help.

Regan pulled Olive to the floor and stretched her out on her back. Olive's body was flaccid and offered no resistance to her maneuvers. She pressed her fingers to Olive's neck and felt a feeble pulse.

She had taken a CPR class years ago, just one class. There had been many pupils; each participant only got a few moments to practice with the CPR dummy. Near the class conclusion, each participant was given an instruction pamphlet and told to continue practicing at home using a child's doll. The instructor knew many wouldn't.

His final sign-off as the students prepared to leave was designed to imprint the class lessons in their minds in an unforgettable way. He assumed John Travolta's famous stance from *Saturday Night Fever*.

"Remember, you're trying to make sure you're keeping them 'Stayin Alive' until help comes," he said as he pressed play on his tape recorder and burst into song.

The instructor was an older, balding, heavyset man who would have had a hard time passing for an aging Elvis. He certainly bore no resemblance to the figure Travolta cut on the ubiquitous posters and DVD jackets, but his laughable performance and instructions did the job. His memorable impression probably saved more lives than anything else he taught that day.

The thump, thump, thump, thump of the movie's theme music began in her head. *Thump, thump, thump, thump, Stayin Alive, thump, thump* ... Regan remembered what it meant at once. She might not recall all the techniques involved, but that was the rhythm for chest compression and breathing she had learned. Press, press, press, press, and when the refrain came up, pause and blow.

Breathing for someone who wasn't required less skill than trying to keep their heart pumping. She opened Olive's mouth and tilted her head back until her chin was elevated. Regan took a deep breath, put her lips to Olive's, and blew. The hand she placed on Olive's chest felt a rise and fall.

The tune continued in her mind and helped her gauge how often to repeat the breathing procedure, but after the first couple of repetitions, the lyrics were replaced by her thoughts and the words of others, set oddly to the music in her head.

Susan's words came first: "I'm not moving in with Olive; she's a monster." *Why would Susan come to visit Olive when she felt that way about her?*

Linda chimed in: "Susan signed a nasty prenup."

Her words were replaced by Byron's: "I ran into her last Valentine's Day," and in turn, Susan's again: "He hasn't had the money to get his pieces in front of the right people ... I'm going to change that."

Susan's sister Casey even had a lyrical say: "Even on my birthday, she barely finished eating lunch before she wanted to leave."

Casey's birthday. Casey's birthday was the day Henry was killed — Regan knew that for sure. Susan couldn't come to the séance because she was going to her sister's birthday party in Carmel.

"Olive confesses to killing all four men." *Susan didn't know about Charlie.*

Her memory of Susan's words stunned her. Had she recalled them sooner, they might have broken her breathing rhythm, but after so many repetitions, the rocking forward, blowing into Olive's mouth, and rocking back for a breath, her movements had become habituated. Reagan continued to make them without conscious thought.

"Sometimes I make it seem like I'm off somewhere — like to my sister's in Carmel — and then I double back."

It was Susan's own words that ended any doubt Regan still had about the murderer. Susan could have left her sister's party quickly after lunch. The séance didn't start until 3:30. If she hurried, Susan had time to drive back to Santa Cruz. *Susan could have been at all three murder scenes.*

Susan helped out with Henry just like Olive did. She knew the household routine just like she knew the property, the house plan, the pool where Henry liked to dangle his feet, and the secluded kitchen way inside the house.

Susan hadn't stopped by to see Olive. She hadn't found Olive and her suicide note. Olive hadn't written one. And she wasn't letting Olive die as an act of misguided kindness. She was killing Olive. She was tidying up. *And now I've become a problem for her, too.*

Regan's realization came just in time. It made her wary and more aware of her surroundings than she had been moments before. A sixth sense alerted her to danger. She caught Susan, who was wielding the fireplace poker over her head, out of the corner of her eye. She threw up her arm defensively and leaned away from the blow as Susan brought the weapon down toward her head.

The pain on the underside of her arm above her elbow wasn't instantaneous, but when it hit, it was agonizing. Reflexive tears filled her eyes. Her defensive move had thrown her off balance, and the onset of tears so thick she could barely see through them added to her instability.

Susan dropped the poker and threw her full weight onto Regan's tilted body. Regan's height and weight didn't give her any advantage over the smaller woman who maneuvered from above her and made full use of Regan's unstable posture.

She crashed to the floor on her back with her legs bent at the knees and her calves bent painfully underneath her. It was a bad position to be in for a fight.

Susan dropped to a straddle on top of her, sitting on her stomach up high enough to compress her diaphragm and make it hard for Regan to catch her breath. Susan's right hand held a syringe.

Regan expected Susan to plunge the needle into her body or her wounded arm, but Susan hesitated, her years of nurses' training made her pause for a second, and out of habit, to depress the syringe plunger just a bit before injecting Regan.

It was all the time she needed. Her adrenaline-filled body overwhelmed her pain. She grabbed Susan's hand with both of hers and twisted the syringe away from her body. She squeezed hard, intent on keeping the needle aimed away and emptying the syringe of its contents.

Susan screamed in the midst of their struggle. Regan didn't realize the needle had penetrated Susan's thigh — all

271

she heard in her adversary's cry was rage.

It seemed to Regan that long minutes went by with the two of them frozen together in that battle pose. She needed to straighten her legs and let her wounded arm rest. More importantly, she needed air that she couldn't get. Her needs distorted time.

It was Susan who gave in first. Her cries gave way to outraged weeping. "What have you done, you stupid cow?" she yowled as she rolled off Regan onto the floor. Susan sat up, sniffled, and wiped spittle from her chin and tears from her eyes with the back of her hand.

"You have to save me," she said with sudden calm. "The syringe was full of morphine, enough to put you down. I'm smaller than you, it will kill me quicker ..." she blinked rapidly and came close to tears once again.

The change in Susan was as abrupt as her earlier transition from pleading, reasoning adult into childlike behavior. Regan was certain Susan was, as she had been then, acting. She squirmed to sit up and braced for another attack.

"In a few minutes I'll be like Olive is now ... I'll lose consciousness and my breathing will slow until it ceases. Eventually my heart will stop. I haven't called 9-1-1 yet. I needed to wait. I needed to be sure you'd be dead and Olive would be too far gone for rescue."

Olive's eyelids flickered as she took another raspy breath.

"I better call now," Susan said with the utmost solemnity. She slid across the floor to the wing chair where Olive had been, reached behind it and produced a purse. She pulled her cell phone out and dialed 9-1-1.

With a nurse's confidence and detachment, she told the

dispatcher how much she weighed, how much morphine she had received, and her age. She hung up without mentioning Olive.

"What about Olive?" Regan shouted at her.

"Forget her." Susan took a deep breath and dismissed Olive once more. "She really is beyond help now.

"If only you hadn't come here." Susan sounded melancholy. "I don't improvise well, you know. I need time to plan. I've always been like that — it's not like Walter thought — he was wrong about me, about my mind not being as quick as it used to be. But if you hadn't ..." Susan's voice dropped until it was barely louder than a whisper, "... killed me ..." she said as she blinked back tears once again, "I think my plan would still have worked.

"I was going to say I found both of you. I'd tell them that Olive must have taken pills and that you must have interrupted her. She couldn't let you stop her, you see, so she bashed you in the head to knock you out and then injected you with liquid morphine.

"Yes, my plan would have worked. It would have seemed like Olive was the one who had been pilfering pills when she worked as a Pink Lady. Morphine tablets, all sorts of drugs, go missing all the time. Many hospitals have problems but nothing is ever done about it; figuring out what happens to drugs might mean pointing fingers at some pretty important people.

"I would have suggested Olive was the one who had been collecting morphine from drips, too, taking the dregs from drip bags as she disposed of them. I would have said she needed time and patience to get enough ... that she might have been getting ready to make another widow. I can tell a convincing story; they would have believed me."

Help was coming but Olive couldn't wait for it. Regan's arm burned with pain as she slid her hand under Olive's neck once again, and although her arm protested the movement, resumed CPR breathing.

"Stop it!" Susan demanded with sudden rage. She gulped air hungrily; her voice sounded full of panic. "You can't save both of us and she's already as good as dead. You have to understand triage; you have to help those with a chance of living."

Susan inhaled rapidly and deeply several times. She calmed down more with each breath, but each time she inhaled, it seemed her breath was a bit more labored.

Regan forced herself to continue her rocking CPR motions with mechanical precision. She tried to become an unfeeling machine propelling air into Olive's lungs with each down stroke; she tried not to listen to her arm screaming for her to stop and hold still.

Each time she raised up to inhale, she looked at Susan to be sure she wasn't reaching for the poker. Susan remained immobile.

"Why?" Regan asked.

"Why Walter, why Mike? Why set up Olive as the murderer?" Susan sounded bitter at the mention of each of their names.

"I really loved Walter and I wanted to have children with him so badly. In a way this is his fault, his and Olive's. Walter already had his own kids when we met and didn't want to have more. It took me years and promises to get him to the altar and to get him to agree to have children with me. Olive came to our wedding; I was the one who invited her. My old friend. And we were related in a way: her husband was a cousin of mine.

"We had a beautiful wedding, small but very nice," Susan's voice was wistful with remembrance. "I was so happy," she inhaled deeply and sighed, "until Olive, as only Olive can, blurted out that it was good we already had Walter's children to love because it wouldn't be a good idea to pass along my genes, not with Huntington's running through my family tree.

"She said that was the decision she and her husband made, and while being childless might disappoint me, I, like she had, would find fulfillment elsewhere.

"That was all it took. Walter jumped on Olive's revelation and said there would be no more children."

Susan grew agitated and breathed rapidly. "Would you stop it, Regan? Rest for a minute." She closed her eyes and fought to regain her composure.

"When I met Byron, I thought I might still have time, be a geriatric mother," she issued a harsh chuckle. "I hadn't developed the disease and I probably would have by then if I was going to — at most, I was probably no more than a carrier — I could explain to any children we had about being tested before they married.

"Regan, please, don't let me die. I'm not a bad person; I don't deserve to die." Panic had returned to Susan's voice. She kept talking as much to calm herself as to explain her actions.

"I needed Walter's money if I was going to give Byron

and me a chance at a real future. Can't you understand? I suggested to Olive it would be a hoot to dress as Death and pass out cards on Halloween. As a joke, I asked her to give Walter one with the day's date on it. She loved the idea. Old fool, I knew she would do it.

"I made up a special card with the time of death on it, too, and put it in my costume pocket. It didn't matter if the time was exactly correct. There would be so much confusion, as long as it was close, in their minds, people would make the time match."

Susan smiled forlornly. "I had a scalpel in another pocket. After Olive did her part and left, I just waited until there was another death figure nearby ... I knew another one would come along ... it's a common enough costume on Halloween.

"In the crush of the crowd, it wasn't hard to lean in next to him ... I knew how to cut a renal artery ... I had surgical training in the war. Walter knew what I had done ... but shock is so immediate from a wound like that ... he couldn't cry out ... I was covered in his blood, but that was to be expected ... since I held him in my arms while he died."

"But why kill Mike and Henry?" Regan asked.

"Why not Mike? He dumped me without a second thought ... when Linda came along. She still loved him ... I could still hurt her. I could get even with both of them ... and more murders would make ... the police stop considering me ... and start focusing on Olive. I put the scalpel and ... an old hot rod magazine in Olive's house," Susan panted.

Susan's breath was coming in gasps but she continued rapidly, almost oblivious to her laboring.

"When Tika's husband was shot ... and there were no

witnesses, I figured ... I might as well add a target card."

"And Henry? Susan, you didn't need to kill him."

"Yes, I did. I planned to put ... another death card in his room to implicate Olive ... the séance was a fantastic gift ... and Olive was so easy to lead ... I suggested she dress up like Death and look in the window ... I made her think it would be funny to scare ... all those silly women. I did it so subtly ... she thought it was her idea.

"Poor Henry," Susan said softly. "His death ... Henry's death was part of the string ... of murdered husbands I created ... but his was truly a mercy killing.

"Regan, I'm having a hard time."

Susan put her hand on Regan's arm. There was no power in her grip. "Please," she gasped, "I'll live if you help me. Olive won't. Please. Help me."

Regan pushed another breath into Olive's lungs. She turned to look full on into Susan's eyes as she rocked back onto her gladiator shoes and filled her own lungs with air.

"No."

Regan ran for the front door as the sirens stopped in Olive's driveway. She barked out information to the firefighters before they cleared the front steps.

"There are two women who've overdosed on morphine. The older woman took pills and was unconscious when I got here, so I don't know how long ago she took them. The last time I checked, she still had a pulse but it was barely there. I've been trying to do CPR for her breathing.

"The younger woman was accidentally ..." her voice faltered. "She was injected a couple of minutes before the 9-1-1 call. She was talking until a few minutes ago. I haven't checked her ... I haven't tried."

"Jason, bring lots of Naloxone; we've got two ODs," the lead firefighter called to the one behind before he pushed by Regan into Olive's house.

Regan recognized the firefighters. They were the same duo who arrived first when Henry drowned. That irony was not lost on her.

She remained outside near the front door, rigidly upright, not looking into the house, trying not to be aware of what was going on inside, but the door was open wide and she couldn't completely close out the firefighter's words.

"The Naloxone should work fast if it's going to, but I still can't get a pulse on this one."

She was spared from hearing more by the blaring of a second siren. Its loud approach paused at the Woods Cove gate while the access code was delivered automatically and the gate swung wide for the ambulance to pass.

The siren's wail grew closer, and as it did, to Regan's ears it ceased to be a man-made sound. The howling siren became the cry of Banshees, the frightful ghostly apparitions of Irish lore her grandmother told her about as a child, Death's hags who sang to announce his presence and who escorted him when he came to claim his due.

She had fought Death's approach, but to no avail. The Banshee's song grew ever louder; Death wouldn't be turned away empty-handed. Regan silently begged him, if he must take someone, to take Susan instead of Olive.

Her legs betrayed her; they were unwilling to support her any longer. She wobbled and leaned against a pillar that supported the front porch roof, hoping it would support her as well. It seemed unable to; she slid down its face and slumped onto the front steps.

Two ambulance paramedics rushed past her into the house. A third paramedic stopped on the steps and squatted down in front of her.

"Ma'am? Are you hurt?"

Regan hadn't noticed her arm since the firefighters' arrival. With the paramedic's question, all the pain she had been ignoring registered at once.

"A little bit."

🏠🏠🏠🏠🏠🏠🏠🏠🏠🏠🏠

Regan's arm was still in a sling. Her humerus bone wasn't fractured but she had injuries to her muscles which required rest and iced massages. The doctor told her she should be as good as new in a couple of weeks.

She took full advantage of her injury to turn over cooking duties to Tom, but after a few days of pizza and hamburgers, his specialties, she was desperate for something else — anything else. When he said he planned to grill for their little dinner party, Regan grinned from ear to ear.

"It's good to see you smiling and meaning it," Tom laughed. "If I had known that was all it would take, I'd have invited friends and offered to grill sooner."

His attempt at light humor stopped her smile. The tears that came so easily at night when, unable to sleep, she sat up petting their cat, Harry, until his purring soothed her, were near. She had to fight hard to keep them from starting.

Sandy and Dave let themselves in when they arrived. They walked through the house to the back patio where Tom had the grill set up so they could enjoy the view of Monterey Bay while he cooked.

Sandy was quick to see what sort of help Tom needed and offered it. "I'll set the table." She followed him inside to get dishes and silverware. Sandy and Tom had once been co-workers and were long-time friends. They worked well together, they bustled happily.

Dave sat down next to Regan. He stared at the view intently, patiently waiting for her to speak first. When she didn't, he broke the silence.

"You OK?" he asked without looking at her.

She managed a smile; it was hardly a bright one, but she hoped it was enough for a good friend who knew her well.

"I'm fine. The swelling has gone down and the bruise is fading. My arm isn't even that sore anymore, but Tom is babying me and I'm letting him."

"That's not what I mean and you know it. Watching the lights go out — it's not easy," he said softly. "How are you, Regan?"

"I'm feeling guilty. I should have tried harder ... done something more." She could feel the sting of rueful tears and blinked rapidly to keep them from escaping.

"There wasn't any more you could have done."

Sandy appeared with a bowl of corn chips and salsa. "Tom suggested this; I'll be right back with other choices."

Sandy returned quickly with a platter of beautifully arranged vegetables, prawns on skewers, and bacon wrapped pineapple chunks. "And my idea of what to eat before dinner," she proclaimed.

They drank wine and complimented Sandy on her contributions until the four of them had almost finished her hors d'oeuvres.

Tom made a couple of trips to the kitchen for garlic bread wrapped in foil and marinating red peppers and baby zucchini from Regan's garden. "The secret is to stop them while they're small," he laughed in reference to the zucchini, "or they'll take over the world." He set a bowl of cut up chicken next to the grill.

The sun was descending toward the ocean in the west. The sunset was blocked by redwood trees, but the fiery display against the bottoms of the puffy clouds across the southern sky made up for what they missed seeing at the water's edge.

They lit candles as the daylight faded and spoke lightly of frivolous things, and watched Regan out of the corners of their eyes. Dave checked his watch when he thought no one was looking.

"Helloow ..." Olive sang out her usual greeting. "I'm so sorry I'm late. I decided to hike up. Dave, you and your lovely wife won't mind driving me to my car in Henry Cowell Park, will you? I started hours ago but it was ever so much farther and steeper than it looked on the map."

Olive held out a bottle of champagne. "It was chilled when I started and in an insulated bag, but I'm afraid it's gotten warm. I do hope you started dinner without me. You know I'm always late, it's a nasty habit I have."

Their little dinner party was complete. Tom set to work grilling the chicken while Olive began a fast-paced account of the latest happenings in her world.

"I thought Byron shouldn't hear about Susan over the phone, so Linda and I went to see him in person. He was quite upset about what she'd done, as you would expect any decent person would be, and began blaming himself for her actions. We soon set him straight about that.

"Well, he is a gorgeous man and so talented, too. He reminds me of my dear husband, Paul. His looks and his talents weren't lost on Linda, and I daresay Linda's mother-in-law would never approve of him as a suitable replacement for her son, another fact I know isn't lost on Linda," Olive whooped.

"Let's just say, I see some hanky-panky in the future, at least I hope so. It would serve her mother-in-law right, too. Linda loved her husband and was a wonderful wife, but that woman never got over that her darling son fell in love with a woman she didn't choose. Linda put up with that old biddy's criticism for her husband's sake for years. Time for some payback, I say.

"Oh, Linda did ask me to let you know, Regan, that she will be wanting to relist her house. She said you were wise the way you only took it off the market temporarily, and that she'll stop by your office tomorrow to sign papers. She hopes it sells quickly so she can move in with me."

"She's not concerned about Mike's ghost?"

"Not anymore," Olive laughed. "Now that she knows it was Susan who switched the shift linkage rods and not me, she's sure he won't be haunting my house. If Mike haunts any residence, Linda thinks it will be his old family home, another reason for a fast sale.

"And speaking of ghosts, Tika wants me to put her house on the market. She finally had Sebastian complete his séance and," Olive chortled, "... oh, that woman has lost her mind ... and she says Charlie told her there's no hidden money.

"It seems he made a killing in the stock market when he was a tax-paying accountant, long before he returned to the family business, and that's where his money came from. So he was allowed to have it, but the four-hundred-thousand dollars the Smiths gave me as final repayment for their house was the last of it; he spent all the rest keeping Tika happy in exile and making sure their daughter's education was funded."

Tom was disbelieving. "Tika got that from a séance?"

"From a séance and the FBI finishing their investigation and filling her in, like they filled in the local authorities," Dave smirked.

"Makes a good story for Tika to tell, though," Olive howled.

"Tika and her daughter will move in with me while their house sells, but I don't expect them to stay. Tika says her roots are calling her and you know her daughter studied cultural anthropology in college and has gotten very involved with the Navajo culture. In fact, she was living on the Big Reservation and working on an advanced degree when Tika reconnected with her. I expect them to move back to New Mexico before long.

"My dear Helen will be joining me permanently, though. Tom, would you give her a call about listing her house as soon as Henry gets planted?"

The rest of them knew Olive, so they were nonplussed by her abruptness; Sandy, however, was unprepared. She tried to hide it, but Olive's language caused her to choke on her wine.

"Which brings me to you, young lady." Olive looked at Regan with the fondness a mother might save for her child. "We all seem to be pussyfooting around how awful you look. You haven't been sleeping well, have you? I know the symptoms of guilt, Regan dear. Believe me, I do. You remind me of myself after my Paul died.

"I felt guilty because I wouldn't help him die after I promised I would. You're feeling guilty because you didn't try to save Susan."

Regan swallowed hard. "She begged me to help her."

"So did Paul."

Olive's words were uncharacteristically gentle and well chosen. She reached out and took Regan's hand. "You couldn't save both of us no matter what you did. I'm so very grateful you chose me.

"Regan, I've been giving it a great deal of thought; I suspect Susan had Huntington's disease."

"What?" Regan asked disbelievingly.

"Susan told me she dropped instruments in Walter's operating room. He thought she was beginning to manifest the disease and demanded she stop working. She said it only happened three times, and she had excuses: she said she was overtired and not focusing properly on her job.

"She was angry at him for suggesting what he did. That was the reason she gave for asking me to help shake him up on Halloween — she said it would be our little joke — she wanted to see how he took being given a death sentence.

"I agreed to help her because at the time I thought Walter was being overbearing. Now I think he may have been right. Susan was just coming into middle age when symptoms are most likely to manifest, and a sudden lack of coordination is one of the first signs of the disease.

"Regan, I choose to believe what happened to Susan was for the best."

"Olive is right, Regan. Take my word as a member of the law enforcement community. Susan probably would have gotten the death penalty, what with committing three murders and two attempted murders. Even if she didn't get that sentence, she would have spent the rest of her life in jail."

"If you mean to include me as one of those attempteds, Dave, that would be a mistake. Oh yes, she gave me the morphine tablets and assured me that I would be convicted of murder — but she didn't force me to take them. Guilt can be a terrible thing to live with.

"You valued my life even though I didn't, Regan. I'm still here because you were willing to make a hard choice. Now I'm so very grateful you saved me. I'm so thankful to be alive and hiking and putting my foot in my mouth — I did notice, Sandy," Olive smiled at Dave's wife, her eyes twinkling, "by the way.

"You gave me a second chance and I have taken advantage of it; one mustn't reject a gift like that. I have finally accepted that like you, I too, did the best I could."

Olive straightened up in her seat and produced one of her big toothy grins, "I'm embracing life anew and am in the market for new widows, it seems. I'll be needing two."

Regan's laugh started slowly but then came easily. She knew with absolute certainty that Olive wasn't a threat to Tom or anyone else.

"Olive, I have to ask you. You've said Tom reminds you of your husband, and that Byron does, and that Dave, who doesn't look like Tom or Byron, does as well. How can all these men, who don't look anything alike, remind you of your husband?"

"I've never shown you a picture of my dear Paul, have I?"

Olive reached into her top and pulled up a long gold chain. At the end of it was a heart shaped gold locket with the letter "P" on it. She opened the locket and leaned toward Regan so the photo inside was illuminated by the candles on the table.

"This is Paul."

The one thing all the men Olive compared her husband to had in common was an abundance of darkish hair. Her locket held a close-up photo of a man with sparse ash-white hair parted too far to the right and swept over the top of his head in an obvious attempt to hide his deeply receding hairline.

His eyes were a watery green, not at all the rich blue of Tom's eyes or the dark brown of Dave's and Byron's eyes. They protruded slightly as if they were being squeezed by the angular cheekbones of his long thin face.

As Olive turned the locket so each dinner guest could see it in turn; those who had, shared discrete mystified glances with one another.

"My Paul was such a gorgeous man," Olive sighed loudly. "Most people might not recognize that from looking at his picture, because photographs didn't capture his most striking features … the features he has in common with you gentlemen … which were, of course, his intelligence, his kindness, and his great sense of decency."

About the author

Nancy Lynn Jarvis was a Santa Cruz, California, Realtor® for more than twenty years. She still owns a real estate company with her husband, Craig, but she says writing is so much fun that she has officially retired from being an active agent.

After earning a BA in behavioral science from San Jose State University, she worked in the advertising department of the San Jose Mercury News. A move to Santa Cruz meant a new job as a librarian and later a stint as the business manager for Shakespeare Santa Cruz at UCSC.

Nancy's work history reflects her philosophy: people should try something radically different every few years. Writing is the latest of her adventures.

She invites you to take a peek into the real estate world through the stories that form the backdrop of her Regan McHenry mysteries. Details and ideas come from Nancy's own experiences and many of her characters are based on associates and clients she has known — at least they may be until they become suspects, or even worse, murderers.

Follow Regan McHenry Real Estate Mysteries on Facebook

or

Visit Nancy Lynn Jarvis' website
www.GoodReadMysteries.com

where you can:

Read the first chapter of the books in the Regan McHenry Mystery Series.

Review reader comments and email your own.

Ask Nancy questions about her books and the next book in the series.

Find out about upcoming events, book club discounts, and arrange for Nancy to talk to your book club or group.

Read or print Regan's recipe for the chocolate chip cookie dough that she and Tom always have ready in their freezer.

Books are available in large print and for your Kindle, iPad, and other e-readers.

Made in the USA
San Bernardino, CA
21 July 2019